FORGET
ME
NOT

ALSO BY STACY WILLINGHAM

Only If You're Lucky

All the Dangerous Things

A Flicker in the Dark

FORGET ME NOT

A NOVEL

STACY WILLINGHAM

MINOTAUR BOOKS
NEW YORK

First published in the United States by Minotaur Books, an imprint of St. Martin's Publishing Group

EU Representative: Macmillan Publishers Ireland Ltd, 1st Floor, The Liffey Trust Centre, 117–126 Sheriff Street Upper, Dublin 1, DO1 YC43

Designed by Omar Chapa

ISBN 9781250887979

For Britt, my everything

It was like I was a tool in the hands of the Devil.

—SUSAN ATKINS, ON CHARLES MANSON, 1976

FORGET
ME
NOT

PROLOGUE

I dream of you sometimes.

Erratic and impulsive, just like in life, I never know when you might show up. When I might close my eyes, attempt to lose myself in the merciful black, only for your face to click into existence like an intrusive thought. Like an unwelcome visitor, your foot wedged in the door, coercing your way inside my mind the way you always did.

The dream, though. It's always the same. Walking into the bathroom at night, bare feet cold on the slick white tile. All the lights off as I stare at my reflection in the vanity mirror—only it's you I see, not me. It's you: haunted, strange, features murky like old bathwater, rippled by time and the lukewarm memories. Eyes like sea glass, foggy and unfocused. The kind we used to collect at the beach. You're eighteen in my dream, the age you were when you disappeared. Forever young, eternally perfect, preserved in amber like an ancient relic. No matter when you come to me, though, always, every time, you stare at me and I stare back. Always, every time, I see your face instead of my own. Every tilt of the head, every twist of the neck, like the mirror is glass and you're right there, right in front of me. Twenty-two years spent trapped on the other side.

Mocking me, miming my movements. Unattainable yet somehow still within reach.

I just wish I knew what you were thinking. I wish I had access to that beautiful brain of yours so I could wade through the folds of it and finally understand.

So I could dissect it, dissect you: Natalie Campbell, my beguiling big sister.

Instead, in my dream, I extend my fingers and you extend them right back. I reach out to touch you, to prove to myself that you're still real, but before I can get to you, before I can feel your skin on mine, you turn to fog in my grip and waft away like the wind.

CHAPTER 1

Sounds of the city slither into the dark bubble of my apartment: cars coughing awake, the impatient honk of a rush-hour horn. I'm listening in the way one might listen to a late-night siren shrieking down the street, a neighbor's angry whispers seeping through the walls. Detached, distant, just barely conscious enough to register that it's early evening, I think, judging by the string of orange light leaking through the crack in my curtains. The overwhelming smell of garlic that permeates my apartment whenever the Chinese restaurant beneath my building gets their dinner rush.

My phone is buzzing across the coffee table again and I try to ignore it but the sound is incessant, pesky as a mosquito, so I roll over on my couch and glance at the screen, a cascade of text messages staring straight back.

Helloooo? Claire?

Are you alive?

I gaze at the words, guilt licking the back of my neck for ignoring Ryan like this. I don't really want to talk to him right now,
I don't want to talk to anyone, but at the same time, I know I owe
him a response. He didn't do anything wrong.

I type at last, flipping onto my back before dropping the phone
on my chest.

> That's too bad

he promptly replies.

> I was just starting to like you.

Despite my mood, it elicits a smile.

> Where are you?

he asks as I glance around my living room, wincing at the take-
out cartons and cloudy glasses. I hadn't noticed it before, but it's
starting to smell a little sour in here. Like old laundry and self-
loathing. I should probably take out the trash.

> Home

I say, watching as an ellipsis appears and disappears. Ryan, apparently, trying to decide how to respond.

> So you're not coming?

I stare at the screen, attempting to decipher what exactly he means when the sting of understanding shoots through my chest followed by a deep wave of shame.

"Shit," I mutter, finally realizing why he's been calling, texting, no doubt waiting for my arrival at the bar down the street. It's Saturday, which means his party is tonight. A party to celebrate his recent promotion.

A party that's been planned for over a month now, one I promised I'd attend.

I sigh, pushing the heels of my palms into my eyes. Then I reach for my phone again, ready to tap out some half-hearted excuse when it buzzes in anticipation, beating me to it.

> It would mean a lot if you did.

I bite the inside of my lip, gnawing hard on a chunk of raised flesh. Then I sit up, head swimming from the sudden movement.

> Of course I'm coming

I finally respond.

> Getting in the shower now.

Studying my toes, dirt and hot water swirling fast down the drain, it's hard not to reflect on the irony of it all. On my attempted rinsing of sins, that frenzied cleansing. Ten whole years spent clawing my way into the investigative unit at *The New York Journal*—a form of atonement, no doubt; a therapist's dream—and the fact that it took ten seconds for me to flush it all away.

All that progress just suddenly gone, slipped straight through my fingers before vanishing completely like the water beneath me.

I'm on the sidewalk thirty minutes later, a cotton dress grazing my knees and strands of wet hair still stuck to my neck. My skin feels slick, a thin film of sweat dampening everything. Growing up in the South, you'd think I'd be used to the summer heat, the general state of discomfort for six months of each year, but July in New York is its own brand of unbearable. I keep my head down as I walk, eyes on my feet as I sidestep the drunken stumblers, the glammed-up girls heading out for a night of indulgence. Narrow heels navigating the sidewalk grates enveloped in clouds of lavender deodorant and honey perfume.

I pass a few bars bulging at the seams, restaurants with diners sitting close over quivering wicks, before finally ducking into the dark entrance of Vern's, a grungy little tavern I know Ryan only picked due to its proximity to my apartment, the minimal effort it would require for me to come.

Which, of course, makes me feel infinitely worse for forgetting.

I step inside, feeling my eyes adjust to the dark before I take a deep breath, the sour smell of spilt beer mixing with the stink of too many people in too small of a space. Then I scan the room slowly, taking in the cheap fluorescent lights hanging from strings on the ceiling, wet napkins stuck to the wood of the bar. There are dollar bills tacked to every inch of the wall, edges curling from the eternal damp. This isn't Ryan's usual scene, a nonchalance so deliberate it feels manufactured.

Like this whole party is his attempt at downplaying it all, the promotion I had been working toward for years being handed to him instead of to me.

I wander in further, ignoring the prying eyes of all my old colleagues. I return a couple sad smiles, keeping my chin parallel to the ground, before finally catching a glimpse of him from across the room, rolled-up sleeves revealing the veins in his forearms. His shirt is untucked, collar yawning wide enough to expose the nominal hair on his chest, and I let myself simply watch for a second. Watch the way he rests his weight onto the edge of the bar, fingers in the air as he attempts to get the bartender's attention.

The way he dips his other hand into his pocket and checks his phone, the subtle disappointment as he slips it back in.

I run a hand through my hair, a half-hearted attempt at composing myself before sidling up beside him and sliding my way onto the stool by his side.

"Hey," I say, giving his shoulder a squeeze. "Sorry I'm late."

Ryan turns toward me, finally, relief and surprise in equal measure. He didn't actually think I'd show up.

"There she is," he says, a pep in his voice as I avert my eyes, pulling my own phone out of my pocket and placing it face up on the bar. There's a moment of silence between us, a handful of seconds when both of us are clearly trying to decide what to say next.

"Thank you for coming," he says at last, and I watch as he starts to pick at a coaster, the cheap cardboard kind that begins to disintegrate once it gets wet.

"Wouldn't miss it," I respond, even though, half an hour ago, that's exactly what I was trying to do.

The bartender appears with a bottle of beer and Ryan pulls it toward himself, ordering another one for me. Then he turns in my direction again, a new expression in his eyes like he's about to come clean with something important, something he's been steeling himself to say, but just as his lips begin to part, a headline uncurls across a grid of TVs. Our noses turning like a pack of bloodhounds picking up scent.

BOYFRIEND FOUND GUILTY IN MURDER OF EIGHTEEN-YEAR-OLD GIRL

I hear a *whoop* from across the room before vaguely registering a second body as it appears beside us, the slap of a hand against

Ryan's broad shoulder. Then there's a murmur of cheers, a round of shots, and I attempt to smile through it all, attempt to soften the perpetually sharp lines of my face, though I'm sure he can tell my expression is strained.

"So, regale me with tales about the life of the liberated," he says at last, turning toward me once we're alone again. "Still everything you hoped it would be?"

"Everything and more," I lie, nodding at the bartender once she arrives with my drink. "Hours are good, the flexibility is nice."

"No more meddling cubemates and cold pot coffee."

"Yeah, that last guy was a real prick."

Ryan chuckles, shakes his head.

"Working on anything interesting?"

I chew on my lip, not sure how to reveal that I've been working on absolutely nothing since the last time we talked. That after putting in a whole decade at *The Journal* only to be passed over for a promotion I was sure would be mine, I had quit in favor of freelance and was secretly starting to think I'd made a mistake. A few weeks of reflection had made me realize I had done it in haste, a bitter distaste for my boss mixing with a profound exhaustion at having spent the last ten years working the police blotter. My stories amounting to nothing more than a summarization of the most mundane murders, the way they usually are.

Another gas station robbery, another pistol-whipped kid just trying to buy drugs.

"I have a few leads," I say, tearing at the beer label with my right hand. I leave out the fact that none of them have gotten back to me; that practically every email I've sent in recent memory has been met with a smothering silence.

"That's great," he says. "One of them is bound to pan out eventually."

I smile, hating the pity in his tone. The fact that we both know it's not true.

"Listen, Claire. I know you're having a hard time with this."

I twist my neck, still distracted by the glimmer of the TVs. There's a mug shot on the screen now, a twenty-something-year-old man dressed in orange, and I watch as the image flips to a truck, police tape wound around the doors as I start to imagine how it might look inside.

Scratch marks on the leather and fingerprints on the dash. Bloodstains like a Pollock painting, luminol everywhere.

"My promotion," Ryan adds, drawing me back. "Everyone here knows it should have been yours."

"Oh," I say, the knot in my chest loosening once I understand what he means. He thinks I'm jealous, and while that is partially true, the particulars are infinitely more complicated than that. "No, Ryan. I'm happy for you."

"Are you sure?" he asks. "Because these last few months, you've been different. Distant."

"Positive," I say. "You deserve it."

He nods, though he doesn't seem convinced.

"Then what is it?" he asks as he twists the glass neck of the bottle between his fingers, a rhythmic *whoosh* on the bar like the blood in my ears.

"What is what?" I ask, playing dumb, though he simply arches an eyebrow, refusing to indulge in my meager attempt at denial.

I stare at him now, trying to decide how to respond as the entirety of our friendship stretches out before me. Ten whole years of misty mornings and red-rimmed eyes, nothing but a particleboard partition between us, until one day I blinked and realized he was the closest thing to a friend I had in the world. It leads to an inevitable intimacy, doing what we do. Surrounding ourselves with stories of death . . . but still, even Ryan doesn't know everything about me.

He knows very little, in fact, when it comes to my past.

I exhale, an oily guilt slipping through my stomach, because no matter how hard I try to justify it all, a lie by omission *is* still a lie. I've known that for a long time.

I open my mouth, my tongue teetering on the edge of another excuse, when I hear the buzz of my phone against the bar top. The glow of the screen drawing both our eyes down.

"You can get that," he says, although his words barely register as I stare at the display. A name I haven't seen in a long, long time.

"It's fine," I mutter, everything suddenly Novocain-numb as I search my mind for the date, for anything else I should have remembered, trying to figure out why I'm getting this call.

My hands stay stuck by my sides, unwilling to move, until the ringing finally stops. Only then do I flex my fingers, wrap them around the bottle to give them something to do.

"If it's important, he'll call back."

Ryan nods, turning toward his beer, but immediately after my phone stops ringing, I watch as the screen lights up again. That grating noise against the old, stripped wood like the sharp chatter of teeth.

"Looks like it's important."

I swallow, watching the device dance across the table as Ryan starts to turn back in my direction, his eyes drilling into the side of my face. I can practically feel his confusion, a climbing curiosity about why I'm refusing to answer the phone, so I force myself to pick it up, hitting Accept before lifting it slowly up to my ear.

"Hello?" I ask, trying to stay calm as I listen to the sound of slow breath through the receiver. There's an uncomfortable stillness between us, thick like two strangers on opposite sides of a door. "Dad, are you there?"

"Hi, Claire."

I exhale at the sound, although his voice sounds different, distant, like he can't quite believe he's calling me, either.

"What is it?" I ask, the alarm continuing to spike in my chest because my father and I do not do small talk; there has to be a reason why he's calling, and whatever it is, I already know it's not good. "Is everything okay?"

I hear him sigh, a long, defeated sound, as I imagine his face on the other side of the line. Fingers massaging his eyes like this conversation is a migraine he's trying to fight off.

"Claire, it's your mother," he says at last. "There's been an accident."

CHAPTER 2

I feel my back lengthen, my posture suddenly ramrod straight as those words, *an accident,* light up my nerves like an electrical shock.

"What do you mean *an accident*?" I ask, registering Ryan perk up beside me. A look of concern flashing across his face. "What kind of accident? What happened?"

"She's fine," my dad says. "But she's a little banged up. She can't walk up the stairs, which, of course, makes navigating the house a bit of a challenge."

"What happened?" I repeat, irritation bubbling up at the way he's directly avoiding my questions. The same thing he's always done.

"She fell through a board on the back deck," he says with another sigh, almost like he's annoyed by the whole thing. "Broke her leg in three places. Sprained her wrist, bruised a few ribs."

I exhale, a sense of relief flooding through me. I'm not close with my mother, either—I haven't been in years—but I realize now that those few seconds of thinking I might have lost her had sent an inexplicable panic through my chest. A surprising sensation I don't know how to explain.

"That deck is a mess," I say, not sure why that's the first thing to pop into my head. "It's been falling apart for years."

"Yeah, well, the house is old," he says. "And you know your mother. Never been one to fix things herself."

We're both quiet, his insinuation, whether intentional or not, digging up old, buried resentment.

"Anyway, it might be good for you to come back for a little. Lend her a hand around the house."

"Come back," I repeat, the idea almost too foreign to fathom. The nonchalance of his statement, like he doesn't understand the scale of what he's actually asking.

"Yes, come home," he reiterates. "Your mother could use some help at home, Claire."

"But I have work—" I start, though I suddenly stop myself, sensing Ryan leaning farther in my direction. Obviously picking up on my lie.

"It would just be a few weeks," he continues. "Can't you write from anywhere?"

I stay quiet, annoyed at his assumption that I can just abandon my life at a moment's notice—as well as the fact that he's more right than he realizes.

"You know she doesn't like asking for help," he says when I don't answer. "The only reason I even know about it myself is because her neighbor called me after she found her trying to drive herself to the hospital."

I sigh, pushing my fingers into the corners of my eyes as I imagine my mother's ratty black Civic juddering down the driveway; clipping a curb before it limped down the street.

"She's gonna kill herself," he adds. "Or someone else, for that matter, if she tries to drive again."

I release my hand, twisting my beer across the counter. Watching the little wet rings start to swirl as I rack my brain for some other excuse.

"She doesn't have anyone else," he continues, apparently switching tactics from logic to guilt.

"Let me think about it," I say, eager to get off the phone before he can start dredging up talk of my sister, all the still-gaping wounds of our past.

"Yeah, sure," he says, palpably relieved that I'm even considering it, and although my parents have been divorced for over twenty years now, it's moments like these when I can tell he still cares.

I glance over at Ryan, managing a half-hearted smile to let him know I'm all right.

"And Claire," my dad adds, drawing my attention back to the phone. "Don't tell her it was my idea, okay?"

I hang up, the voices around me turning to static as my eyes drill hard into the bar. I can practically feel my skin buzzing as the thought of going back snakes its way through my system, my limbs suddenly heavy like they're filled with sand.

"Well, I'll be damned."

I blink back to the room, the loud clack of billiard balls in the background as a new voice cuts its way through the fog.

"I was starting to think you weren't going to show up."

"Mike," I say, squaring my shoulders as I attempt to shake off that conversation, my former boss materializing by my side.

"Haven't seen your byline in a while," he says, reedy lips twisting into a smirk as I feel his broad arms brush up against mine. He's standing too close, a habit he's had since the moment I met him, and I fan out my elbows in an attempt to take up more space.

"Doesn't mean I'm not working on anything."

I watch his smile stretch before he plucks a straw from the caddy and bends it in half, using the sharp edge to pick at his teeth. His skin is a caramelized brown, his hair slightly shorter than it was a few months ago. The thin gray strands buzzed so close I can see the spherical shape of his skull.

"You know, you can always come back," he says next, his voice dipped low like he's doing me a favor. The leathery scent of cigar stuck to his tongue. "Your desk is still there, all sad and empty."

"That won't be necessary, but thanks for the offer."

He stares at me for a second before shaking his head, a disillusioned little bob like he can't understand. Then he turns toward Ryan before slapping his hand against the base of his neck, the intensity of the blow jolting Ryan's whole body forward.

"This guy," he says, shaking his shoulder with too much force. I glance to the side, noticing a flush creeping into Ryan's cheeks that he tries to mask by taking a swig of his beer. "Gave him a promotion and you'd think someone died with the way he's been moping around."

I force a small smile, my attention lingering on the slope of his jaw as he swallows; the familiarity of it, the reliable shape. He has his usual five-o'clock shadow, although I know he shaved this morning. He shaves every morning. Back at the office, I always made fun of the way he looked so different in the evenings, thick black stubble shading the skin of his cheeks, the stretch of his neck. His face a sundial showing the passage of time, physical proof we were working too late.

"You been following this thing?"

My gaze drifts over to Mike again, then back to the TVs, talking heads now condemning a dead girl for dating a guy who wasn't her age. For sending him selfies, for low-cut tops.

"Here and there," I say, attempting to downplay the fact that not only have I been following it, but that I've been watching it unfold with a sad obsession: the clothes, the car. The attractive young girl and the older man who killed her for reasons nobody could begin to explain.

"Sick shit," Mike continues, although he almost sounds pleased. "Anyway, think it over. Pride won't get you a paycheck, you know."

He ruffles my hair and I watch in silence as he walks away, a quiet anger simmering beneath my skin.

"Are you all right?" Ryan asks after Mike is gone, his voice soft like he's embarrassed for us both.

"Yeah, screw him," I say, bringing my beer back to my lips. "There's no way I'm crawling back now."

"I don't mean that," he says, before gesturing down to my phone on the bar. "I mean *that*."

"Oh," I say, remembering that conversation with my dad now, the cold dread starting to sink back in. "Yeah, it's fine."

"What was that about? Sounded serious."

"It's my mom," I respond. "She's okay, but my dad's trying to get me to go home for a while."

Ryan nods, both of us eyeing all the bottles lined up against the wall as he lifts the beer in his hand, gesturing to the bartender to deliver two more.

"I get the feeling you don't want to go."

I exhale, trying to work out how to explain as I think about the moment Ryan and I met, both of us settling into adjacent desks at *The Journal* during our shared first day on the job. The way he had asked about my past, my family, and me blurting out my little white lie.

I have a sister, I had said, Natalie's porcelain face, so still and white, blazing through my mind like a forensic flash. *But we haven't spoken in years.*

It wasn't a conscious decision, keeping her from him. At least, in the beginning it wasn't. I just wanted to be normal. I wanted to answer his routine questions with nice, polite answers—but then we got close, closer than I had ever expected, and it started to feel like the time had passed. He had accepted my vague explanation, did the nice thing and decided not to pry. I could tell he wanted to, though, and sometimes I could sense him tiptoeing toward it, slowly starting to work up the nerve, but I never let him get close enough.

I always deflected, changed the subject. Pushed my sister back into the box in the recesses of my mind, the place she's lived for the last twenty-two years until night falls and she comes crawling back out.

"No," I say at last, fingernails picking at the glass lip. "I don't want to go."

"Why not?" he asks, and I down my beer in one long gulp, the answer too knotty to fully untangle. Too complex to form into words.

"It's been a while. I'm just having a hard time processing it all."

"How long?" he asks, softer now as he senses we're working toward something big, something serious. Something we should have discussed a long time ago.

"Since I graduated high school," I admit, nodding at the bartender as she delivers our drinks. "Fifteen years."

"Claire," he says, lowering his bottle as he takes me in. "What the hell."

"I'm not close with my parents. Clearly."

"What happened?" he asks as my leg starts to bounce on the top rung of the stool. I know I'm stalling, dragging my feet, but the second the words slip from my lips, there will be no reeling them back in. They'll be out in the open, unrestrained, this secret I've kept from him for ten whole years taking on a life of its own. Ryan will look at me differently, I know he will—but at the same time, it might be nice to ease the burden, to have another person to share in my pain. The truth has been living on the tip of my tongue for so long . . . but now, between the call from my father and the story on the news, the door is ever-so-slightly cracked open.

All I have to do is step through.

"Here," I say at last, picking up my cell before I can change my mind. Then I open the browser and type *Natalie Campbell* before hitting Search. The articles are old but there are plenty to pick from so I click one at random and thrust it toward him, my heart in my throat as he grabs my phone. "Read this and you'll understand."

CHAPTER 3

I stumble home well after midnight, a warm buzz carrying me through the streets of the city and the hoppy remnants of beer on my breath.

I peel off my clothes as soon as I step inside, my dress puddling onto the floor with the rest of my laundry. It's hot in here, my window unit barely able to keep up with the humidity hovering on the other side; even so, the gush of mildly cooler air in my apartment still chills the sweat stuck to my skin and I can feel it raise in reaction, fleshy little bumps responding to its touch.

I step around the clutter, bare feet navigating the spaces like I'm dancing through land mines, and plop down on my couch, grabbing my laptop from the far end of the cushion. Then I open the lid and tap at the keys, the glow of the screen illuminating my face like a flashlight as I type my sister's name back into the browser, selecting the same result as before and watching as the headline appears on the screen.

BOYFRIEND ARRESTED FOR MURDER OF
MISSING GIRL

I close my eyes, imagining Ryan's pupils flicking back and forth while he read. The gentle drop of his jaw as comprehension clicked and the way he lowered my phone slowly, the sounds of the party suspended around us like we were suddenly the last ones left.

"Why didn't you tell me?" he asked, a whisper of disbelief in his voice once he realized the scale of what I'd been keeping. The real reason for my mood over these last few months. Grief is not a rational thing, I know it doesn't make much sense, but even though there are two decades of distance between these two cases—even though the story on the news now is not related to this story on my screen, to what happened to Natalie—the parallels between them have dug up so many old memories it's been a bleak reminder of all the ways the world hasn't changed.

How we're all still dancing to the same, sick song. Little ballerinas spinning in circles. Constantly moving but going nowhere at all.

"I don't know," I admitted at last. "I guess I try not to think about it."

"For ten years?" he probed, eyes narrowing as he took me in. "You've tried not to think about it for ten whole years?"

I stayed quiet, not sure what to say.

"Your sister was murdered, Claire."

My eyes snap open, an instinctive flinch at the thought of that word like a finger grazing against a hot stove. *Presumed dead* is the technical term, but at this point, it's a trivial change.

I begin to scroll now, taking in this article from August 2002. I know it's not smart, traveling down this long, dark road, but I'm just drunk enough to be feeling a little too wistful. An emotional cutting I know I'll regret. There's a mug shot on the right side of the screen, the name in the caption identifying the man as Jeffrey Slater, my older sister's secret boyfriend. The one none of us knew that she had. She had kept him from everyone, hid him like a bad habit she knew would come back to bite, and I lean in closer, my nose practically touching the glass as my eyes bore into the lines of his face. He had been attractive, no doubt about that, although it had been in that weathered sort of way: too-tan skin and sandy blond hair pulled into a bun at the nape of his neck. Muddy tattoos peeking out from beneath the collar of his shirt and a boyish quality to his lips, tipped up at the edges, even though he had been twenty-eight at the time of his arrest.

Ten whole years older than her.

I keep scrolling, forcing myself to move on to the words. Then I skim the article, beginning to end, even though I know there's nothing new in here. Nothing novel has come out about my sister's case since Jeffrey was arrested, twenty-two years of anniversary articles with regurgitated details, an occasional blitz of fresh results when some podcaster catches a whiff and attempts to make it shiny again. Still, I rehash it all as I read about the clues, the car, the traces of Natalie pushed into his passenger seat: a thick blond hair with the root still attached, her fingerprint smudged on the passenger door. And all of that could have been explained, of course, except for the shirt soaked in her blood balled up in the glove box.

That had been the proverbial nail in the coffin. The reason he got life without the possibility of parole.

I glance down, eyeing the ominously edited pictures of our childhood home. Natalie's window in the distance, cracked like a shell. At first, the cops insisted she'd just run away. They thought she'd be back in a few days.

She probably spent the night at a friend's house or something, one of the detectives had said, a man by the name of Eric DiNello who had grown up with my mother, the small-town stereotype of every-one knowing everyone just a simple fact of life. *You know how girls can be.*

I blink a few times, my body floating like it's been flung two decades into the past. Like I'm suddenly eleven again, legs kicking in the air as the detectives sat us down at our dining room table and tried to walk my mother off her mental ledge. Their theory had stuck around for at least a few days, especially once we realized a bag was missing. A black duffel bag Natalie kept in her closet. That, plus the lack of a body, had made it easy to hold out hope, but we were eventually told she probably died in that car, her DNA paint-ing a grim picture of how her last minutes might have played out: the two of them fighting, screaming. Natalie capable of saying the most terrible things, her tongue a razor that knew just where to cut until her hand reached out and grabbed at the handle the moment Jeffrey's reached out and grabbed at her hair.

Until she tried to leave and he yanked her head back before slamming it forward, blinking to find her body go limp. Fingers shaking with wet blood on his hands.

I click out of the article and launch a new window, trying to force my mind to switch gears. I log in to my bank account, my chest squeezing when I eye the number glaring back, dangerously low. Journalists don't make much—especially at mid-tier papers like *The New York Journal,* especially after two months with no paycheck—and I do some quick math in my head, realizing that, in another two months, I'll be down to single digits.

"Fuck," I mutter, pushing my fingers into my eyes, feeling the sockets. Letting the world get blissfully blurry before forcing myself to pull my hands back.

I think of my old colleagues back at the bar; their pity-soaked smiles, pinched and tight, as I wound my way through the parting crowd. My former boss, that petty patronization cloaked as concern, and the fact that I've spent the last eight weeks in a vicious cycle of rage and regret. Maybe a month away could be good for my psyche; maybe a break from the city, from the pressures of trying to make it all on my own, could spark something new in my mind. Besides, if I spend the rest of the summer back home, I could rent out my apartment. Put a little more money in my pocket. Give myself a safety net so I won't have to drain my savings completely.

I pick up my phone and click over to Contacts, tapping my mom's number before starting a new text. Then I stare at the blank screen for a second, the cursor pulsing like a ticking clock, a beating heart. The sight of it sending a sharp chill down my spine. My parents are still in Claxton, that small fishing town on the South Carolinian coast. After their divorce, my dad moved into a new house, of course, but my mom still lives in the exact same one in which we grew up and I don't know how she does it, to be honest. I don't know how she can keep walking past Natalie's bedroom, peeking inside.

Her twin bed forever unslept in, a closet full of clothes forever unworn.

I take a deep breath, forcing my thumbs to dance away at the screen. Then I type a few words, delete them. Rephrase, type something else, as I remember my dad's plea not to mention his name before finally settling on something casual, vague.

> Thinking about coming home for a visit. Any chance my room is open?

I shoot off the text and close my eyes, my jugular pulsing hard in my neck. I realize, after I've sent it, that it's one in the morning and my mom is probably asleep—that, and she's notoriously bad about checking her phone, anyway; it can sometimes take days for her to get back to a text—so I open my eyes and stand up quick, ready to make my way to bed when I feel the phone vibrate in my hand.

I look down, the screen suddenly bright in my palm as my mom's number appears on the display, a generic *M* in place of a picture because I didn't have any recent ones to use.

I swipe up, holding my breath as I read her response.

Would love to have you. The room is yours.

CHAPTER 4

I know I'm close by the scents seeping in through the open windows: salt, mud, the sticky film of the air itself gripping to my skin like drying glue. I rolled them down an hour ago, once I started to approach the coast, the exhaust from the city replaced by aromas I know deep down in my bones.

I can feel my hair whipping in the wind, strands getting stuck to the wet of my lips, the corners of my eyes. My phone perched in my cup holder, Google Maps narrating each turn because I've forgotten how to find my way home.

It's funny, the things the brain chooses to recall. I can't for the life of me remember street names but I instinctually know the tide is low solely based on the smell.

I take a left, the map now telling me I'm five minutes away. The sky is peach pink, a little bubble of orange barely visible on the horizon, and I watch as it shimmers against the water like the Earth itself is holding a mirror. Despite my fifteen years away, it's a warmly familiar sight: the water, the reeds, the shade of green that glows so bright it looks practically neon at dusk. Comforting like an old stuffed animal, a childhood blanket wrapped warm around my shoulders.

I had forgotten, until this moment, that there are good things about this place, too. That it isn't all synonymous with death.

I take a right, my car winding down a street that looks vaguely familiar like recognizing a face from my past but not being able to place the name. It's so surreal to be back here, so haunting and strange, and I feel myself twitch as my phone rings through the speakers, the sudden sound pulling me out of my trance.

"Hey, Claire. Your renter is here," Ryan says as soon as I answer. "I just dropped off the keys."

"Thank you." I exhale, a physical relief at this last piece of my plan clicking into place. I had found a tenant in record time, some intern in town for the summer, so after a flurry of deep cleaning, a couple hours spent hiding the evidence of my recent decay, I had collected my three thousand dollars and left the place in pristine condition with a request for Ryan to occasionally pick up my mail. "I really appreciate it."

"Sure, any time."

His voice cracks and I glance down at my screen, realizing I only have one bar of service. Claxton is in the middle of nowhere, a tiny little town surrounded by nothing but other small towns. The reception out here is probably terrible, a problem that hadn't even occurred to me when I was a kid.

"Hey, look, I've been thinking a lot about what you told me at Vern's," he continues, his voice a little hesitant now, a little embarrassed, like he isn't sure if he should keep talking. "And I just wanted to say that I think this will be good. Healing."

"*Healing*," I repeat, only half listening as my eye catches a glimpse of the next road sign, my old street now coming into view.

"You having a reason to finally go home."

I stay silent, not sure how to respond.

"Have you ever heard of exposure therapy?" he asks, and I can't help but smirk. Ryan has always been into this kind of thing: wellness blogs and self-help books, happiness podcasts and name-dropping his therapist in casual conversation. Like every small tragedy is an opportunity to *grow*. "Avoiding the thing you're afraid of only gives it more power."

"I'm not *afraid*—" I start to argue, my denial trailing off once I realize my hands are clasped too tight on the wheel.

I study the whites of my knuckles, their gentle shake.

"Yeah, I know," he says, trying to backtrack, and I'm grateful he can't see the way I've relaxed their grip, flexing my fingers to loosen them back up. "I just mean that you haven't been home in fifteen years. That's a lot of emotional weight. But if you expose yourself to it, little by little, maybe it can start to release its control."

I push down my turn signal, distracted as my old house comes into view. It's exactly as I remember it, brick by brick, almost as if time has been paralyzed in this little corner of the world. I can see the same tuft of weeds pushing its way through the pavement, the one I used to trip over when I ran up the driveway before coming down hard on stinging palms. There's the familiar tangle of jasmine crawling its way up the walls, the citronella my mom planted to scare away the mosquitos. Rows of gap-toothed blinds covering the windows, the same slats still missing after all these years . . . although it does feel slightly smaller, somehow. Like the cartilage is wearing, shrinking down. The bones of the place shriveling with age.

"Claire?" Ryan asks when I don't respond.

"Yeah, sorry, I'm having a hard time hearing you," I lie, realizing I've been holding all the air deep in my throat, an old superstition like the place is a graveyard and I'm afraid it might come to life if I breathe. "The service out here. It's not the best."

"Oh, sure. I'll let you go then," he says. "But you can do this, Claire. I know you can."

I hang up, my body on autopilot as I round the cul-de-sac curve. Then I pull into the driveway and kill the engine before catching a glimpse of the live oak in the back. It's the same one Natalie used to climb down when she snuck out at night, its thick, long branches like twisting tentacles barely visible from behind the roof. There's a slurry of feelings coursing their way through my veins now, a weightlessness like I've been injected with some strange drug. It's the mental image of my mother, I think: sitting inside and holding her breath, just like me, because guilt and grief have turned us into strangers. The fact that she's probably spent the last few days preparing for my arrival—hobbling around the house positioning pillows, running a dust rag over all the same spots— while simultaneously wondering when I would back out. If I'm being honest, I almost did. Multiple times. It would have been easy. I could have told her something came up at work, an assignment big enough to keep me in the city; or, better yet, I could have just never responded to her text back. I could have ignored it, the parental equivalent to a drunk text I was suddenly ashamed of in the harsh light of morning. She wouldn't have pushed it; I know she wouldn't have. Instead, we both would have let the possibility of seeing each other simply slip away, dissolving completely like a salt tab in water.

Turning into a murky memory that, with time, would leave nothing behind but a bad taste.

I catch a glimpse of movement now, the flutter of a curtain behind one of the windows, and I know she's there, just on the other side. Watching me idle in front of the house. There's a pinch of something strange in my chest at the sight, a cousin to the fear I had felt when my father first called. Shame, maybe, remembering as I listened to his final few words. His voice dipped into a whisper like the thing he was about to say next was too sad to admit out loud.

She doesn't have anyone else.

The truth is, he's right. My mother doesn't have anyone else. Her parents died young, a car crash that claimed them long before I was born. She's a divorced only child with no extended family at all and it feels so juvenile now, sitting here like this. Her only remaining daughter avoiding her like the plague. My mom and I have had our disagreements in the past. We've had our spats. With the benefit of hindsight and a fully formed brain, something I certainly didn't have at eleven, I've realized there were things back then she should have done differently. She was the adult, it was her job to keep her kids safe . . . but at the same time, I know I'm far from blameless.

I did a lot of things I'm not proud of, too.

I exhale, my head starting to swim as I feel the bony fingers of fear crawl their way up my neck. Then I open the door and step outside, fighting the phantom sensation of two cold hands clasped tight around it.

Their gentle caress across exposed skin before closing softly and starting to squeeze.

CHAPTER 5

My mother comes to the door with a bottle of wine in one hand and a full glass in the other, ruby-red liquid threatening to spill over the lip.

"To celebrate your return," she says by way of a greeting, hoisting it high, though I glance at the bottle, already half gone, and can't help but wonder how long she's been drinking. She's never needed much of a reason before.

"Hi, Mom," I say, pulling her in for a reluctant hug. There's a black brace on her leg that makes her body tilt at a harsh angle; another on her wrist that digs into my spine.

"Welcome home, Claire," she says at last, both of us letting go as soon as we can.

I step back, taking the free seconds to scan her face. I can't help but register the way fifteen years have changed the lines of it. Everything looks deeper, settled in, soft like the well-worn surface of a leather couch, with permanent wrinkles and a dark stain to her skin. She looks thinner, too, flesh hanging off her bones like a mannequin modeling clothing two sizes too big, but although her hair is longer and streaked with gray, it's still the same honey blond she passed down to her daughters.

"I couldn't believe it when I got your text," she adds.

"I couldn't believe it when I sent it," I admit.

She smiles at me, a red tint to her teeth, and I step into the living room, looking around as two large duffels hang heavy at my sides, a single briefcase slung over one shoulder. It feels like stepping through a time warp, the doorway a portal to the world of my past.

"So, your father told you."

I twist around, eyeing her from across the room.

"You didn't ask about the braces," she says, gesturing down to her leg, her wrist. "You didn't even seem surprised."

I bite my tongue, realizing my mistake.

"*Thinking about coming home for a visit?*" she asks, parroting my text with an expression that looks mildly amused. "Since when have you ever done that?"

"He was only trying to help," I say, turning back around as I clock all the same furniture in all the same places, a sense of surreality descending upon me until my eyes land on a cluster of pictures hanging prominently on the wall. The biggest one square in the center slightly loose like a wobbly tooth.

I take a step closer, all the memories I've tried so hard to forget washing over me now with a staggering strength. There are a few pictures of my mom and dad only, sepia-toned snapshots from when they met in the seventies; rosier days before life got so thorny and they eventually drifted apart. Next to those is a shot of us all at the beach, gangly girl legs and a crumbling sandcastle off in the distance. I take in our diapers and pigtails, our missing front teeth. Natalie in kindergarten, third grade, fifth grade. High school. The slow march of time as her face shifts with age, a baby-faced kid to an awkward adolescent; a teenager with braces to, at last, her senior-year picture.

The last school picture she'd ever take. The oldest age she'd ever be.

"Why do you still have these?" I ask, barely realizing I said it out loud as I zero in on the frame in the middle. A family portrait I remember getting done at the mall. Then I bring my fingers to the glass, remnants of dust brushing off on my skin as I lean in close, eyes resting on the necklace nestled into the dip of my sister's throat. It's her birthstone, a peridot, held in place by a dainty gold chain—although I know it's not a real gem. It's not real gold, either, because I bought it for her for her sixteenth birthday from one of those vending machine jewelry dispensers. It had cost me a quarter, I was only nine, but she told me she loved it and she wore it everywhere until that last summer, when she finally took it off.

I look away, eyes stinging as I think about the very first time I saw her without it. The moment I realized she had outgrown it in the same way she had outgrown me.

"Why would I not?" my mom asks at last. "It's our family."

I turn around, cocking my eyebrow. This is the kind of delusional behavior I've come to expect from my mother—blindly displaying the photos of a family that was so violently ripped apart—although I suppose I'm not one to talk. According to Ryan, avoidance is a coping mechanism. I know I must have learned it from somewhere.

"I'll just put these upstairs," I say instead, pointing to my bags. She nods, gesturing to the steps like I could have forgotten my way, and I start to ascend, holding my breath as I reach the landing. Then I glance down the hall, toward the two doors situated side by side. Natalie's room to the left, mine to the right. The small sliver of wall that separates the two. The doors are both shut and I say a small *thank you* as I think about how I'll simply breeze past her bedroom, spend the whole summer ignoring it completely and convincing myself it's not even there, when Ryan's words once again enter my mind uninvited. Soft and serene like a whisper in the night.

Avoiding the thing you're afraid of only gives it more power.

I chew on my cheek, taking a few tentative steps forward before dropping my bags in the center of the hall and closing the last handful of feet. I don't want to go in there, my skin crawling as I imagine how it might look inside. The room a casket I'd prefer to keep closed . . . but at the same time, maybe Ryan is right.

Maybe my avoidance has only made this all worse, Natalie's absence pulsing like a neglected tumor. Pinching my nerves, twisting my senses. A sickness that's grown too big to ignore.

I take a deep breath, placing my hand on the knob before turning it gently and peeking inside. Nothing has changed in here, nothing at all. The walls are still the same pale pink, her twin bed still pushed against the one that we shared. There's a white desk in the corner, her closet door closed—though I imagine that, if I opened it, I'd probably still find all her clothes tucked inside. The familiar smell of her skin forever caked into the fabric wafting up like a shove, pushing me back.

I step deeper into the room, leaving the door open behind me and feeling, strangely, like the floor is tilting. Then I walk toward her bed, letting the tips of my fingers trail across the comforter before glancing out the window, the latch on the bottom firmly flipped shut.

I twist around, finally facing the other side of the room.

"Okay," I whisper, my heart starting to creep into my throat as I eye the old desk, the paint in the middle weathered and worn. "See? This is okay."

I will my legs to keep moving before pulling out the chair and lowering myself down. My hands feel damp, but still, I extend my arms, placing my palms firmly on the table. Ryan's words gently forcing me forward.

But if you expose yourself to it, little by little, maybe it can start to release its control.

I look down, studying my chewed-up cuticles, my ravaged nails, as my mind starts to scan all the nights I would lie rigid in bed, pretending to sleep, but instead listening to my sister's movements in this very room through the wall: her window sliding open, the scrape of her jeans as she slinked her way out. My own body easing out of the sheets before creeping into her bedroom behind her and helping myself to her stuff like a bottomless buffet.

I can still see the glow of the moon through her window as I tried on her makeup, sticky pink lipstick that never stayed in the lines. The smell of her sweatshirt as I slipped it over my head, limbs swimming in fabric six sizes too big.

"Goddamn it," I mutter, closing my eyes. All the old recollections sweeping me away like a riptide I know I'm not strong enough to fight. We had been seven years apart, the gap too great to have much in common, but I looked up to her. I envied her. In so many ways, I longed to be her, but despite how alike we looked, how many times people pegged us as sisters with our butter-blond hair and wide doll eyes, lurking just beneath the superficial surface of it all, once you drilled into our respective cores, Natalie and I were opposites in every way that mattered. Our personalities so different, the disparities so vast, it was hard to believe we were even related at all.

I push my palms into my sockets, letting it hurt for a few seconds before I remove them. Then I look down at the desk, suddenly desperate to keep digging as I realize I'm still thirsty for information about my big sister.

A sister who it felt like I lost long before I actually did.

I stare at the knob on the top drawer before grabbing it without thinking, pulling it open to find the usual clutter: notebooks and pencils, highlighter and tape. A collection of pushpins and paper clips and metallic gel pens next to a barrette I remember her painting with nail polish once, the sparkly pink now dull and chipped. I close that drawer, moving on to the next one. School supplies and report cards, binders and files, and I sift through it all with a ravenous urgency, the last two decades spent starving myself of all these details now catching up to me with an insatiable strength. I can't believe my mom kept all this stuff, but at the same time, I'm not actually surprised. Judging by the state of the house downstairs, the way it still looks exactly the same, it makes sense that she would keep this room untouched, too—although I know it isn't from some sense of nostalgia, some maternal need to preserve Natalie's memory like a shadow box displaying all of her things. Instead, it's her inability to deal with it all. A deep-seated delusion that if she keeps this door permanently shut, keeps polishing those pictures hanging up on the wall, then she can keep pretending that nothing has changed.

I push a stack of paper to the side, trying to ignore the fact that this is a delusion I apparently inherited, too, considering I've been doing the exact same thing.

I shrug the thought away, my attention now drawn to the bottom of the drawer. There's a shoebox nestled into the back, hidden beneath the papers I just removed, and I twist my head, trying to place it from all the other times I've snooped through her things. There's no way to be sure if I've seen this before—it's been fifteen years since I was last here—so I lean down and grab the soft sides, the corners torn from too much use. The box is old, clearly, and I slide it onto my lap before slowly lifting the lid like I'm afraid there might be something in there that bites.

Instead, my eyes are met with a collection of photographs. The old, shiny kind developed from disposable cameras or rolls of film.

I move the lid to the side and pick up the stack, my fingers sticking to the glossy paper. A pinch in my chest when I see the one on top. It's a picture of our parents, significantly younger, the two of them standing on the steps of our porch. They had been high school sweethearts, apparently inseparable since the age of sixteen, though they look a little older than that here. And they look happy, truly, my dad grinning into the camera as he hugs my mom from behind.

I turn the shot over, their names and the date written in pencil. This was taken before Natalie and I were born, back when they first moved into this house, and I feel my eyes sting at the thought. This proof that their marriage wasn't always so stale.

I move the image to the back and continue to flip. The rest seem to be pictures of Natalie and her friends, mostly. Pictures I've never seen before. Her tan lines and freckles tell me they were taken sometime in the summer and I spy a tangle of thin limbs laying out on a dock, a couple shots from a house party with a red plastic cup clutched in her hand. A few of the prints have those thick yellow streaks on the sides, like the film was faulty or the lighting was weird; others have fleshy little orbs in the upper right-hand corner like someone's thumb was partially covering the lens, but the one thing that's consistent is the size of her smile.

A smile I haven't thought of in years.

"Claire?"

I look to the side, to the wide-open door, my mom's voice traveling from down the hall fracturing the reverie like cracking glass.

"You doing okay up there?"

"Fine," I yell, my eyes on the pictures again. To the way Natalie looks so happy, so *free*. The exact opposite of how my mind insists on remembering her as she haunts my dreams from the vanity mirror.

"Come on down!" she calls again. *"This wine isn't going to drink itself!"*

I place the box onto the desk, ready to nestle the images back into the drawer when something in the corner catches my eye. It's a little black tube barely bigger than a battery and I lean down slowly, picking it up and feeling the gentle weight in my hand as I realize, with a jolt, that it's a roll of old film.

A roll of old film that was never developed.

CHAPTER 6

I round the stairwell to find my mom sitting on the couch, nursing her wine, an expectant smile snaked across her lips. I can't tell if it's the same glass she answered the door with or if she's already helped herself to another but there is a second one on the coffee table now, presumably for me, filled less than an inch to the brim.

"Have you eaten?" she asks, taking a sip.

I shake my head, walking to the couch and taking a seat beside her. The shoebox nestled under one arm and the roll of film still clutched in my hand.

"I don't have much," she says, looking around, as if she's just realized. "I probably should have ordered something."

I smile, placing the film on the side table before reaching for my glass and taking a drink. This, too, is the kind of thing I've come to expect from my mother. Once my sister was gone, she used to parent me like an afterthought. An inconvenient postscript tacked on to her day. I can't even count the number of times I showed up to school without any supplies, without lunch. Neglect casual enough to shrug off as oblivion, like it was normal for a mother to forget to feed her kid.

"We can get a pizza," I say.

"Pizza sounds good," she muses, though she doesn't make a move and I know I'll probably end up ordering it. "How's work?" she asks instead, the perfunctory question when nobody knows what else to say. Sort of like commenting on the weather, it's a safe topic. Most of the time, anyway.

"Work is fine," I lie, avoiding her eyes.

"I still don't know how you can stomach that job. It's a grisly profession."

I take another sip, refusing to answer. My parents have never understood why I do what I do, the fact that I marinate in murder for forty hours a week. More than that, really, because it's impossible not to take this job home with me. Not to see the faces of victims in crowded rooms, hear their names in casual conversation. Stew on the fact that their entire lives had to be whittled down to two sentences in the middle of a mid-tier newspaper, my allotted word count reducing them to their dreariest parts. So I simply recounted their age, their profession. The fact that they died by the hands of a driver so drunk they fell asleep at the wheel or an accidental overdose of laced cocaine. And that's another reason why I had quit, to be honest: I've been desperate for the freedom to tell my own stories. To show that human beings, like Natalie, are so much more than their final moments. That the days that they lived deserve just as much attention as the day that they died . . . but at the same time, I would be lying if I didn't admit there was another piece to it. That there's something about the inevitability of death that somehow soothes me, makes me feel better. Reminds me that if Jeffrey hadn't gotten to my sister, something else would have.

Sooner or later, it always does.

"Are they letting you work remote now?" my mom asks next,

pushing her way through the stubborn silence. "That seems to be the thing these days."

I pick at my cuticle, still thinking about how it's not that unusual, really, why I chose this job of mine. In fact, it makes perfect sense. I like the quest for answers, the ability to scrape together fragments of fact and create a narrative that's logical and true.

"What have you been writing about—?"

"I found something in Natalie's bedroom," I blurt out, unable to take it any longer. Her probing questions, my little lies. My mom doesn't know that I'm not actually employed and, to be honest, I don't want her to find out. I don't want her to know that I have nothing to go back to, no concrete end to my stay—but mostly, I just really want to get back to those pictures.

To the memory of my sister's face, so flushed and alive. Flip through the rest I haven't yet seen.

"A shoebox full of old photos," I continue, removing the lid before balancing the box square on my lap. It feels strange, my sudden eagerness to revisit the past after all the years I've spent trying to bottle it up. I suppose it's because the dam has finally burst—this house, her room, two decades of pressure steadily building—and now I can't stop the memories from pummeling through. "I went in there, just to look around, and I think . . . I think they might have been from that summer."

My mom stares at me, her expression blank.

"Look," I say, eager to show her how good they are, how happy she was, because I know that's not the way my mom remembers Natalie, either.

I know she remembers the screaming, the crying. Her daughter of that summer like a shadow self that somehow broke loose; a rabid animal with froth and fangs.

"See?" I say, grabbing the picture nestled on top. It's of Natalie and a girl in the middle of the woods, probably from one of those parties out in the boonies where they could drink and never get caught. There are bottles of beer littered in the distance, a single cigarette dangling from between her two fingers, and a flash of metal peeking out from the corner. Some kid's car parked in the brush.

"Oh, wow," my mom says, reaching out to grab the image.

She must see it too, then. The Natalie from before. The one that's gotten lost in the midst of this mess.

"That's Bethany Wheeler," she continues, pointing at the second girl as she brings the picture up to her face. "Do you remember her?"

I squint. Of course, I remember Bethany Wheeler. She was tall and blond with bright hazel eyes and I had been jealous of the way she and my sister had clicked, a built-in best friend I could never quite grasp.

"God, she used to be here all the time," my mom says, tilting her head. "I wonder what she's up to now."

I think of Bethany, the way she followed my sister around like a dependent pet. Natalie liked to save people, outcasts she found and tucked under her wing, but the two of them had been truly inseparable for a while. My mother is right: she was always here, digging through our freezer before perching herself on the edge of the counter. Tongue Popsicle-pink as she asked about my day. I could always tell she felt bad for me, too. For the way I was always alone.

I go back to the stack and continue to flip.

"I haven't seen her since that summer," my mom continues as I feel my eyes start to water, my gaze zeroing in on another face from my past—only this time, it's the face of Jeffrey Slater, his arm flung around my sister's shoulder as she throws her head back in delirious laughter. All the soft spots of her neck exposed.

"I think she got a little strange," she adds, still staring at Bethany. "Started getting tattoos."

I swallow, taking in the first and only picture I've ever seen of my sister and Jeffrey together, although despite the fact she kept their relationship hidden, I had an inkling that summer that she was seeing someone. Little clues I picked up on when I was alone in her bedroom: the smell of boy on her sweater, sandalwood and sweat, when I slipped it over my head. The spray of small flowers I once found crushed in the pocket, bursts of blue petals with yellow suns in the center. Stems tied together like a daisy chain.

I move the picture to the back, eager to hide it, because the rest of these memories seem to be good ones. I don't want the presence of Jeffrey to taint them all.

"Look at this one," I say instead, the picture on top of Natalie and me now, the two of us perched on the edge of a gnarled wood fence. There's a stretch of placid water sparkling in the background, strings of Spanish moss framing the shot. "I think this is from when she worked at that vineyard."

My mom turns toward the photo, her expression hardening into something I can't quite read.

"Do you remember?" I nudge, noticing the rows of vines stretching into the distance, a little blue bucket gripped tight in my hand. "In the beginning of that summer? Picking grapes?"

I smile now, the memory of the moment coursing through me.

"She was so embarrassed when we showed up," I continue. Thinking of how we decided to surprise her that day—Mom, Dad, and me—their clunky old station wagon trundling down that clay dirt road. The place was on an island, I remember; a quaint and quiet little corner of the South with a smattering of small houses and a single-pump gas station. One lonely restaurant with rocking chairs creaking on an old wooden porch. It was the only area around here that hadn't yet been touched by the development taking over the neighboring towns and I remember that drive feeling like we were gliding into a different world, a different life.

That was also the last good day we'd all spend together before our parents told us about their divorce.

I close my mouth and look up at my mother, a bleak comprehension squeezing my chest as the stiffness in her expression suddenly makes sense. She must be thinking it, too. The way things changed right after this. The fact that Natalie quit that job shortly after our visit, a rebellion spurred on by their separation devouring everything good in our lives.

"What was that place called again?" I ask, picking up another picture as I try to break through the mounting silence, still not ready to put these away.

"Galloway Farm," she says, a quiet sadness seeping into her voice.

I look down at the photo, this one of us standing in a grassy aisle. Wild vines on either side of our bodies and smears of smashed grapes staining the soles of our shoes.

"Is it still there?"

"I assume so," she responds. "I still see their stuff at the grocery store."

I flip to the last picture, this time one of my sister alone. She has a grape shoved up her nose and she's making a face, crossing her eyes, the kind of goofy demeanor I forgot she even had. There are a few other people in the background of this one—other workers, I assume—but I blur them out, her presence alone overpowering them all. The image is overexposed, giving her skin a ghostly glow, but she still looks so alive, more alive than I've ever remembered her, and like with that sunset as I drove in, the warm nostalgia that surged its way through me, the sight of her like this reminds me that this place wasn't always so bad. That there were happy moments, too, before life bared its teeth, and I wish we could go back to this moment, this day.

I wish I could erase what came next and stop time right here, freeze it in place before she could get hurt.

"So, about that pizza," my mom says, jerking me from the memory, and I turn just in time to watch her down the rest of her wine, reaching for the bottle to pour herself more. "Do you know of anywhere good?"

CHAPTER 7

Sleep does not come easily here.

I spend the first few hours lying rigid in bed, eyes wide in the dark, the sour taste of wine on my tongue and a tinny ringing deep in my ears.

I forgot how quiet this place is. How much I've relied on the city's white noise to drown out my thoughts, my own bodily sounds, so instead, I listen to the ringing, to the way it grows louder as the minutes stretch on. The silence around me so heavy and charged it feels like a physical thing, thick and meaty. My mind on the countless other nights I used to do just this.

I stare at the ceiling, the childhood canopy suspended above me like an intricate web, sticky and strong, before I flip to the side, next training my eyes on the wall that Natalie and I shared. After venturing into her bedroom earlier, trailing my fingers across the cold sheets, I'm now painfully aware of how empty her bed is, the absence of her body tucked safely inside radiating like an echo in a barren room.

I squeeze my lids shut, listening in the same way I listened before. Still desperate to hear all those same sounds: her breath low and slow like she was hiding something or the quiet flick of the pages when she read herself to sleep, the scrape of her furniture on the nights she stayed awake.

I drift off eventually, sometime past two, a restless dip out of consciousness until I twitch and find myself in the bathroom down the hall. It's pitch-black except for the glow of the moon through the sole window by the sink; the tile cold on my feet and the vanity mirror luminescent in the dark. I don't know what I'm doing in here, I can't even remember the walk from my room, but I stare at my reflection until slowly, like a ripple traveling through water, I see Natalie's face instead of my own.

I bunch my forehead, tilting my head to the left, to the right. Observing as my sister does the same. Her neck is long and lean like a porcelain swan's; her skin wraith-pale like a smudge on the mirror. Then I start to reach out and that's when something new happens, something strange. Her lips begin to shudder into a smirk and I look down at my palms, vaguely aware of a pillowcase clutched tight in my fingers. Little frills on the edges, the exact same one from my childhood bed. I don't remember bringing it in here, I have no idea why I did, but when I look back at the mirror, Natalie is holding it, too, and I watch as she lifts it higher, placing it snugly over her head. My hands and her hands pulling it tight from the back, the fabric now flush against her face. I can't see anything anymore, all I can see is black black black, but I can imagine the indents of her eyes, the dip of her mouth as she tries to inhale. The cloth of the pillowcase making it impossible to breathe.

Now she's choking, and I'm choking, ragged little gulps like I'm underwater, my lungs on fire. My entire body begging for air.

I come to with a gasp, my hands grabbing madly at my own face. I'm still in bed, dripping in sweat, my mind stuck in that same dream again—but there really is something covering my mouth, some kind of gossamer fabric stuffed in like a gag, and when I finally grip it and pull it away I realize it's the canopy, mosquito netting covering my face like a cobweb. It must have fallen somehow. I must have rolled over the fabric in my sleep, pulling at the old hook on the ceiling until it gave out after two decades of neglect.

I exhale, breathing deeply, relief flooding my lungs as my hand instinctively reaches for my heart. The entire thing is draped across my body, a gauzy sarcophagus trapping me inside, and I rip the mesh from my chest. Throwing it into a wad on the floor before glancing at my phone resting on the table.

It's just past six.

I got barely four hours of sleep, but I know I won't be getting any more after that, so I decide to get up, peeling myself from the mattress before making my way into the hall in the dark. The house is silent, my mom's still asleep, though I notice her bedroom door is open because she's been staying in the guest room downstairs, her leg making it impossible to walk up the steps. Still, I keep the lights off as I descend to the first floor before turning into the kitchen.

Only then do I flip on the light, rooting around in the cabinets until I find the mugs and coffee. Then I bring them to the machine, measure out a few scoops, and lean back against the sink as it brews.

I take a deep breath, pushing the stale air out through pursed lips as I try to slow my still-hammering heart. The truth is, I always feel strange when I awake from that dream—off-kilter and queasy, like putting on the wrong glasses, viewing the world through a warped lens—but it's even worse now, being back in this house. Now, it feels like Natalie is watching me, somehow. Like she's trapped in the walls. Glassy eyes following me around, waiting to see what I might do next.

I glance to the side, taking in the raw-wood cabinets and linoleum floors. The scent of strong coffee curling under my nose. Then my eyes land on the same table my mom and I sat at that morning, the very first morning we realized Natalie was gone: me picking at my cereal as the same smell of coffee soaked the air. Natalie used to sleep in, especially on Sundays, but then noon rolled around and it started to feel strange she hadn't come down.

I imagine my mother standing up, the squeak of her chair before she ascended the stairs and the gentle noise of her knuckles as they knocked on the door. It was such a timid sound it was almost embarrassing, like she thought of her own daughter as some curled-up viper ready to strike on the other side . . . but then there was no answer and the knock grew louder, more incessant. Her voice urgent as she commanded her to come out.

Next came that scream, Natalie's name. The sharp clatter as she dropped her mug on the ground and me slinking up the steps to find my mother alone in an empty bedroom. No movement at all except for the gentle dance of the curtains, a wide-open window letting in the wind.

A *beep* from the coffee maker cuts through the thought, the pot in front of me filled to the brim. I blink away the memory and fill up my mug, blowing on the steam before glancing out the back window, taking in the gaping hole on the porch. The wood is clearly rotten out there, the boards simply buckling after years of neglect, and I turn away quickly, stifling my judgment before making my way into the living room and lowering myself onto the couch.

I bring the mug to my lips, taking a small sip before I look to the side. The shoebox is still there, the roll of old film sitting beside it, so I put the mug down and grab the film next, twisting it slow between my fingers.

I open the box, ready to place the film inside when a muffled sound steals my attention.

"I don't care, Alan. You should have asked me first."

I freeze, staring in the direction of my mother's voice traveling through the thin walls. She's clearly awake, on the phone with my father, and while I know I shouldn't eavesdrop like this, I'm way too curious to turn away now, so I drop in the film and slide the box shut before making my way to the other side of the room.

"Yes, but this is my *house now,"* she continues as I creep into the hallway, red runner lolling like a tongue in a throat. The door to the guest room is closed, a thin ribbon of light spilling onto the carpet, and I hold my breath as I lean in close, acutely aware that they're talking about me.

"I know," she says, her shadow pacing across the crack in the door. *"But I don't need her here."*

I clench my jaw, a familiar hurt bubbling up from the depths of my chest as this entire encounter calls to mind that summer they separated. The way my mother would routinely retreat to her bedroom, the quiet click of the door as I stood still in the hall. Her seeping soft sobs I would pretend not to hear.

The way I immediately started to curl in on myself while Natalie did the opposite and started to lash out.

"I told you already," she adds. *"I can take care of myself."*

I twist around, eager to get away before she can hang up and find me. Then I sneak up the stairs, getting dressed quickly before charging back into the living room and grabbing the shoebox, making my way toward the front door.

CHAPTER 8

It's still early, just past eight, a golden glow illuminating the water and a quiet stillness as the world wakes up.

I'm back in my car, my phone returned to its spot in the cup holder as a map once again leads me through the streets of my past. After twenty minutes of driving, the voice in my speakers has announced my arrival, so I pull into an empty spot on the street as I read the sign of the small shop opposite my pollen-caked windshield. Claxton is still small, still relatively old-fashioned, and although chain restaurants are now erected where mom-and-pops used to be, the corner store I used to go to for candy replaced by a Starbucks that looks oddly out of place, a few of the original shops still seem to be in business, including the one I'm sitting in front of right now.

I put my car in park before opening the shoebox and grabbing the film, stepping onto the asphalt, and walking inside.

"Hi," I say, making my way toward a man tinkering with something behind a counter. The place smells like hot metal and dust and I smile as I approach, a collection of cameras and technical equipment taking up every inch of the wall. "I was hoping I could get this developed."

I push the film across the counter, watching as he grabs it and deposits the roll in his palm.

"I read online that you specialize in that," I add. "Better than a drugstore or something."

The man stays quiet, two rodent eyes magnified behind his wire-rimmed glasses.

"This is old," he says at last, twisting it between his fingers like he's found something sacred. "*Really* old."

"Yeah," I say, nodding. Thinking about the pictures in that box, twenty-two years, and realizing, for the first time, that it might actually be impossible to recover these now. I have no idea how long film keeps, what the images would even look like if we could get them developed. "It got lost in some clutter, but I guess I was wondering, I was *hoping*—"

"Sure, yeah, I can do it," the man says, squinting as he pulls at the tape. "It'll take some time, though."

"That's fine," I say, glancing at my watch. "A couple hours?"

"Try a couple days," he says. "Maybe a week."

"A *week*?"

"You have to be delicate with film this fragile. Make sure it doesn't get damaged in the process."

I stare at him, chewing impatiently on the side of my lip.

"It might need some color correction if the dyes have broken down," he continues. "The pictures might be faded, or grainy, or—"

"Okay," I say, cutting him off. Realizing that time isn't really the issue; that unfortunately, right now, I have all the time in the world. "That's fine. Just do what you can."

"All right," the man says, slipping the roll somewhere out of sight. This place is a mess, no obvious attempts at organization, and I try to swallow the twist of discomfort in my chest as I watch the film disappear, the anxiety of trusting a stranger with what could very well be some of my sister's final moments making my palms itch with fear. "Just leave your number and I'll call when it's ready."

I nod, jotting down the digits before forcing myself to walk back to the car. Then I slide inside and crank the engine, eyeing the clock as it blinks back to life. It's only 8:20, the entire day, the entire *month,* stretching out before me like a long walk to the gallows, and I know I'm not ready to go home yet. I'm not ready to spend the afternoon sitting in my bedroom, avoiding my mom. Still bitter about the things I just overheard, an entire lifetime of resentment building as the two of us dance around our problems in that way we've always done—except this time, without the benefit of eight hundred miles of distance between us. I need to keep busy, I need to *do* something, and I glance over at the passenger seat, that box of old photos still propped up on the fabric.

Then I lean over and peer inside, the picture of Natalie and that grape resting on top.

CHAPTER 9

I'm bumping down a dirt lane thirty minutes later, pinpricks of light streaming through the trees giving the day an ethereal shine. After a few more miles of nothing but water on either side of the road, I reach a fork with a single wooden sign carved with the words GALLOWAY FARM pointing to the right.

I follow the sign, feeling the tires of my Corolla kicking up dust as I turn.

It wasn't a deliberate decision, coming here. I can't identify the exact moment I decided to punch the name into the GPS; the instant my hands gripped the wheel, taking all the proper turns. It was more of a knowing, a chest-deep awareness as soon as I glanced at that picture and took a long look at my sister's expression. A desperate desire to keep that girl close uncurling in my stomach like the stretching tendrils of a wild vine.

I bounce down a few more miles of road now, the live oaks on either side forming a twisted bridge with their branches; streamers of Spanish moss like a decorative archway beckoning me in.

It's a gorgeous sight, just like I remember, although it feels a little unkempt now, a little neglected. Patches of overgrown grass peppered with weeds; algae floating across dollops of marshland, a boggy breadcrumb trail leading up to the creek itself. Just like how my house had looked smaller when I first pulled up, how certain places of the past seem to shrivel with time, the nostalgic glow of Galloway has been slightly snuffed out after my years away and I can't help but wonder if it always looked like this, if my memory had simply buffed out the harsh edges, or if it has more recently descended into a state of disrepair.

I approach an ivy-clad fence with a house now visible in the distance. It's giant and white, two stories overlooking the water and a wraparound porch with a row of gliders rocking gently for no one. There's what looks like a small guesthouse to the left, essentially a miniature version of the main house beside it, and a shed off to the right made of old, chipped wood.

I creep up the drive, a produce garden tucked away to one side and the vineyard in view just behind it, perfect rows of muscadine grapes hanging loose and messy on the vines. There's a line of trees on the edge of it all, a swath of forest that looks wild and untamed, and a single clothesline stretched across the lawn. Drying shirts swaying gently in the breeze.

I ease to a stop, realizing, with a sense of dumb awareness, that I have no idea if this place is even open. My mom said they're still in business, but it's private property . . . which I'm currently trespassing on. Someone *lives* here, clearly, and they must have heard my approaching car, seen the plume of disturbed dust in the distance, because just as I tap again on the gas, trying to find a spot to turn around, I watch as a man emerges through the door, jogging down the stairs to meet me out front.

I cuss under my breath, rolling down my window before plastering on a smile.

"Good morning," I say, my hands still gripped to the wheel. "I'm so sorry to disturb you."

"Morning," he says, looking at me with a puzzled stare. He's slightly older than me—late thirties, maybe; early forties at the latest—crow's-feet by his temples and a head full of hair peppered with gray, though he's tan, handsome. A solid jaw and robin's-egg eyes the same blue as the brightening sky. "You don't look like an Elijah."

"Sorry?" I ask, not understanding.

"You here for the job posting? Elijah McCrae?"

"Oh, no," I say. "I hate to disappoint, but that's not me."

"I wouldn't call this a disappointment," he says, smiling warmly. "What can I help you with?"

"I was just here to look around, but I didn't realize how early it is. I doubt you're even open yet."

"We're not actually open to the public anymore," the man says, and I watch as he twists around, his palm rubbing his neck as his eyes land back on the house. "We stopped that a while back."

"Oh, I'm so sorry," I say again, cheeks flushing. Wondering how many times I can say the word *sorry* in the span of one minute.

"It's fine," he says. "It was just a lot of unnecessary maintenance. The owners, Marcia and Mitchell. They're getting a little too old for that."

"I'll just turn around then, get out of your hair—"

"What's your name?" he asks, cutting me off. Head cocked to the side like he's trying to place me, this uninvited visitor who just barged into his place of work.

I watch as he leans his forearms against my window and I glance down, taking in their chestnut brown with a spray of blond hair bleached from the sun. He's wearing jeans and a gray T-shirt, tan work boots that look well past their prime.

"Claire," I say at last.

"Claire," he repeats, rolling my name around on his tongue like he's trying to taste it, savor the sound for a little bit longer. "Nice to meet you, Claire. I'm Liam."

He thrusts his right arm through the window and I grab his hand and give it a shake. It's rough, calluses peppering his palm like malignant growths. His fingernails are dirty, but the rest of him is clean, and I get the sense that's just a part of him. Soil pushed into the cracks of his skin, the land leaving a permanent mark.

"I'd be happy to show you around," he continues. "Since our friend Elijah appears to be a no-show."

I glance at the clock. It's not even nine.

"He was supposed to be here at seven," Liam says, reading my mind. "We get an early start around here. Best to beat the heat."

"I really don't want to impose—" I say, gesturing again to the road behind me.

"Not at all," he says. "Park over there and I'll walk you around."

I follow his finger as he points to the side of the house and I nod, smile, rolling up my window before pulling into the makeshift spot. I'm grateful for the invitation, it's a kind gesture, but it still feels like I'm intruding, charging into someone else's home before nine o'clock in the morning. Nevertheless, I am in the South. A part of the country where manners matter, almost ad nauseam. Turning him down at this point would feel even ruder than showing up in the first place, so I kill the engine, looking down at the picture on my passenger seat before folding it twice and stuffing it into my pocket.

Then I get out of the car, meeting Liam in front of the clothesline.

"Welcome to Galloway," he says as I approach, grinning with his arms spread open wide. "Founded in 1984, we grow and sell all kinds of produce, but we specialize in the grapes. Have you ever had one of these?"

He walks me over to the nearest trellis and I look down, noticing the clusters hanging heavy from the vines. They're muscadines, large and plum purple to the point of appearing a bloody black, and I watch as he picks one at random, squeezing it gently between his fingers.

"A few times," I say, nodding. Watching as he sticks it into his mouth, gnawing aggressively before spitting out the seed. Then he gestures to the vine, motioning for me to take one, too, so I follow his lead and pluck my own. A little red orb that looks like a speckled marble, a swollen eye.

"They're about ready to be picked," Liam says. "Hence the need for our friend, Elijah."

I push the berry into my mouth, the skin tough between my teeth. It bursts with a saccharine gush that coats my throat and I close my eyes, my body immediately transported back to that summer. To the way Natalie used to come home with a giant bag of scuppernongs we'd eat on the dock, popping grapes like candy before sucking on the seeds and spitting them out. Counting ripples in water like rings in a tree.

Somehow, I had forgotten all about that.

"They're usually not ready until August," Liam continues, his voice forcing me back to the present. "But we've had an exceptionally hot spring. Some are ready now; the rest will be in a few weeks."

"How many workers do you have?"

He gestures to himself, a dirty finger digging into his chest.

"I'm the main caretaker," he says. "I tend to the place year-round, everything that requires real knowledge of the vine. We bring on one more seasonal worker in the summer to help with the harvest."

"That's it?" I ask, looking back at the vineyard. The place is easily a dozen acres, the rows extending so far into the distance it's hard to see the end of them.

"That's it," he repeats. "Harvesting is a job, for sure, but it's fairly monotonous. Doesn't require a lot of skill, to be honest. Just two working hands."

I open my mouth, suddenly compelled to tell him about Natalie and her time here, ask what happened to the high school kids they used to hire for cheap. After so many years of stuffing her memory deep down in my chest, of never uttering a word of her existence, I can feel the temptation to talk about her gurgling up my throat like bile, urgent and sharp . . . but then I close it again, thinking twice. Remembering how that went during the years I still lived here, seven long years before I graduated and ran away to the city. Thanks to the trial and sensational headlines, the name *Natalie Campbell* tended to produce an uncomfortable reaction: awkward silences, a swell of apologies. Good conversation suddenly stilted because I knew, from that moment on, that every time the person I was talking to looked at me, they weren't actually seeing me at all. Not really, anyway. Not anymore. They were seeing her. They were thinking of her and her final moments, wondering how it all played out. Curious about what kind of girl would foster a relationship with a man ten years her senior; what she could have done to deserve what she got.

"It's a pretty sweet gig," Liam continues, and I direct my attention back toward him as I realize he probably wouldn't know, anyway. I doubt he even worked here back then. "We used to hire a handful of seasonals, give 'em each a couple hours a week, but now, with only one, we can put them up in the guesthouse. Have them work longer days."

He points over to the cottage in the corner, the one that looks like a miniature replica of the main house behind us. It's only one story, and I can tell it's quite small, but still, it's gorgeous, like a boutique dollhouse. Perfectly square and entirely white; a small porch in the front, facing the water, and a single glider angled to the view.

"I ran the numbers a while back," he continues. "It turned out to be cheaper, believe it or not. Got the job done a lot faster, too."

"Your workers stay *there*?" I ask, impressed with the digs.

"Free food and housing." Liam nods. "Plus, five hundred bucks a week."

"How long does harvesting take?"

"About a month, give or take."

"Two thousand dollars to spend a month on a vineyard," I say, doing the math in my head. "That is a sweet gig."

"Apparently Elijah didn't think so." Liam grins at me, nudging my shoulder as we keep walking. "We've got goats, chickens," he continues, gesturing to a coop behind the house I didn't notice when I drove in. "Fresh eggs every morning. The garden has just about every fruit and vegetable you can think of. Herbs over there."

"Why would you ever leave?" I wonder out loud as I take the place in. My initial impression from the car, that sense of neglect, has been replaced entirely in the ten minutes I've been here. Instead, the place feels loved, lived in. A well-worn cardigan peppered with holes.

I look at Liam, waiting for a response that never arrives.

"What do you think about hiring me?" I ask, the words tumbling out before I can stop them as my gaze darts back to the guesthouse, my mind wandering to time spent on that porch.

A mug of coffee in the mornings while the sun slowly rises over the water. A glass of wine in the evenings as the sweat of a day's work dries salt on the skin.

"I'm here for the summer without much to do."

Liam turns to me, finally, and I can see the cogs spinning slowly, this stranger sizing me up as we stand side by side. I don't know much about farms, or grapes for that matter, but ever since overhearing my mother this morning, admonishing my father for bringing me here, I've been debating if I should actually stay. She made it abundantly clear that she doesn't need me—though I can't go back to my apartment, either, not without giving back the three thousand dollars I desperately need—but *here,* at Galloway, I could have a place of my own and a slow Southern summer. I could keep busy, spend time outside, and work with my hands. Not only that, but I could earn an extra two grand *on top* of the sublet money.

That's five thousand dollars to get me through these next couple of months. My first real chunk of money since I quit.

"Do you have any experience working on a vineyard?" Liam asks.

I think about going back home, having to walk by Natalie's bedroom night after night.

Lying on my comforter, trying to sleep. The nightmares growing progressively worse and the memories lurking like mice in the walls.

"No," I admit, remembering that day we all came here, little blue bucket clenched tight in my palms. "But I do have two working hands."

I hold them up and smile, watching as Liam grins in return.

"Well played."

"I work hard," I continue, a sudden urgency in my voice as I realize I want this, badly. So much more than I initially thought. "I'm a fast learner. And I wake up early. Clearly."

I shoot him a self-conscious smile, hoping he can't tell how desperate I am.

"Let me run it by Mitchell," he says at last, chewing his lip. "Give me two minutes."

He gestures back to the house and I nod, watching as he jogs back up the stairs before disappearing through the screen door with a slap. Then I wander over to the water as I wait, letting the breeze rustle my hair. My hand venturing over to my pocket before digging out the picture folded up in my jeans.

I open it slowly, my finger trailing down the crease cutting clean across Natalie's throat. A faint sting in my eyes as I take in her smile. Back at our house, all her good moments have been painted over with the reality of what happened like an antique too tarnished to see the beauty beneath—but *here,* in this picturesque place we so briefly shared, the memories of her are still happy, still good.

Here, in my mind, she's still alive.

I close my eyes, inhaling deeply. Finally feeling calm for the first time in days. Then I hear a door open behind me and I twist around, expecting to see Liam back on the porch—but instead, it's a different man with a shock of gray hair and a long, drawn face. Even from this distance, I can see the curve of his cheekbones, crabapple round and dotted with sunspots like the flesh has started to rot. He's older, certainly, but his bone structure is still so deftly defined his face looks like a statue cut from cold, hard stone.

He walks to the edge of the stairs and peers down, both hands shoved deep in his pockets.

"I hear you're here for a job," he says, and I immediately understand that I'm looking at Mitchell, the primary owner of Galloway Farm. His voice is rough and gravelly, a bullfrog croak that hints at a youth full of swallowing smoke.

I peg him in his sixties, which makes sense, considering this place is forty years old.

"Yes, sir," I say. That word, *sir,* slipping from my lips without my conscious permission. I don't know why I said it, why I felt the need to address him like that, but something about the man commands attention. Some hidden aura that seems to have made everything around us come to a stop: the birds, the wind, all of it suddenly nervous and still like the world itself is holding its breath.

Or maybe it's just my old Southern upbringing; that programmed politeness peeking out from some long-dormant place.

"I'm Claire."

I swallow, purposefully leaving out my last name, and I wonder if he's going to ask me for it. I wonder, if I tell him, if he'd recognize it at all. Surely he wouldn't—he's probably employed hundreds of workers over the years—and we stand still for a second, my body rigid as he takes me in. I'm suddenly self-conscious under his scrutiny and I start to fidget, my fingers digging into my palms, until slowly, he smiles, and I feel my shoulders relax a little.

"Claire," he repeats, the soft sound of my name on his tongue melting the tension I've been carrying around like a puddle of wax in the searing sun. "Welcome to the Farm."

CHAPTER 10

I'm back at Galloway by the end of the day, this time with both of my bags by my side.

Mitchell had requested the afternoon to get ready, suggesting I come back after dinner to get settled, and I had agreed. Eyes darting to Liam as he watched through the window, feeling a little dizzy at how quickly things changed.

"Are you sure you'll be all right?" I had asked my mother, loitering on the porch as the sun started to set, the live oak's large branches casting shapes on the lawn. In the late-afternoon light, they almost looked like fingers, arched and arthritic. An outstretched hand hovering over us both.

"Oh, sure," she said, flicking her wrist like I was a gnat she was shooing away. "As long as you're good to drive through the night."

I hadn't even been home long enough to unpack—less than twenty-four hours, in fact—a realization that made me feel dimly guilty the second I stepped into my bedroom, eyeing my bags in their same spots on the floor. Still, my mom believed me when I told her I was going back to the city; that something came up at work I couldn't turn down. I didn't want to admit where I was really going. That I was staying in the state, barely an hour away. The thought of another night in that house enough to make my skin itch, my past a rash that would never heal. Of course, I considered the fact that I might bump into her somewhere around town—at a coffee shop, maybe; in the aisles of the grocery store. A month is a long time to be hanging around, and Galloway is only forty-five minutes away . . . but then I remembered she rarely leaves the house.

My mom's practically a recluse, choosing to exist inside her bubble of the past instead of real life. Besides, she can't drive. She's essentially housebound.

"And your neighbor said she'd check in?" I continued, glancing down at her leg as I second-guessed, once again, if I was doing the right thing.

"Claire, I'll be fine," she said as she crossed her arms tight, an unexpected sadness settling over my shoulders, because even though I knew she wouldn't ask me to stay, it stung that she was letting me go so easily. The child in me apparently still starved for affection, a burning thirst that could never be quenched.

I'm standing in front of the Galloway main house, twilight casting everything in a yellow glow. It looks so strange outside, the goldenrod sky reflecting off the water; goliath trees covered in moss and dripping vines visible in the distance. The air is bloated and still, an eerie stagnation like before a tornado, and I grab my phone out of my pocket, snapping a few pictures before I pick up my things and walk up the porch steps, realizing I'm not exactly sure what to do next. I know they're expecting me, I assume I should knock, so I rap a few times on the door and stand still as I wait, the sound of footsteps echoing from somewhere deep inside the house.

I stare down at the door, squinting in the dusk as I take in the brass knob. A cursive *M* embellished on the surface that looks like an old, weathered antique.

I reach out to touch it, the pad of my finger drawn to the curves, but then the door suddenly swings open and my attention snaps up, my eyes on Liam on the other side of the screen.

"Welcome back," he says, one shoulder leaning against the frame, and I feel an inexplicable relief at his presence. I barely know the man, but there's something about him that feels familiar. An inherent comfort in a friendly face. "Come on in," he continues, opening the screen door and gesturing for me to follow. "Marcia and Mitchell are just inside."

I step into the house and let him lead me to the foyer, stealing glances at various rooms as we walk. Despite the grand exterior, the inside of the house is somewhat dated, the way older homes usually are, but still, it's nice. Cozy. Patterned wallpaper with little white daises and doily coasters on shiny wood desks. It smells like masked aging, the sensory equivalent of slathering makeup over liver spots, dots of concealer under baggy brown eyes.

I catch a whiff of burnt dust and some kind of citrus. Antiseptic and hand cream, lavender and lime, and then the hallway spills into the living room and I eye a late-middle-aged woman slouched in a chair in the corner. Her eyes are closed, one long braid draped over her shoulder, and I stop in my tracks, standing at what feels like a safe distance as I take in her hands folded into a neat little knot in her lap. Her skin looks tissue-paper thin, speckled like a sparrow's egg, and I feel a twinge of something strange deep in my chest.

Discomfort, overt voyeurism, even though I know I was invited to be here.

"Tea?"

I twist around, spotting Mitchell as he walks out of the kitchen with two steaming mugs clenched in his hands. He thrusts one in my direction without waiting for me to respond, so I take it, not wanting to be rude, even though it feels a little too hot for tea. My skin still slick from the outside air.

"Let's sit over there," he says. "Get to know each other a bit."

I follow, taking a seat in the chair opposite his.

"This is Marcia," he says, gesturing to the woman as her thin lids fly open. It makes me jump, the sudden movement, and I watch as her neck slowly turns, cloudy eyes blinking like they're fighting their way through a blanket of fog.

"Hi, Marcia," I say, slightly taken aback by her appearance. It might be because she's seemingly just woken up, her eyes still coated in that miasma of sleep, but while Mitchell looks quite good for his age, Marcia appears to be somewhat ill. "Thank you for inviting me into your home."

I smile, waiting for a response that never arrives.

"Where are you from?" Mitchell asks as Marcia blinks at me again, agonizingly slow. There's a certain emptiness in her eyes, two pinprick pupils with the hue around them a lackluster gray like all her color is fading away.

I force myself to turn back toward him, trying to decide how to respond.

"New York," I say at last. "Manhattan."

"Manhattan," he repeats, a low whistle whining through his front teeth. "And what brought a city girl like you to our little vineyard on Ladmadaw Island?"

"Oh," I say, twisting my hands around the mug, feeling the pinch of warmth on my palms. I don't want to go into the whole story—my mom, her accident; finding those pictures of Natalie here and feeling like an intruder in my own home—so I strip the answer down to its most basic truth. "I needed a change of scenery. For the summer, you know. Nice, open space. I don't get much of that in the city."

"Change of scenery," he repeats before lowering his voice, leaning in close. "In my experience, that usually means you're running from something."

He lifts his eyebrows like the two of us are sharing some kind of secret and I feel another flush deep in my chest, a warm sensation like this man somehow understands me even though I know we've only just met.

"It's nothing like that," I lie, attempting a smile, though he's still quiet, still staring, like he's genuinely waiting for me to explain.

"I grew up nearby," I say, looking down at the mug in my hands. Steam is pouring from the surface of the liquid and while it still seems too hot to drink, I'm suddenly eager for something to do, to have a reason for my lips to stop moving and toss the conversational ball back in his court. "About forty-five minutes away."

I lift the mug and take a small sip, wincing when I feel my tongue touch the scalding water.

"And what do you do in New York," Mitchell asks, "that lets you take the whole month off?"

I look back at him, realizing I'm not sure how to respond to that, either. Just like how talk of my sister invites unwanted questions, pitying looks followed by a long, dead pause, telling people I'm a journalist—especially a journalist on the hunt for a story—can often dredge up opinions I'd rather not know.

"This and that," I say, internally cringing at the terrible response. "I like to dabble around."

"Dabble around," he repeats, smiling.

"Why don't we let Claire get settled in for the night," Liam interjects, and I spin around in my chair, registering him leaning against the kitchen counter. Biting softly into a peach. "She has a big day tomorrow. Learning the ropes."

I turn back toward Mitchell, his inquisitive eyes still trained on me. He stays silent for another few seconds before he nods in resignation, standing up and pulling at a silver ring on his jeans.

"Your key," he says, detaching one in the middle before thrusting it in my direction. "This will get you into the guesthouse."

I hold out my hand, the subtle weight of it as he drops it onto my palm, ushering a physical relief into my chest, because this isn't *just* a key, this tangible thing that's finally mine. Instead, it's a place to live, it's five thousand dollars.

It's a summer away from both the city and home; a chance to reset in a place I once shared with my sister. Maybe even a chance to *heal,* like Ryan had said.

"Thank you," I say, looking next at my mug, barely touched. I don't want to be rude, leaving it behind virtually undrunk, so I down as much as I can, the hot pinch of the liquid like nails on my throat.

I stand up, placing the half-empty cup on the table.

"I appreciate the opportunity, truly. And I'll stay out of your way, I promise."

"Oh, please, no," Mitchell says as he rests his hand on the small of my back, guiding my body onto the porch. "I want you to think of this as your home now, too."

CHAPTER 11

Sleep consumes me, the warm embrace of it sudden and unexpected after leaving the porch and walking to the guesthouse,
the night thick and heavy like velvet plush. Without any streetlights
or nearby houses, there had been no ambient light to lead the way.
No obtrusive noises like the honking of horns, the backfiring of
cars. The music drifting in from some nearby party or the whispers
of neighbors, voices muffled and low. Instead, all I could hear was
a cloud of cicadas screaming in the trees, the occasional flip of a fin
coming from the direction of the water.

An entirely different kind of silence, both foreign and familiar
at the exact same time.

It's morning now, six A.M., hazy light streaming through two
tiny windows and flecks of dust floating aimlessly in the sunbeams.
I wake up groggy, unsure of where I am, one of those disheveled
arousals that's immediately disorienting—and then it hits me, like
recalling a dream.

I'm in the guesthouse at Galloway Farm, my new home for the next month.

I sit up slow, blinking a few times as I think about how I had pushed the key into the door last night, twisting it slowly before letting myself in. The way my body had beelined straight to the bed, collapsing hard onto sharp metal springs. I hadn't realized how tired I'd been, how much of a toll the last few days had taken on both my body and mind. I could keep sleeping, I *want* to keep sleeping, but the cabin is growing warm with the mounting sun and I can already feel my skin getting slick with sweat so I climb out of bed and look down at the mattress, the damp outline of my body caked to the sheets.

I glance at my phone on the side table and reach for it quickly, a jerk reaction, until I notice the exclamation point in the upper right corner.

I have no service. Not even a single blinking bar.

I drop my hands; defeated, but not entirely surprised. Google Maps had worked to get me here, but the service was unsteady once I got on the island. This place is small, rustic. Smaller than Claxton, if that's even possible. I don't actually recall seeing any phone lines on my way in and I make a mental note to ask Liam about the internet the next time I see him.

Surely they have Wi-Fi. I can get connected with that.

I put my phone back down before walking to the windows and pushing them open, the wind whipping off the water still stifling hot. Then I head into the kitchenette, the distance between everything only a handful of feet. The guesthouse is nice, but old, and undeniably tiny. It's even smaller than my apartment back in the city but I can't deny the view is better. I can see the marsh through the windows; bright green reeds and curtains of moss swaying gently in the barely there breeze. A runway of dock, long and lean and stained from the sun.

Then I scan the kitchen, taking in all the things Mitchell left me to use.

There's a knife block on the counter, a container of utensils right next to the stove. I notice a percolator in the corner and move to fill it up with hot water from the tap; then I locate the coffee in a cabinet and spoon some into the filter, sifting through a few more cupboards while it brews. I eventually find what I'm looking for: a collection of mugs, all ceramic and white, and I grab one at random before walking to the fridge and opening the door. Then I catalogue the contents: a glass jug of milk, a dozen fresh eggs. A loaf of seeded bread and all the typical condiments; a bowl of bright berries that look freshly picked.

It's all so welcoming, so homey, so harshly at odds with those first few hours at home with my mother, and I can't help but smile as I imagine Mitchell stocking the place with all the necessities. The mental image so genuine and warm.

I close the fridge, filling my mug and easing my body onto the floor, legs crossed as I start unpacking my bags. I load some clothes into a small dresser before hanging a few shirts in the closet beside it. I put away my toiletries, dropping my toothbrush in the little glass holder; shampoo in the shower, face wash perched on the edge of the sink. I unpack my laptop next, positioning it on the small desk opposite my bed and plugging it into the nearest outlet. Then I fish the picture of Natalie out of my pocket and open the desk drawer, getting ready to drop it in along with my notebook when something inside catches my attention.

I lean down, reading the sentence scratched into the far-right corner.

Lily was here.

I run my fingers across the words, the surface smooth from years of use, as I wonder, vaguely, who Lily might be. Then I place my things inside and slide the drawer shut, chalking it up to just a piece of old furniture. There are a million different people who could have left that mark; a million different reasons for why it could be there. Maybe the desk was bought secondhand, passed down from a friend. Or maybe Lily was a worker, just like me, who decided, in a flash, to scratch her name into something as she unpacked her things.

Once my bags are empty, I find cleaning supplies in the kitchenette and wipe the place down, the morning light emphasizing the finest glimmer of dust on everything. I don't have much to unpack, but by the time I'm settled, the coffee is gone and the cottage is sweltering, the summer sun beating down hard on the roof.

I stand in the center of the room and dab the sweat from my lip, hands on my hips as I survey my surroundings. There has to be air-conditioning in here. I can sense it, just barely, the faintest draft breaking up the stillness of the air around me. It didn't feel terrible when I stumbled in last night, but at the same time, I had slept on top of the sheets. I was bone-tired, too exhausted to be roused awake by anything—that, and I'm so accustomed to my apartment in the city, the constant mugginess that never really goes away. I'm used to existing in a state of general discomfort, but here, in the South, the heat is something else entirely. I've almost forgotten how oppressive it is, how exhausting, a siphon sucking the energy straight from my veins. Especially as we creep deeper into the summer, the temperature ticking into the triple digits, I know I'm in for a miserable month if I can't get a little movement in here.

Suddenly, I think of the dust. All those motes I could see swirling around in the light; the faint film of it in the kitchen before I wiped the counters clean.

I drop down to the floor and survey the walls, noticing an air vent partially obscured by the back leg of my bed. Then I crawl toward it, pushing my bed to the side so the vent is fully exposed before curling my fingers around the edge and jiggling the cover.

It pops loose, a gush of cold air pushing its way out. It's absolutely filthy inside, inches of gray grime accumulated on each side. The cover slats are clogged with it, which is probably why nothing was getting through before, so I stand up and make my way back into the kitchen, wetting a paper towel before running it over the metal. Then I walk back to the vent and start wiping the dust from the inside walls. I lean in farther, as far as I can go, until my hand bumps against something shoved deep in the back. Something thick and hard with a fabric cover and deckle-edged paper.

It's a book, unmistakably. There's a book in there.

I crane my neck, squinting as I look into the hole. I can make out the shadow of it cowering like an animal trapped in a cave; some nocturnal thing curled up in the dark. Then I wrap my fingers around the edges, grime and cobwebs clinging to the pages and stretching slowly as I pull it out. It's old and worn, a deep maroon with no title at all, and I blow on it carefully, a plume of dust erupting from the fabric before I brush away what's left with the towel.

I part the covers, the gentle crack of the spine indicating that it hasn't been opened in quite some time. Then I flip to the very first page, eyeing the lines filled with cursive. Sweeping strokes that feel elegant and old-fashioned.

I guess I'll start with my name, Marcia, because most days, my name feels like the only thing that's mine.

I stop reading, my eyes hovering blankly over the page. This isn't a book, then. It's a diary. It's *Marcia's* diary. Marcia, Mitchell's wife. The woman I met last night, sunken-in and ambiguously ill. I assumed the book was old based on its appearance: the tattered cover and delicate pages, brittle like bones and crumbling at the edges. Some of the ink is so faded I can barely make out the words, but the date in the upper right-hand corner confirms it for me.

November 9, 1983.

This first entry is forty-one years old, when the woman next door was still just a girl.

I look down at the words, continuing to read.

Technically, it's Marcia Rayburn, and even though someone else gave me my name, I'm still the only person I know who has it so I cling to it like I bestowed it myself.

I pause again, hesitating as I attempt to swallow the discomfort lodged deep in my throat. This is a clear invasion of privacy. I should put this down, put it back in the vent—or, better yet, I should return it. Give it to Mitchell and let him know what I found. I'm sure they would love to see it, it's probably been lost for decades at this point . . . but at the same time, curiosity overcomes me. I can't help myself.

I keep going.

I'm seventeen years old. Almost eighteen, actually, in just a few weeks. I can't wait to turn eighteen because that means I'm finally an adult. That means, at last, I can do what I want. My parents act like they own me now: my body, my time, all of it strictly watched and regulated. They control who I see, what I read, so in a lot of ways, this little book is my tiny rebellion.

    It's exciting, isn't it? Keeping a secret.

I smile, my weight sinking deeper into my legs on the floor. Those final few lines sounding so much like my sister.

The truth is, I got this diary because I have another secret. A secret for my secrets, I guess you could say, only this other secret might

burst right out of me if I don't tell someone soon. And I can't tell
someone, I can't tell <u>anyone</u>, so this feels like the safest solution.
A way to get the words out while still keeping them to myself.

I turn the page, surprised to feel a little lump in my throat. The
buzz of the text pushing me forward, my curiosity suddenly too big
to contain. I realize now, somehow for the first time, that Marcia
didn't speak a single word last night. She just sat there, eyes wide
and blank, staring as Mitchell and I talked just beside her. I have
no idea what she sounds like, I don't have a voice to overlay on top
of her words, so instead, I use Natalie's, imagining all those little
mutinies that made her feel so alive.

Pushing up that window at night, shimmying her way down
that branch in the dark.

I met a boy. There, I said it! I can't stop smiling as I write these
words. But he's not just any boy. He is THE boy. The boy of my
dreams, but my parents wouldn't approve of him AT ALL.

My smile widens at the teenage dramatics: AT ALL, written in
caps, underlined five times for emphasis.

His name is Mitchell, the diary continues, and it feels so strange
to picture my hosts like this. They're older now, weathered skin
and watering eyes, but Marcia's words make me realize they weren't
always that way.

In the beginning, they were kids. Just two kids who stumbled
in love.

And here, dear diary, is how we met.

CHAPTER 12

It was a cool evening. Cool for Draper, at least, screen door cracked to let in the breeze as Marcia recited her scripture slowly in the living room. Pressed dress grazing the skin of her ankles, hair draped down to the small of her back.

"Ye should be humble, and be submissive, and gentle," she said as she attempted to keep her voice balanced and calm. "Easy to be entreated; full of patience and long-suffering."

Her dad was in a rocking chair to her left, hands clasped tight as he closed his eyes and nodded gently, the familiar words a silky balm soothing some damaged part of his soul.

"Being temperate in all things," she continued, ignoring the nervous beating in her neck she hoped her father couldn't see. Instead, she focused on the tick of the clock on the wall like a metronome, holding her steady. Keeping her still. Her mother in the kitchen, scrubbing the dishes. The gentle clink of the plates and the familiar flick of a candle flame breathing softly in the barely there breeze. "Being diligent in keeping the commandments of God at all times."

"Good," her father said, opening his eyes. "That's very good, Marcia."

She smiled, raised her gaze slightly, that gush of pleasure in her chest leaking out slowly, filling her up. She hated that feeling; her latent desire for approval. No matter how hard she tried to tamp it down, keep it contained, it always reared up when she heard those words, *very good,* the need to receive them as real and necessary as food, as water. The very sustenance that sustained her hammered into her slowly, deliberately, since as early as she could recall.

Ye should be humble, and be submissive, and gentle.
Easy to be entreated; full of patience and long-suffering.

"Go ahead and get ready for bed," her father said next, jerking his neck to the stairs. Then she watched as he took off his glasses, those thick black rims that darkened his eyes, and rubbed the lenses against his shirt, one by one, before putting them back on. "Don't forget to say your prayers."

It wasn't even dark out, but of course, she nodded, closing the book and slipping it back into its hallowed spot on the shelf. Then she ducked into the kitchen and gave her mother a peck before ascending the carpeted steps as quickly and quietly as she possibly could. Her heartbeat hard in her neck, hot blood rushing like a river in her ears.

Slipping into her bedroom and twisting the lock on the door behind her, a quiet click she hoped her father couldn't hear.

Two hours later, she was on the sidewalk, walking quickly through the brisk night air. Her parents were asleep, they kept early hours, and it was dark, finally, but only just. The darkness didn't bother

her, though; she was only a few blocks from her destination, anyway. She had lived in this bubble of South Carolina her entire life. She had these streets memorized, could probably walk them blind. Her school was two blocks south of here; her church, four blocks east. It was a small community, tightly knit, which was precisely part of the problem.

If she ran into anyone she knew out here, anyone she recognized, her parents would surely find out in the morning.

A flashing marquee signaled her arrival and she walked up to the box office with practiced confidence, forcing her chin to stay parallel to the ground.

"One for *Romeo and Juliet,* please."

She pushed over two rumpled bills as the clerk slipped her the ticket; then she hurried into the theater, found a seat in the back. Waited for the lights to dim and the darkness to descend and the screen to light up with forbidden stories of love and passion; violence and death.

Temperate in all things, she thought, the words rearing up uninvited like a stranger was sitting in the row behind her, leaning forward. Whispering it softly into her ear. This certainly wasn't temperate; of course she knew that. But the older she got, the more she felt herself starting to change. Starting to question things. Starting to wonder if she really believed the commandments that came trickling out of her mouth each night or if they were empty shells, drained of all meaning.

Starting to wonder if there was even a difference.

But if stories were a sin, she couldn't bring herself to care. It's not like she was drinking or doing drugs; she had never been with a boy, though she was embarrassed to admit that the thoughts were there. The fantasies bubbling up from the pit of her stomach every time she saw those movie stars on their promotional posters, the bands of boys on their vinyl covers. Bands she wasn't even allowed to listen to. This, in comparison, seemed so mild. A fleeting break from reality, a few hours of fiction.

What could possibly be the harm in that?

Still, she wouldn't dare tell her father. She knew how he felt about books and movies, music and art. The way those things polluted young minds, distracted them from the stuff that actually mattered. He didn't even believe in going to college, waxing on about the liberal brainwashing of America's youth.

He doth not dwell in unholy temples, she thought, the chisel picking away slowly at the supple edges of her pliable mind. *Neither can filthiness or anything which is unclean be received into the kingdom of God.*

She pushed the words out again, listening as the sound started to trickle out of the speakers. The glow of the screen reflecting back in her eyes. Then she smothered the guilt the way she had practiced so many times, snuffing it out like stomping down hard on a kindling flame, and began to lose herself in the unfolding story, tumbling slowly down the warm, black hole. Observing as two teenagers met behind masks, an illicit love beginning to bloom that was made so much sweeter by the fact that it was something forbidden. Star-crossed lovers doomed from the start.

She watched as Juliet ingested that vial of poison, plunged a dagger deep into her heart.

Would it be better to die, she wondered, *than not be allowed to live at all?*

Leaving the theater, it was the plume of smoke that caught her attention. It erupted from nowhere like a fat, hazy cloud and she coughed, hand waving, before glancing to the side at the person in the shadows. His body leaning hard against the brick wall.

"Excuse me," she said, a rare moment of nerve, but the boy just looked at her, subtly amused.

"You want a drag?"

He reached his arm out, handing her a cigarette that looked

hand-rolled, but she simply stared, mute. Eyes wide as if he were holding a gun.

"I don't smoke," she said at last.

"That's too bad."

He went back to it, those thick lips sucking it down. He had a mop of brown hair that was abnormally long; scruff on his cheeks like those pictures of hippies she used to see on the news. She knew bad things happened out there, out in other parts of the country; her parents didn't let her watch TV, of course, but she caught glimpses sometimes when she hid on the stairs. Besides, they told her all about the horrors of the world, the litany of things that could go wrong. They made sure she knew about violent men and the chaos they craved: a killer in California who left ciphers for the press, a guy in Chicago with bodies in his crawlspace. There was even a man named Ted who drove across the country, targeting young girls just like her. Still, all that seemed so far removed. Draper felt immune, bubble-wrapped, but the mere presence of this person before her felt like a sharp needle poke, the sphere of safety suddenly popping. The wide-open world bleeding its way in. And it should have scared her, she supposed, based on the way her father talked, but instead, she felt a little shiver of excitement trail its way up her spine.

A subtle curiosity, like finding a foreign coin in a handful of change.

"You shouldn't be out here this late by yourself," the man said, regarding her more carefully now. She listened to the crackle of his cigarette, the gentle exhale as he blew the smoke out. It smelled different, rancid, like the tobacco inside had started to decay. "It's not safe."

"I'll be fine," she said, her heartbeat picking up as his big brown eyes took her in. It felt like he was sizing her up, making some kind of calculation in his mind. A predator suddenly locked in on its prey.

"What's your name?"

She hesitated, arms stuck by her sides as she let him judge her the way men judged livestock at the county fair, lips licking as they assessed their worth. Why couldn't she walk away? She should be getting home. She needed to get back to her room, get tucked into bed, but for some reason, her shoes stayed planted on the ground beneath her like the soles themselves had fused into the concrete.

"Marcia," she said at last.

"Marcia," he repeated. "You're very pretty, Marcia. Especially those eyes."

She felt her cheeks flush hot and she crossed her arms, suddenly unsure of what to do with her hands.

"I get the feeling you don't hear that enough."

She tilted her head. He was older than her, certainly. Maybe late twenties, early thirties at the latest, and she realized, distantly, that this might be dangerous, the two of them alone in a cold, dark corner. But it was more of a suggestion than anything, one she quickly flicked away. Instead, she felt the static of excitement growing slowly, a crackling in her skin like someone, somewhere, had flipped a switch and her body had been awakened from some long-dormant slumber. Bundles of cells buzzing back to life.

"I'm Mitchell," he said, not waiting for her to ask.

"Mitchell," she repeated. "You're not from around here, are you, Mitchell?"

She didn't know why she said it, but there was something about him that was so different, so strange. Dirty jeans and a rumpled cream Henley, the open buttons at the top revealing a tuft of curly brown hair. His voice was gentle but rough, elusive but friendly, and she had the sudden urge to rip off her mask and let this stranger see her fully. Nobody had ever seen her fully before. She, herself, had never seen herself fully. And how could she? Her life, up until that point, had been one never-ending series of sameness. The same thing, day after day, like a movie with no plot. A book with the same words repeated across each page. And it was suffocating, really, the idea of this being *it*. The whole point of it all.

"I'm not from around anywhere," he said at last.

"How is that possible?"

He just shrugged, took another drag. But when he went to toss the roach onto the ground, stub the remainder of it out with his foot, she found herself stepping forward, her hand reaching out to touch his arm. Grabbing his wrist, taking it from him.

Letting the smoke fill her up as he watched in the dark.

CHAPTER 13

I jump at the sudden sound of knocking: a person outside, their fist hard on the door.

I had settled back into bed earlier, subconsciously moving from my spot on the floor as if my feet had developed a mind of their own. My eyes felt glued to the page before me; to Marcia's quaint cursive, her bleeding blue pen. Gentle loops and fluid strokes as my back sank deeper into the pillows, cracked-open spine perched against my propped-up knees.

I hear the knock again, more urgent this time, and it's as if the noise has jolted me from some sort of trance. I leap from the bed, shoving the diary beneath the sheets. I don't know why I hid it—it was a simple reflex, not even a conscious thought—but I do know that I've read enough of it by now for my interest to be piqued.

I don't want to give it up. I want to keep going.

I smooth down my shirt, run my hands through my hair, and open the door to find Mitchell standing on the other side.

"I hope I didn't wake you," he says, his eyes darting to the digital clock in the kitchen. Somehow, it's just past ten, and I'm suddenly self-conscious about him thinking me too languid, this woman he hired to keep his home running seemingly sleeping until its late morning.

"No," I say quickly, trying to orient myself. Feeling like I was just startled awake from some vast, vivid dream. I had been so consumed in Marcia's story, this illicit glimpse I had been given into these two people with whom I'm now sharing a home, I hadn't even noticed the hours tick by, though I can tell that the cottage feels cooler. The marsh is higher. "Not at all. I was just getting settled."

"I figured I'd show you the property," he says. "Go over your duties before it gets too hot."

"Sounds great," I say, plastering on a smile as I try to keep my thoughts from wandering back to the book. To the Mitchell I was just with, forty-one years younger: longer hair, slimmer frame, some spellbinding quality to him I caught the faintest glimpse of last night as he stood on the porch, assessing me slowly. "Just let me get dressed."

We start with the garden: romaine lettuce, mustard greens. Bell peppers in all colors and tomato plants that are practically my height, little red welts dotting the leaves like a rash.

"We grow all our own produce," Mitchell says, and I watch as he grabs a snap pea, breaking it from the stem before biting down with a satisfying crunch. "Herbs are over there. Berries in the corner. We'll need help with the weeds and watering."

"Sure," I say. "Simple enough."

"Make sure you harvest first thing in the morning," he directs. "If you neglect the crop, it'll die on the vine."

"Of course," I say, wondering if that was a subtle stab about the time.

"And help yourself to whatever you want," he continues. "Make a list of things you need from the store, but anything fresh, just take it from here."

"Oh, I can do my own shopping—" I start to say, but Mitchell cuts me off.

"I head to town every day to deliver the produce. Doesn't make sense for you to go, too."

"I really don't mind."

"One of the benefits we offer is free food and board," he argues. "There's only one gas station on the island, and it's obscenely expensive."

I think about the drive in, both yesterday and that summer with my parents twenty-two years ago. The single-pump station as soon as I entered the island and the long stretch of road for miles thereafter. It does seem like a waste, retracing his footsteps. Spending my own money on groceries and gas when Mitchell is offering to do it himself. Not only that, but there's also the concern about running into my mother. Even though I don't think she ventures out much, even though her leg means she shouldn't drive, I wouldn't put it past her. She tried to do it before. Besides, it's been fifteen years since I was last here. I don't actually know her routine, the places she frequents—and then, of course, are all the other people who I could run into. Old neighbors and classmates, people who would inevitably gossip about my return.

It might actually be wise for me to lay low for the summer, avoid unnecessary outings where I could be seen.

"But of course, if you *insist*—" Mitchell continues, drawing me back.

"No," I say suddenly, cutting him off. "No, that's very generous of you. Thank you. I'll make a list."

"Chickens are in the coop over here," he continues, nodding, and I follow as he leads me to a giant wood structure, six massive birds plucking around in the mulch. "They lay once a day. Just pop in in the morning and grab the eggs. Don't forget to lock the gate."

"Got it," I say, trying to make a mental list, but I really should be writing this down.

"Supplies are in the shed," he continues at a dizzying speed. I watch as he opens the two double doors, musk hitting me like a solid wall. "Feed, gardening gloves. Rakes, shovels, fertilizer, pesticides. Anything you might need for the whole property is here."

I scan the room, taking it in. The place is musty and neglected, a stark contrast to the house and guesthouse, though I suppose it's simply worn down from years of use. The proximity to the water and the hot, humid air. I follow Mitchell deeper inside, the wood spongy beneath my feet and an inexplicable shudder running down my spine as I stare at all the tools with sharp metal tips; the smell of rust and old, wet dirt. There's a giant barrel with packets of seeds, chains hanging from nails on the wall, and I wonder if I might be in a little over my head here. I don't even know what half these tools are. My only experience with this kind of thing are my weak attempts at caring for the potted plants in my apartment: a rubber plant I water once a month, if I remember. A snake plant I don't water at all. I hadn't thought much about the work, to be honest, when I asked Liam to bring me on. Instead, I had been drawn to the place itself, the idea of having a space of my own.

That guesthouse the answer to all my problems and the memories of my sister clouding my judgment, blotting out everything else.

"The grapes," Mitchell continues, snapping me back, "will be taking up most of your time."

"Of course," I say, blinking out of the daydream. "The grapes."

"We've got muscadines and scuppernongs," he continues, and I let him lead me out of the shed, latching the double doors behind us and tugging them twice to ensure they're closed. He ignores the

padlock hanging open on the handle and we walk toward the edge
of the vineyard, coming to a stop next to the nearest trellis.

"Harvesting will be time consuming and labor intensive," he
says, and I watch as he plucks a grape from the vine. "We don't use
machines out here. We do it the old-fashioned way."

"And what is the old-fashioned way?" I ask.

"You pick them," he says, like it should have been obvious.
"One by one."

"By *hand*?" I ask, eyes bulging as I look beyond Mitchell and the
trellis before us, scanning my way down the rows of vines. It feels like
standing at the entrance of a giant hedge maze, the plants extending
out so far in the distance I can barely see the end of it.

"By hand," he repeats. "Of course, you'll have Liam to help."

My mind flashes back to Liam again; his big biceps and large,
tan hands. The grime permanently stuck to his nails and those dirty
brown boots holding on by a thread. I had assumed, back when he
mentioned they had pivoted to bringing on only one other worker,
that that meant they had found a more efficient way to handle the
harvest.

Having twenty people picking by hand is one thing; having just
two, given the size of this place, seems to be slightly insane.

"I think you'll find it rewarding," Mitchell continues, maybe
picking up on my hesitation. "Therapeutic, out here in nature.
Nothin' at all but you and your thoughts."

I attempt a smile, though I'm still not convinced. Besides, me
and my thoughts are a dangerous combination. We've never gotten
along when left alone together—but then I imagine Natalie from
that summer, her manic smile and big, bright eyes. The bloody
little nicks I'd always see on her skin, evidence of the hours she
spent digging through vines, and I feel a shiver at the thought of
us spending our summers in the exact same way, in the exact same
place.

Like swimming through a cold spot, sharp and brisk, the idea itself an unexpected thrill.

I try to shrug off the irony—the fact that, twenty-two years later, I still want to know what it must have been like to be her—and instead focus on the fact that it makes me feel closer to her, somehow. Closer than I've ever felt before.

"I'm sure I will," I say at last, because if she did it like this, then I can, too.

CHAPTER 14

The guesthouse is cold by the time I'm back, my hairline damp with sweat and an angry red burn stinging the back of my neck.

I sit down on the edge of the bed, my body sinking into the mattress and a weariness settling into my bones. We didn't even do any work today. We only walked the grounds, a slow, leisurely pace, but still, I'm tired. The intensity of the sun and the sheer size of this place. The magnitude of what exactly I signed up for and the slow stretch of summer pulling like taffy, long and lazy and only just the start.

I look down at my legs, at the crust of dirt flecked across my ankles. A small smattering of welts like a cluster of bites. I reach down and absentmindedly scratch, my nails dragging across the skin as I feel the wet slick of blood, the sting of ripped flesh. Then I stand up and walk to the desk, grabbing a piece of paper from my briefcase and starting a basic list for Mitchell.

I jot down *sunscreen* and *bug spray,* my pen hovering over the page until my eyes are drawn to the laptop asleep by my side. The screen is dark, but still, it's tempting, so I tap at the keys, deciding to check my email before being hit with an error message.

I already forgot: I'm not connected to the internet.

It strikes me as strange, suddenly, how blindly reliant we are on technology. How much has changed since 2002. How we go about our lives swiping and dragging, clicking and tapping, and how back when Natalie disappeared, none of this stuff even existed. There was no digital trail pointing directly to Jeffrey. No online footprint for us to follow, no damning messages for the cops to scour. We couldn't search her browser history or learn about her life from various apps. People had to talk to one another, face-to-face. The world was so much simpler in so many ways and it might actually be nice to stay disconnected for a bit, to use this month to fully reset.

I lean back, letting myself daydream about a summer without my phone, without email. Without idly scrolling to numb my mind. It's nice, the thought, but I know I need to be able to check in on my tenant, access my inbox in case I hear back from my leads, so I glance around now, letting the thought melt away as I look for a password written somewhere. A modem or a router. As I wonder if this place even has internet at all. It *has* to have internet—how could anyone these days survive without internet?—and I stand up when I can't find anything, making my way back to the door and deciding to walk to the main house and ask.

I place my hand on the knob, pulling it open before jumping straight back as a startled sound erupts from the depths of my throat.

"Hi," Liam says, smiling uncomfortably on the other side of the door. He looks timid and embarrassed, a sharp contrast to the way he appeared just yesterday. All confident and sure as he walked me around. "Didn't mean to scare you."

"Hi," I echo, embarrassed myself by my skittishness, my nerves.

I look down, realizing my hand is clutching the base of my throat, and I remove it quickly. Wiping my palms on the sides of my jeans. "No, sorry. I just wasn't expecting you. Can I help you with something?"

I feel my body tilt into the doorframe, trying to hide the mess inside.

"I brought you lunch," he says, holding up two brown paper bags. "Actually, I brought *us* lunch. I thought you might be hungry?"

He says it like a question, the end of his sentence trailing off in high pitch, and I think I register a subtle blush in his cheeks. A shyness peeking through I hadn't noticed before.

"Starving," I say, and as if on cue, I can feel my stomach rumble as I realize I haven't had a proper meal since that pizza back home, back with my mom, almost two days ago now.

I step back outside, closing the door and looking down to find a straw basket pushed against the siding. There's a blanket folded neatly inside; a strainer of freshly washed berries I assume he just picked.

"I thought we could have a picnic," he says. "Sit outside somewhere in the shade."

I smile, the two of us taking off in the direction of the vineyard, no sounds between us except for the crunching of grass and occasional zip of a mosquito. It isn't awkward, though. The lingering silence. Instead, it's oddly refreshing; a comfortable kind of companionship like we've known each other for years instead of hours.

We stop once Liam finds a spot beneath a live oak and I watch as he unfolds the blanket, draping it gently across the ground. Then I plop down, too, pretzeling my legs and opening the basket before pulling out two bottles of beer.

"Drinking on the job?" I ask with a teasing smile.

"It's five o'clock somewhere."

I twist off the caps and thrust a bottle in his direction, clanking mine against his before taking a sip. It's cold, hoppy, and feels incredible on my throat. Then I swallow, exhale, and allow myself to close my eyes, tip my head back, and simply sit with the silence for a second. Something I haven't done in a long, long time.

"It's nice, isn't it?"

I open my eyes to find Liam staring, that wary little smirk emerging back on his face.

"Very nice," I say, tucking my hair behind my ear. "Have you worked here long?"

Liam nods as he unpacks the brown bags: two sandwiches in plastic, oddly shaped carrots he pulled from the garden. Then he hands me my sandwich and I unwrap it quickly, taking a large, ravenous bite.

"How do you handle it all on your own?" I ask next, gesturing to the grapes and the garden; the animals in their pens and the shed out back. "This place is so big."

"It's manageable," he says. "In the off-season, at least."

I watch as he takes a long swig of his beer, the tendons in his neck pulling as he swallows.

"I won't lie to you, though. I'm enjoying the company."

He smiles at me, the crow's-feet by his eyes setting even deeper, and maybe it's because he's in his element now, the afternoon glow of this picturesque place, but something about Liam strikes me as even more attractive than he was just yesterday.

I watch as his Adam's apple bobs in the dip of his throat; the dark tan of his arms and the way the veins bulge in his biceps, a kind of rugged appeal I hadn't noticed before.

"You got a boyfriend back home?" he asks, eyebrows lifting with insinuation. I feel my cheeks turn hot, wondering if he caught me staring, though I doubt he can see the blush creeping in. I'm already flushed from the sun, my face warm and pink. "Any visitors we should be expecting?"

"I'm . . . sorry?" I ask, taken aback by the change in topic.

"If so, you should probably let him know," he says, going back to his sandwich. "Mitchell. He doesn't really like unexpected company."

"Oh, no," I say, my face feeling hot again. At my mistake, my assumption that he was asking because he was actually interested, but also because a flash of Ryan has suddenly entered my mind along with a wave of guilt that feels unexpected and strange. "He won't have to worry about that. It's just me."

"That's surprising," Liam says, and I watch as he ducks his head, like he hadn't meant to say that out loud. "Just, you know. You're very pretty."

I smile at him, charmed by the compliment.

"Eight million people in New York City and I still haven't managed to meet the right one."

Liam smirks, turning his attention back toward the vineyard.

"Well, I'm sorry to say you won't find many prospects on the island, either."

"What is the population out here, anyway?" I ask, my teeth snapping into a carrot.

"A couple hundred," he says. "If that. The center of town is about ten miles away, but there's not much there other than a general store and a diner. You and I might be the youngest two people on this whole spit of land."

He holds his beer out with a cheeky grin and I tip mine against his, smiling back.

We're quiet for a while, the moment between us heavy and charged. I'm still sipping my beer, eyes trained on an egret wading in the distance, when Liam's voice starts up again—only this time, it sounds different, strained.

"Listen, I don't mean to pry," he starts, and when I turn to face him, I can tell he's deliberately not looking at me, staring intently at the grass beneath. "But I have to ask. Last night, I overheard you talking about your occupation. *This and that.*"

He turns to me, finally, eyebrows raised.

"What, exactly, does that mean?"

"Oh." I laugh, trying to sound blithe. Thinking of the way he had been eyeing me last night, that suspicious stare as he stood in the kitchen.

The way he swooped in when Mitchell kept prying like he could tell I couldn't come up with a valid response.

"I guess it means I might be between jobs."

"Well yeah, I gathered that," he says. "Why else would you be here."

I stay quiet, mentally flipping through all the possible excuses.

"It's just that I'm in charge of the labor around here," he continues. "Which also means I'm in charge of *you*. So I have to have at least a general idea of your background, you know. Of who you are."

I gaze down at the blanket beneath us, pupils tracing the patterned fabric.

"You don't need to tell me your whole life story or anything," he continues. "Places like this don't exactly do things by the book. We've employed plenty of people with shady pasts—"

"I don't have a shady past," I snap, suddenly defensive as I lift my head.

"I didn't mean to imply that you do," he says, raising his hands in mock surrender. "You just gotta give me something."

He looks at me, his eyes puppy-round, and I realize, at last, that it's a fair question. These people hardly know anything about me, yet they've graciously invited me to live in their home. They're saving me this summer, whether they know it or not, and it feels like I owe them at least a kernel of truth.

"I'm a journalist," I say at last, deciding, in a flash, to just come clean. That I don't want to deal with an entire summer of lies, tip-toeing around my only coworker and friend. "I quit two months ago to go freelance, but I haven't been having the best of luck."

I look down to find my fingers pulling at the beer label, little wet rips scattered in the grass.

"I don't really know why I kept it from him," I continue. "Mitchell, I mean. I guess I'm embarrassed I haven't published any-thing in a while. Plus, I didn't want him to think I'd be poking around or something. Snooping through their stuff."

I feel another flash of heat on my cheeks; the irony of Marcia's diary sitting on my bed, concealed in the sheets, not at all lost on me.

"People can be wary of journalists," I add, clocking the way Liam is nodding slowly, his eyes squinting in the glare of the sun.

"Right," he says at last. "They can be a little paranoid."

"Paranoid," I echo, nudging him to go on.

"About their privacy. I guess you can say they're . . . protective. Of their privacy."

"Of course," I say, that word, *privacy,* cutting like an insect sting, venomous and sharp, as Marcia's diary pulses through my mind like a migraine. My blatant violation of keeping it to read.

"I wouldn't mention that," he says, and I'm suddenly confused, wondering how he could possibly know I've been reading her di-ary, when I realize he's not talking about the diary. Of course he's not. He's still talking about my job. "I mean, I wouldn't tell them what you do."

"Okay . . ." I say, slightly perplexed about why my profession would be such an issue. I suppose, in recent years, that plenty of people have become distrustful of the news, wary of the media, and I start to wonder if maybe I was right to hide it from them.

Maybe Marcia and Mitchell *are* the suspicious kind and Liam is simply saving me the headache.

"I won't mention it," I add, feeling a swell of gratitude at having someone to look out for me here. "Thanks for the heads-up."

"Sure thing," he says as he turns toward the water, his eyes trained on a spot in the distance. For a second, it looks like he's about to say something else, his mouth parting only an inch, but then he shakes his head, a gentle twitch like he changed his mind, before bringing the bottle back to his lips and downing the rest in one fell swoop.

CHAPTER 15

I'm back in the guesthouse a few hours later, the gush of cold air cooling my skin and a yellow Post-it Note stuck to my finger.

"Wi-Fi," Liam repeated when I asked for it earlier, eyes on the ground as he packed up the basket.

"Yeah," I said before hesitating a second, turning toward him. "You do have internet here, don't you?"

"Sure," he replied, rubbing his hand against the back of his head. "But the modem is in the main house. The signal's gonna be weak in your cabin, if it even reaches at all. I can't promise how good it'll be."

"I'd still like to try," I said. "If you don't mind. I can't just be totally cut off out here."

"No, of course not," he had said, laughing like the suggestion was crazy. "I'll grab it for you on our way back up."

I walk over to my desk now and stick the note onto the surface, opening my laptop and tapping the keys. Then I look down at the paper, an alphabet soup of letters and numbers. The network and password are scribbled in pen, the kind that comes programmed when you first set it up. It doesn't surprise me—Marcia and Mitchell don't strike me as the kind of people who would update their password; I kind of doubt, based on their lifestyle, that they would even know how—so I tap on the network and type the password in, the wheel spinning slowly as I wait until that familiar little icon appears in the corner.

I'm connected, but barely. There's a single bar there, but it's better than nothing.

I grab my phone next, doing the same thing until a bar pops up in the corner there, too. Immediately, it starts emitting the faintest *ding,* over and over, the sound of incoming texts flooding the cabin as increasingly more concerned questions start to trickle in from Ryan.

> Picked up your mail and caught your tenant throwing a party. That didn't take long.

> Are you getting my texts? I'm green for some reason.

> Hey, is everything all right? Tried calling and went straight to voicemail.

I tap at the display, ready to respond, but before I can get a full sentence out, I feel the phone start to buzz in my hand, Ryan's face appearing on the screen.

He's calling again, and I take a deep breath, swiping to answer.

"Man, you're a hard woman to get in touch with," he says as soon as I pick up. It's clearly in jest, although I sense a substantial relief in his voice like he was actually starting to worry about my well-being. "What have you been doing over there?"

"Sorry," I say, pushing a strand of damp hair from my eyes. "My service has been spotty."

"Right, you mentioned that," he says, mildly embarrassed at his overreaction as I remember my lie from back in the car, claiming I couldn't hear him because I didn't want to deal with the things he was trying to say.

I open my mouth again, about to fill him in on the last twenty-four hours, when he starts talking again, cutting me off.

"Well listen, I just wanted to tell you I'm proud of you, Claire. I know this is hard, what you're doing."

I fall silent, the update immediately dying on my lips.

"I could tell the other day that you don't want to be there. But you're doing it," he says. "You're being the bigger person, helping your mom, and that's huge. It really is."

"Yeah," I say, a deep shame descending upon me as I glance around the guesthouse with a pair of fresh eyes, this place I escaped to after a single bad night at home. It's no different than how I ran away to the city the second I graduated. How I mock my own mother for avoiding her problems when here I am, mere miles down the road, living my life in the exact same way.

"Don't get me wrong," he continues, maybe mistaking my silence for offense. "I'm painfully bored without you here, but I do think this will be good. Healthy."

I close my mouth, swallowing hard.

"Anyway, I just wanted to tell you I'm glad you're there. In case you're still questioning it."

"Thanks," I say, deciding, in this moment, that I'm not going to tell him where I actually am. Not yet, anyway. "That means a lot."

"Yeah, sure," he says as I imagine his skin flushing scarlet the way it always does when he lets his emotions slip through. Then he clears his throat, changes the subject. "Your apartment, on the other hand, might have to be fumigated when you get home."

"I can't even be mad," I say, sitting down at the desk before wedging the phone between my shoulder and ear. "I probably should have done that before I let her move in."

Ryan laughs, a sound that emerges from the depths of his chest, and I'm reminded again of that strange surge of guilt I felt in the vineyard, the flash of his face that appeared in my mind the second Liam asked about a boyfriend back home. It wasn't a lie when I told him I was single; Ryan and I have only ever been friends. I can't blame it on work anymore, although it might have subconsciously started that way, neither of us wanting to muddy the waters of a brand-new job by hooking up with a coworker. Besides, I have all the obvious problems that inevitably come with a past as complicated as mine.

Trust issues, attachment issues. A chronic sense of self-loathing I can never seem to shake.

Ryan is still talking when I reach for my laptop and open my inbox, skimming the handful of new emails that just came through. There are a couple bills, mostly spam. Still nothing at all from my various leads.

I sigh, a long, defeated sound as I push my fingers into my eyes.

"Everything all right?" he asks as I lift my head, realizing I must have cut him off.

"Yeah, fine," I say, glancing back at the bed as all my real-life stressors come barreling back, wondering if it's too late to catch a quick nap—but then I eye the diary, that flash of maroon, peeking out from beneath the white sheet.

I stand up, the book like a rope looped around my waist as it draws my body across the room.

"But I should probably go," I add as I slide onto the mattress, the diary's hard edge cutting into my leg. "I'm still trying to get settled over here."

Not a lie, exactly. Another half-truth as I choose my words carefully, though that doesn't make me feel any better.

We say goodbye, hanging up with a promise to check in soon. Then I pull the book out, my fingers sweeping slow across the cover as I push away the thoughts of these four weeks ending, my five thousand dollars only lasting so long. Ever since the moment I stepped into this place, it's been so easy to let reality slip away for a while. This forbidden garden I could crawl into forever choking out all my worries like a pest getting smothered by an invasive vine.

I whip the sheets back and place the book on my lap, the soft snap of the spine when I part the covers like the cracking of knuckles before I settle back in.

CHAPTER 16

DECEMBER 1983

Marcia opened her eyes to find Mitchell staring straight at her, his pupils stretched wide like two gaping black holes.

She couldn't remember falling asleep. She could only remember lying there, in the back of his camper, a bitter cold as their limbs lay tangled and the dull heat radiating from the surface of his skin like a fire in the wild, her only source of warmth.

"What are you looking at?" she asked as she burrowed herself deeper into his side. Her head felt thick and heavy, swaddled in sleep. Her brain bubble-wrapped in a blanket of fog.

"You," he replied, his fingers crawling their way up her leg. "You're the most beautiful girl I've ever seen."

She smiled, thinking back to their first night at the theater. The two of them strolling down the walk in the dark until they came to a stop in front of her house. She could practically feel him watching from the street as she snuck back in, the hall cold and quiet as she crept up the stairs. Silently passing her parents' bedroom and listening to her father's rhythmic snores.

Then she had slid into bed, pulled the covers up to her chin. Trained her eyes on the ceiling as she lay still in the dark, her body beating as Mitchell's voice whirled around in her mind.

You're very pretty, Marcia. I get the feeling you don't hear that enough.

In truth, he was right. Rarely had Marcia ever been called pretty. She was gangly and plain with long hair and an even longer hemline; chewed-up cuticles and a mousy demeanor that made her easy to overlook. She knew a lot of it had to do with her parents, how strict they were, the whole town of Draper aware of their rules and therefore uninclined to get too close—but at the same time, she didn't do herself any favors, either. Instead of attempting to meet people, find some friends, she was like a finicky flower that closed up in the dark. While the other kids were dabbling in the kinds of things teenagers ought to be dabbling in—sex and drugs, freedom and fun—Marcia kept her nose out of everything but a book.

But it wasn't because she wasn't curious about it all. It was because she was Marcia Rayburn, daughter of William Rayburn, and that's what was expected of her.

It was because she spent her adolescence getting poked and prodded, ribbed and roused, cafeteria boys making fun of her smothering necklines and unshaven armpits. Her naïveté about the way the world worked. It was because she wasn't allowed to do anything to draw attention to herself—*Modesty is an attitude of propriety and decency in dress, grooming, language, and behavior*—to let in desire or unholy stares . . . but instead of pushing back against all those constricting commandments, pushing away, she leaned in to them as far as she could.

She had leaned in so far that she'd disappeared.

"What is it?" Mitchell asked as she blinked back to the present, his expression obscured by the inky black night. "What's on your mind?"

"Nothing," she said, rolling to face him. "Just thinking about when we met."

She could barely see a foot in front of her face, but somehow, she could still sense the intensity of his stare breaking through. His undivided attention on her making her head spin like that smoke she'd inhaled, her skin static like a crackling wire. It was the same way he had stared that night in the alley, the same stare that made her feel so helplessly high. That's why, when she woke up the next morning, the entire encounter had felt like a hallucination, a wavy mirage, and she was sure she'd never see him again . . . but then the next night, something caught her eye through the living room window.

An idling camper just down the street, smoke billowing out from the exhaust.

You're not from around here, are you?

She remembered squinting in the dark, recalling the feeling of her heart in her throat as she took a step closer, asked him those questions. The tendons bulging beneath the skin of his neck as he sucked his cigarette down.

I'm not from around anywhere.

He had come back for her, she realized. And he had come back almost every night since.

She shivered at the memory, leaning over to grab the sweatshirt she noticed wedged between the wall and the bed.

"What did you study at Berkeley?" she asked, fanning it out as she clocked the word stitched on the front. Ever since their meeting four weeks ago, she had managed to learn a few things about him—albeit it had been slowly, methodically. Like putting together a jigsaw puzzle, the picture emerging piece by piece. Most notably, she now knew he lived in that camper, oblong and orange. The same burnt orange as her parents' living room couch. It was an eyesore of a thing, hard not to notice, but she supposed the inside was all that mattered: a yellow plaid sofa and brown shag carpet next to a kitchenette and cubbyhole bathroom. A single bed situated way in the back.

"Psychology," he said after a beat of silence.

"Psychology," she repeated, still slightly enveloped in the miasma of sleep. She hadn't known he had gone to college, though she had been curious about the camper's California plates. Found herself rapt by the tales he'd told about the opposite coast.

"People," he clarified, his fingers twisting through the fine strands of her hair. "I studied people."

She scooted in closer, her skin tingling with warmth, with want, with whatever was inside those cigarettes she always found him rolling himself. It had surprised her, at first, how quickly he was able to open her up. Ger her comfortable enough to try new things, his fingers caressing her body with such delicate care she felt like a piece of glass, fine and fragile and easy to crack. He was patient with her, though. Gentle. He walked her through it, coaxing her slowly out of her shell until she found herself yearning for him whenever he was away.

All day, she thought about when she would see him again: sitting at her desk at school, staring out the window at the bleak, gray sky.

"I wish I could go to college," she said as she imagined him with a backpack slung over one shoulder, sauntering his way into some class. She often found herself feeling envious of the experiences he had that she would never get to share, but at the same time, fantasies of some other life had always consumed her, long before the two of them had met. She always thought about moving away, finding a job, but it felt so foreign, so impossible to grasp. Her life had been on the same set path since she was a child, almost as if her parents had twisted a crank in her back and simply set her down, her feet programmed to walk in whatever direction they wanted her to go. She wasn't capable of pivoting on her own, of turning herself around and forging a new future. If they had it their way, which they always did, she would be married before she turned twenty-one. Probably someone from the church, someone her father would pick. She wouldn't be surprised if he had picked someone already, and Marcia suddenly imagined herself growing old like her mother, a dish towel permanently flung over one shoulder as she stood in the kitchen, a pinched smile on her lips.

"You don't want to go to college," Mitchell said, his voice breaking the thought like a snapping twig. "College is a scam."

She twisted her neck, straining to see his expression in the dark. That sounded like something her father would say.

"You can learn everything you need to learn out there," he continued. "Out in the world."

She was quiet, teeth digging into her bottom lip as she thought of just how little she knew. It was embarrassing, really. Her lack of experience. Her entire existence whittled down to this one small town. All the same people in all the same places.

"Society is a trap," he continued, eyes on the ceiling. The ripping fabric and smears of black smoke. "A cage they use to corral and control. Independence is the only true form of freedom. You know that, right? You understand that?"

She thought of her parents, her teachers. The passages she recited like clockwork each night, all of it beaten into her as indisputable fact.

"Of course," she said, immediately hearing the uncertainty in her voice.

They both fell quiet, no movement between them except for the occasional plume of warm, thick breath. Then she heard him sigh—a deep, disappointed sound—before he reached out his hand, trailing his finger across her cheek.

"I've known so many girls like you. Girls who are lonely, girls who are lost."

She felt a catch in her throat, ashamed he had picked up on it so easily. The very essence of her as something aimless and adrift.

She hadn't known it was that obvious.

"But I *see* you," he continued, his hand moving down her throat before pushing a finger deep into her chest. "I see who you are. At your core."

"I know you do," she said as she felt a sharp pain between her ribs—but it was a good pain. The kind of pain she sometimes felt when they came together, an aching pleasure that felt so intense, she thought her body might tear in two. She had never known anyone like him. He was a mirror, a pane of smooth glass that reflected back her own insecurities. Liquid smoke that seeped inside her so quickly, filling in her hollow grooves.

Marcia squeezed his fingers, watching as Mitchell smiled in the dark. His breath warm as he leaned in close. Then he cupped her cheek with his free hand, his thumb rubbing against her smooth skin.

"You're ready," he said, a conviction in his voice she didn't quite understand.

"Ready for what?" she asked, eyebrows bunching as she watched him turn back around, staring at the ceiling as if talking to himself.

"To meet the others."

CHAPTER 17

It's early morning and I'm standing outside, watching the sun rise slow over the water. The color trickling into the cotton-candy clouds like the slow bloom of a flower as it turns its face toward the light.

There's a mug of coffee pushed hot in my hands and I inhale it slowly, the bitter smell of the beans keeping my breath soft and steady. The air is dewy, but my eyes are dry, every flip of lids feeling like sandpaper scratching the surface.

I stifle a yawn, pushing my hand flush to my mouth. I slept terribly last night.

Lying in bed, not nearly as exhausted as I was the first time I collapsed onto those sheets, I had noticed that the mattress was hard, metal springs stabbing the flesh of my back. The quilt was scratchy, the pillows limp, but it was the diary that kept me awake. I had stayed up reading for entirely too long, all of Marcia's memories so vivid and real it felt like cracking open her skull and dipping into her brain. Wading through the murky inner workings of an eighteen-year-old girl.

I look down at the water now, the tips of my shoes at the edge of the dock as I stare down at my own reflection. Then I kick a pebble over the ledge, the rippling liquid twisting my features into a face that appears distorted and strange.

I turn around and start my walk back, eyes on the guesthouse and my mind on the diary safely tucked into the back of the desk. Earlier this morning, after hours spent reading through my hosts' most intimate moments, I had started to feel like something of a voyeur. A Peeping Tom at the edge of their window, helping myself to their private lives. I had read about Marcia losing her virginity, recounting every subsequent encounter in more detail than I have any right to know. She had seemed so young, so naïve, that even though she had been eighteen—technically legal, a certifiable adult—it felt wrong imagining the things they did together, her mind more immature than her body itself.

I lift the coffee to my lips, draining it completely as I will my brain to stay awake. Of course, I'm still interested in all that I'm reading. There's still so much I want to know. The diary is hundreds of pages, every single one filled front to back, and I'm tempted to keep going, to finish the whole thing . . . but at the same time, it's starting to feel wrong, finding it all out like this.

I'm starting to wonder if I should just *ask,* learn more about them the regular way.

I'm getting ready to head inside when a gust of wind whips off the water, a strange new scent traveling with it. I lift my nose, inhaling deeply as I try to place it. It isn't pluff mud, that familiar odor of curdling decay. Instead, it smells like something rancid and sour.

It smells, I realize, like death that's fresh.

I step off the dock before walking toward the edge of the water, the scent getting stronger the closer I get. The bank is peppered with plants, bushy shrubs and swaying reeds, and my eye catches on something red in the distance. A tuft of fur blowing in the briny breeze.

I squint, realizing it's an animal, maybe a fox, lying motionless on the rim of the marsh. It's definitely dead, and I'm still staring at its limp little body when a noise from behind makes me jump.

I twist around, recognizing the slap of the screen door from the main house behind me. Marcia is on the porch now, making her way to one of the gliders and easing herself gently down. She's in a white bathrobe, that same braid draped over her shoulder, and I raise my arm to wave in her direction—but instead of smiling or waving back, all she does is stare straight ahead. Almost as if she can't see me at all.

I feel a twist in my chest, a subtle unease about how she hasn't spoken a single word since I got here. She's barely even acknowledged my existence . . . although maybe I caught her at a bad time. She seemed out of it that first night, groggy like I had woken her up, so I decide to walk over now, wondering if maybe this is my chance.

I close the distance in less than a minute, climbing the porch stairs two at a time.

"Gorgeous morning," I say, my empty mug still clutched in my hand. I register a twitch of a smile, a gentle nod, but still, she says nothing. "Are you always up this early?" I ask, switching tactics. A direct question, after all, requires a response. A fairly obvious but helpful trick I learned after ten years of interviews. "It's barely light out."

She nods again, still refusing to engage, and I take the opportunity to scrutinize her more carefully, feeling another rush of remorse at reading her words. Of course, she's not the same person she was when she wrote them; forty-one years is an incredibly long time. She probably doesn't even remember that diary, the things she thought when she was only eighteen, but I can't help but wonder how she would feel if she knew that I had it.

Like sneaking through a stranger's medicine cabinet, thumbing my way through a pile of clothes, it's a blatant invasion. Helping myself to a person's private thoughts.

"You know, I was just thinking about how we haven't had a chance to get to know each other yet," I try again, making my way across the porch. "I know I only just got here, but I'd love to hear how you and Mitchell got together."

I raise my eyebrows, hoping that if I can get her to tell me the story herself, maybe I won't feel so guilty about all this knowledge I shouldn't already have.

She turns to me, finally meeting my stare.

"You don't want to listen to that."

"I do," I say, slightly taken aback at the sound of her voice; entirely lucid but low and melodious, not at all what I was expecting. "I'd love to know how you created this place."

She regards me cautiously, her eyes that light, liquid gray, and I wonder if maybe she's just being modest. Like the kind of people who bat away compliments, too insecure to accept the praise.

"We were young when we met," she concedes at last, and I feel a small thrill in getting a little bit closer, prying away this piece of the truth.

"Liam told me you started Galloway in the eighties."

"We lucked into the land." She nods. "We've always been very . . . self-sustaining."

I open my mouth, prepared to ask another question, when I hear the screen door slap again. Then I twist around in the direction of the noise, eyeing Mitchell as he walks toward us with two large mugs steaming hot in his hands.

"Good morning," I say, flashing a smile as I wait for him to shoot one back, though his expression stays vacant so I simply watch as he walks. His body cutting clean across the porch like a shark breaching the water, silent and sleek and a little unsettling. "Marcia was just telling me the story of how you two started this place."

"Oh, was she?" he asks, eyebrows raising in amusement. "And what, exactly, did she say?"

I turn back toward Marcia, a gentle swallow as her eyes dart to the ground.

"We didn't get far," I say after a long stretch of silence, my gaze now boring into her hands. Her grip has tightened around the armrests, the thin skin on the top threatening to tear, and I feel the inexplicable urge to backpedal, something about Mitchell's expression and Marcia's sudden silence making me uneasy. "I'm just so impressed by everything you've built."

I look up at Mitchell now, my own skin bristling at the way he seems to be assessing me carefully. Then he hands Marcia a mug, his eyes never once leaving mine. After a few seconds, the prolonged staring is too much to bear so I lower my gaze again, instead staring at the mug in her hand. It's the same white, ceramic mug as the ones in my cabin, the very same one as what I'm holding right now, and I watch as she takes a tentative sip, the herbal smell wafting in my direction making my hair stand on edge.

"Well, don't let me disturb your morning," I say at last, gesturing to the vineyard and suddenly desperate to get off of this porch. Mitchell nods, Marcia's eyes still stuck to their spot on the floor, and while I know I haven't done anything wrong—at least, nothing they know about, my mind back on the diary again—it still feels like I've broken some cardinal rule. Like Mitchell just caught me snooping through his things and he's waiting for me to drop to my knees, beg for forgiveness.

Like I somehow just got Marcia in trouble, even though she never told me a thing.

CHAPTER 18

I dedicate the morning to my list of chores: feeding the chickens, scattering fistfuls of feed across their pen and refilling their water from the hose by the house. Then I collect the eggs, dipping my hands into their nests and tucking them inside a lined basket before bringing it to the shed like Mitchell had asked.

I unhook the padlock, stepping inside. The stuffy scent stuck in my nostrils as I place the basket on the closest counter, eyeing all the tools hanging up on the walls. Something about this room still makes me uncomfortable, some unnerving air to it I can't quite place, and I let my gaze wander around for a while before grabbing a set of shears and turning back around, shutting the doors swiftly behind me like I'm trying to lock some evil aura inside.

I head into the garden, picking what's ripe before tossing everything into a strainer. Rinsing the fruits and vegetables clean. Then I weed and water, fertilize and feed, the morning passing by in a dreamy haze as the heat of the day slowly mounts until I feel the familiar sting of sweat on my skin. I've tried to keep busy, keep my head down, but after what feels like at least a few hours, I chance a glance back at the main house, relieved to find the porch is empty. Marcia and Mitchell nowhere to be found.

I exhale, immediately more relaxed now that I'm not being watched—because Mitchell *had* been watching me earlier. He had been watching intently. Even after Marcia had left, standing up to make her way back to the house, he had stayed behind, rocking slowly on the porch with his eyes on my back as I puttered around. I told myself he was just making sure I was doing everything correctly, given that this is my first real day, and while I've been trying not to read too much into his sudden hostility—I had been warned, after all, that Marcia and Mitchell are private people; that I shouldn't expect to get too close—the secrecy is strange, their blatant refusal to answer innocent questions.

The way Mitchell seemed both amused and angry when he saw Marcia and me talking, walking outside as if to break us apart.

I make my way to the side of the house, the only spot where I can find some shade, and twist the bib attached to the hose, bringing the stream of water up to my lips. It isn't cold, it isn't even cool, but I take a few sips anyway, making a mental note as I drink to talk to Liam about it all later. I'm sure he knows more about our hosts—some little detail that might be useful, something that could help explain—and I think back to our conversation yesterday, his cryptic warning as we sat beneath the trees.

I guess you can say they're protective, he had said, looking at me with a strange mixture of affection and remorse like he was happy I was here, grateful for the company, but also suddenly sorry I came. *Protective of their privacy.*

I turn the hose off, wiping the water from my chin with the back of my hand before resting it on the side of my hip, deciding it's time to take a small break. Then I look around slowly, my attention now directed to the side of the house, because despite

Mitchell's abruptly odd behavior, I can't help but admire what he's done with the place. In addition to the herbs and produce I've been instructed to pick, there are plants and wildflowers covering almost every inch. I recognize the basic ones—the ones with easy names like lavender and lilac, black-eyed Susans and sunflowers stretching their necks to the sky—but there are also plenty of plants I've never seen before, a plethora of things I can't even name. There's a whole secret garden over here, away from everything, and I trail my fingers across the various flowers, their petals soft as silk to the touch.

I lean in, take a deep breath.

"You ever taste that?"

I twist around, surprised to find Liam standing behind me. He's smiling wide, catching me in this private moment. I hadn't even heard him walk up.

"Honeysuckle," he elaborates, gesturing to the plant in my hand when I don't respond. "It's good."

"No," I say at last. "Can't say that I have."

He scoffs, though it's a teasing sound. I can tell by his growing grin, the way he takes a step closer with his chin tucked low.

"And you call yourself a Southern girl."

"Do I?" I ask, watching as he walks even closer, toward the plant I was just touching. A giant green shrub with little white flowers sprayed across the surface. I had been drawn to the smell of it, the subtle sweetness, and I watch as he plucks one of the flowers and brings it up to his lips. "I don't recall saying that."

"You grew up around here, right?" he asks, sucking the stem.

"I did," I agree, remembering how I blurted that out during my first night here. A desperate attempt to break the mounting silence.

"Which part?"

"Claxton," I say, trying to figure out how to change the subject before he can connect too many dots. I have no idea if Liam has heard of Natalie Campbell, a former Galloway worker who disappeared, but the fact that she was my sister seems like something I should have disclosed back when he was asking about my past.

"Though I wouldn't call myself Southern anymore," I add. "This is my first time back in years."

"Well, you know what they say."

"What do they say?"

"You can take the girl out of the South . . ."

He smiles again, trailing off, and I can't help but smile back. Relieved the name of my hometown didn't ring any bells.

"Here, try it," he says, grabbing another. "Use your fingers to squeeze the stem."

I follow his lead, snapping a flower of my own and squeezing the tip at the bottom of the bloom. Then I pull the stem out, a little bead of nectar erupting from the opening before touching it to my tongue, the bubble bursting with a honied gush.

"It's good, right?"

"It is good," I say, savoring the sweetness before picking another.

"You can do all kinds of things with honeysuckle," he continues, watching as I scrape the flower with my teeth. "Put 'em in salads, boil 'em in tea. Those little blue berries are edible, too."

I look at the berries peppering the shrub, oblong like blueberries stretched into a tube. Then I pick one from the stem before popping it into my mouth, suddenly more comfortable with Liam here.

"Just don't go blindly eating stuff around here," he adds. "Not if you don't know what it is."

"Mitchell said I could eat whatever I want," I counter, teasing him back. Of course I know better than to eat random things growing out in the wild but Liam keeps talking, not reading my tone.

"Yeah, over there," he says, gesturing to the produce. "All of that is edible. But some of the other stuff around here is toxic."

"Like what?" I ask, glancing down at the shrub like it just sprang teeth.

"Mostly out there, out by the water," he says, turning to face the marsh behind us as I remember what I saw this morning, that still little body blowing in the breeze. "Marshland grows all kinds of things."

"So you're telling me not to make my dinner with the poison ivy I saw by the guesthouse," I say, smirking.

"Yes, that's right. Try to avoid that."

"Got it." I smile. "Thanks for the tip."

Liam winks at me, that cheeky grin, and I feel a familiar flush in my chest. The same one I felt just yesterday, during our picnic, when we had been ribbing each other like we'd been friends for years.

"By the way," I say. "I noticed something by the dock this morning. It was an animal, and I'm pretty sure it was dead."

Liam is quiet for a beat before twisting around, letting his gaze follow mine.

"It looked like a fox."

"Yeah, that can happen," he says simply. "I'll take care of it."

We stay silent, my eyes still squinting into the distance.

"Anyway," he says, slapping his legs as I look to the edge of the vineyard, a couple wheelbarrows next to a towering stack of blue buckets waiting for us to fill them all up. "The grapes are ready whenever you are."

CHAPTER 19

I can barely feel my fingers by the time I get back.

We had been picking for hours, until early evening, when Liam decided we were done for the day.

"Let's pack it up," he had said, probably noticing how my body had started to sag; my shoulders hunched, the subtle crick in my neck. "You're going to be pretty sore in the morning."

It had been daunting, standing there. Looking down at the buckets I had filled and realizing just how much more there was to go. Glancing at my hands, the dirt and dried blood. Mosquito bites peppering my ankles and the stinging sunburn on the back of my neck. After a while, though, it had become rote: my fingers burrowing between the leaves, finding the grapes that were ready to pick—swollen and ripe, skin thick like a callus—and plucking them briskly from the stem. Liam had told me to watch where I walked, warning of snakes and spiders that liked to lurk in the brush; then he taught me how to strap the harvest bucket onto my chest, eliminating the need to carry it around. Still, it was physical work—grueling, even—spending all that time on my feet.

Even so, I found that I liked it, strangely enough. The sun on my cheeks and the breeze on my face so vastly different than my life back in the city. The stale air of my apartment and the fluorescent glow of my laptop screen leaving me depleted in an entirely different way.

"So, what do you know about Mitchell?" I had asked after a long stretch of silence, still unable to peel my mind from him. I didn't want to appear too eager so I had waited a while, instead inquiring about the business and nodding politely as Liam spent the better part of an hour spewing out facts about taxonomy and pathology; how they sell grapes by the basket to grocery stores and farmer's markets, but also as jellies and jams and to wineries around the coast.

"What do you want to know?"

"Anything, really," I said. "I can't seem to get a read on him."

"You're not the only one," he responded, smiling vaguely. Continuing to pick.

I thought hard about how to word my next question, careful not to reveal too much from the diary and all this knowledge I shouldn't already have. Marcia hadn't given me any information, either, but then I remembered what she said about the vineyard. About how they had *lucked into the land*.

"How did he come across Galloway?" I asked. "Is it family owned?"

"No, he bought it back in the eighties."

"How many acres?"

"Close to fifty," Liam had said, turning to face me. "Give or take."

"*Fifty?*" I asked, glancing around. "I didn't realize it was that big."

"A lot of it is the woods out back," he said, gesturing to the tree line on the side of the house. "The marsh, too."

"But how could he afford that?" I asked next, realizing, too late, that I may have tipped my cards too much. "I mean, he must have been young when he bought it," I added, trying to feign ignorance as I remembered how Marcia had guessed at Mitchell's age on the night they met. "In his late twenties?"

Liam stared at me, his expression blank before he turned back toward the vines.

"Something like that," he said at last. "Land was cheap back then. A lot cheaper than it is today."

I nodded, falling quiet, something about it not sitting right. Based on all the things Marcia had written, it didn't seem like Mitchell came from money. He lived in a camper he parked around town.

"Why grapes?" I asked at last, looking back at the trellis, but Liam just shrugged.

"He's good with plants."

I unlock the door to the guesthouse now, my feet swollen and throbbing in my shoes. Then I step inside, an object in the kitchen stealing my attention. Something that wasn't there when I left.

I walk closer, eyeing a large basket perched on the counter. It looks like a picnic basket, woven straw with a cloth lining inside, and I peer over the lip once I'm close enough to see, realizing it's all the things from my list: bug spray and sunscreen, a few other supplies I requested from the store. I remember giving the list to Liam, swapping it for that sticky note with the network and password scribbled in ink, but what I *can't* remember is if I locked my door this morning.

I rack my brain, replaying the events of the day: sipping my coffee on the dock before trying to talk to Marcia on the porch, Mitchell walking outside and breaking us up. It's possible I forgot, my mind pulled in so many directions, but I'm slightly unsettled at the thought of someone coming into my space uninvited—still, maybe Mitchell just didn't want to leave it outside. There's food in here, perishables that would attract animals and bugs, so I shrug away the unease and walk back to my laptop, opening the lid and tapping it awake.

I navigate to the county website first, simultaneously pulling up Google Maps on my phone. Then I find Galloway's address from the first time I drove here and type it into the property records page now loaded onto my screen. I hit Enter, leaning back in my chair as I wait. The connection in this corner is painfully slow so I drum my fingers against the keys, watching the little timer spin as I attempt to justify my own nosiness, still not sure why I care so much about these details that probably don't even matter at all. Maybe it's my profession, an entire decade of being trained to be curious and dig for answers. A phantom itch that's now begging to be scratched. Or maybe it's pure boredom—the long, lonely hours of the last few months spent trapped inside my own wandering mind—but something about all this just doesn't feel right. It's an instinct, barely there, but based on that diary, Mitchell was practically penniless when he met Marcia in 1983 . . . although somehow, less than a year later, he managed to make enough money to buy fifty acres of land.

Petty as it may be, I want to know how.

The results appear and I lean forward, taking in the information on the screen—and there it is, right in front of me. The land was acquired by Mitchell Galloway on October 3, 1984, for a deed price of forty-five thousand dollars. It all seems perfectly legal and I let out a low whistle, doing the math in my head. In today's market, this land has to be worth at least a couple million. They could sell it and make a fortune—though, of course, they live here, too. It's their home, their livelihood.

I scroll down some more, looking for information on the previous owners. Before Mitchell, it was owned by a man named Steven Montague, and before that, Andrew Montague.

So it *had* been family land, before, for some reason, it was sold to Mitchell.

I flip back to Google, typing in the name *Steven Montague* and hitting Enter, already knowing it won't get me anywhere. The search terms are too vague, but I don't have anything else to go on so I scroll through a few pages, just to be safe. It's mostly LinkedIn profiles and random obituaries, a few mug shots and an attorney's office out in Washington state. None of them seem relevant so I pull my notebook out of the desk and flip it open to a clean page, scribbling the name at the top of the paper and making a note to revisit it later.

Maybe the diary knows who he is.

I shrug off the thought, fighting the urge to dip back into its pages and instead turning toward the laptop again, typing in *Mitchell Galloway* next. There are a few relevant results, mostly articles about the vineyard. A nice fluff piece from a few years back about how this place is a hidden Southern staple, a reminder of the simple pleasures in life. Still, I can't find anything of value, anything that might shed some light on his past, and I'm about to close my computer and figure out what I should do for dinner when my arm suddenly stops in midair as I realize there's still one person I haven't yet searched.

I lift the lid again, replaying our strange interaction this morning, before typing *Marcia Galloway* into the search bar and watching as the cursor blinks on the screen.

I chew on my lip as I think back to the diary again, the only real details about her I have. Then I hit Delete and rephrase my search to *Marcia Rayburn,* her maiden name, before adding *Draper, South Carolina* in at the end.

I hit Enter, waiting impatiently as the results load. It takes too long—twenty seconds, at least—but a new page finally appears and I feel my eyes widen when I see what's there. A handful of articles now fill the screen, and while their headlines vary, the gist is the same, so I click one at random and hold my breath as it loads. The link bringing me to an archived page of *The Draper Daily Herald* dated March 18, 1984.

I lean forward, trying to wrap my mind around the words on the screen.

DRAPER, SOUTH CAROLINA, TEEN GOES MISSING
RAYBURN FAMILY DESPERATE FOR ANSWERS

CHAPTER 20

A creeping unease slinks up my spine as I continue to stare at the headline, my gaze traveling next to the black-and-white picture printed beneath. It's a portrait of a family, grainy and old. The caption identifying them as William, Jane, and Marcia Rayburn.

Beneath that, a short article.

Local family William and Jane Rayburn are requesting the public's assistance in the continued search for their daughter, Marcia, who disappeared from her bedroom in the middle of the night on Thursday, March 15. According to the family, Marcia was last seen by her parents the night before. They state she retreated to her room as usual, but in the morning, they grew concerned when she never appeared.

When her mother went upstairs to check on her, she found nothing in her room but an open window.

I blink, that familiar sense of déjà vu like my body is submerged in lukewarm water, waves of recollection caressing my skin as I relive that morning in August 2002: my mom and me sitting at the kitchen table, the rhythmic clink of my cereal spoon and the moment she finally succumbed to the silence.

Ascending those stairs, that gentle knock. Her panicked scream splintering the stillness and the clatter of her mug when she realized Natalie was gone.

I continue to read.

No note was left behind, nor were there signs of a struggle or break-in. However, when pressed about whether anything appeared out of place, the Rayburns admitted to a missing duffel bag, as well as a recent change in behavior from Marcia.

Despite this, they do not believe she left of her own accord.

I swallow, picturing the black bag that disappeared from Natalie's closet. Her sour stare as she glowered at our mother, the slam of her door like a slap to the face.

"Marcia is a good, righteous girl," William Rayburn said in a recent press conference held by the Draper City Police Department. "She had no reason to leave like this. She was loved. She was happy."

I stare at the screen for so long the lines of text start to blur in my vision before clicking back to the search results and opening up a couple more. It's a futile exercise; I know I won't be able to find anything else. The articles are scarce and they're all from local papers, as well as all published in 1984. Marcia's disappearance didn't appear to gain much traction outside of a small cluster of towns and I suppose that, without the prevalence of the internet, it was a lot harder back then for news to travel. Despite all its flaws, that is one strength I can't deny: the world is better at sharing knowledge now.

If Marcia had vanished a couple decades later, her picture would have been plastered all over the place. She would have gone viral, her name probably trending, instead of withering into oblivion after only a month.

I lean back, my mind starting to swim as I think about the diary again, her blatant desire to get away. She had written about leaving, dreamed of going to college and finding a job, so maybe she simply ran away with Mitchell and got in touch after. She could have called, could have written a letter. Could have somehow let her parents know that she was okay. I bet they were humiliated once they realized their "good, righteous girl" skipped town on her own—especially that she skipped town with a *boy*—so they kept it a secret, allowed the attention to simply dissolve away . . . but then I glance back at the screen, another result catching my attention. This one dated from 1985.

ONE YEAR LATER, MARCIA RAYBURN STILL UNFOUND

I click on the link and scan the scant article, the image, this time, of William and Jane only. They're standing in front of their house and holding a picture of their daughter, their expressions solemn. Practically blank. They look older here, so much older than in their family portrait from only a year before. I can see it in the lines of their faces, the ache in their eyes. William has a beard, Jane's hair is entirely gray, and I suddenly think of my mother again, how she's aged in such a bone-deep way. There's a weariness to her that's infused into everything: her eyes sunken in and shoulders slumped down like the weight of the world is too much to hold. Her smile empty like the muscles remember how to go through the motions but there is no feeling there. No emotion at all.

I zoom in on my screen, looking at the picture of Marcia they're holding. It's pixelated after my attempt to enlarge the framed shot but she still seems so young, so vibrant, her expression exposing a certain lust for life that feels so far removed from the way she is now. Her hair is long and straight and draped over her shoulders, her eyes the same amorphous gray, and I try to reconcile her adolescent face with the older one I saw just this morning. It's hard to compare them, how changed they are, and it makes me wonder what Natalie might look like if she was actually given the chance to grow up. If I would be able to see past the creases and scars, the alterations etched in after twenty-two years of time spent apart, and I realize with a pinch of guilt that it's possible I wouldn't even recognize her if I were to pass her on the sidewalk.

If she's somehow still out there, if she's still alive, she could pass as a stranger to me. After all this time, she *would* be a stranger.

I lean forward, the tips of my fingers grazing the digital picture on the screen as I imagine a young Marcia scribbling into the book I now have, filling up its empty pages with a story an outsider would one day read. It's a bit jarring, I think. All the different ways time changes a person. How the years distort both flesh and memories until everything is too wrinkled to smooth back out—and then it dawns on me swiftly, an insight that jolts me so hard it feels like the Earth has been knocked off its axis. All this unwanted power I suddenly have.

It's the realization that, to the rest of the world, Marcia Rayburn is still missing. She's an unsolved mystery, her life an ellipsis with no tangible end, but I know where she is. I know what happened.

Other than Mitchell, I might just be the only person who does.

CHAPTER 21

A numbness has started to creep into my limbs from these strange revelations I can't understand.

I stand up and peel off my clothes before floating into the bathroom and stepping into the shower, twisting the knob to the hottest setting and letting the water burn me raw. Then I grab a washcloth and start to scrub at the dirt on my arms, the dried mud caked to the creases of my knees. Scratching my nails through a bar of old soap like I can rinse all this knowledge straight from my skin.

I step out a few minutes later, my body buzzing like a severed nerve. My mind is foggy from the heat, from the fact that I now have to make a decision on what to do next.

I walk over to the dresser and change into a pair of shorts and a clean T-shirt, toweling off my hair as I make my way back to the desk. Then I stand in the center of the room, looking around in a strange kind of daze. On the one hand, I could do nothing. I could go back to the city or still stay for the summer, simply going about each day as if none of this happened. I could try to forget I ever found that diary, wiggled my fingers into their business and uncovered these things I should not know. After all, these people invited me into their home, their *lives,* and now here I am, digging around. Exhuming all the skeletons buried deep in their past. I realize now that I've been running on autopilot, that always-oiled urge to put the pieces cleanly together taking over the second I sniffed out something strange, but there could be an innocent explanation for this. Maybe Marcia disappeared for a reason, a reason I don't yet understand.

Maybe she doesn't actually *want* to be found . . . but at the same time, I already know I won't let this go.

I turn around, toward the guesthouse windows, the sky outside a deep, bruised blue. I can barely see it from here, the ambient light fading fast, but I let the main house materialize in my mind as I imagine those looming white columns and restless chairs. The phantom presence of Marcia on the porch, just this morning, sipping slowly from a mug of hot tea. It's so hard to wrap my mind around it: the fact that, just across the yard, on the other side of the grass, lives a woman who no longer exists. A woman who has spent the last forty-one years hidden in plain sight, tucked away in the same state where she once vanished.

So far away, yet still within reach.

I ease back into the desk chair, hoping to uncover a little more before I have to decide what I should do. Then I reach for my laptop, returning to the first article I found.

DRAPER, SOUTH CAROLINA, TEEN GOES MISSING
RAYBURN FAMILY DESPERATE FOR ANSWERS

I flip back to the map, typing in *Draper, South Carolina* and watching as a pin slowly drops. Of course, I've heard of Draper before. Growing up around here, I have a general idea of where things are, the names of all the neighboring towns. I know it's a farming community; mostly large fields and wide, open space. Inland, rural. Full of conservative Christians with political posters in their yards year-round. Now, though, I can see that it's a little over one hundred miles away, and I click over to the second article now, my eyes on the picture of William and Jane as I take in their ranch house in the background. Four blurry numbers bolted to the stairs.

I zoom in further, squinting at the address. I can make out the numbers 1629 and I turn toward my notepad, about to scribble it down when I realize it's pointless without a street name to go with it . . . but then I remember the diary again, Marcia's very first entry when she described her walk to the theater, the fear that she would run into someone she knew. She had called her town a bubble, tightly knit, mentioning her school was only two blocks south of her house—her church, four blocks east—so I switch back to the map again, zooming in to Draper's Main Street. Suddenly grateful she grew up in a place I can crawl in a matter of minutes.

I roam around now, finding my bearings as I click across various locations. Acutely aware of how much has likely changed in such a long stretch of time. I'm reminded again of my drive through Claxton, all the growth that took over my own tiny town, though there still seems to be only one high school in Draper, apparently founded in 1966, so I touch the icon with the tip of my finger, tracing my way two blocks north. Then I search for a church, knowing, in a place like this, that I'm likely to find quite a few. As predicted, there are several across various denominations: Presbyterian, Catholic, Southern Baptist. They're scattered all over town, making it impossible to narrow it down, but I continue to comb through my memories, recounting all the clues Marcia inadvertently dropped. Her talk of the scriptures and the way she dressed.

He doth not dwell in unholy temples. Neither can filthiness or anything which is unclean be received into the kingdom of God.

I tap my fingers against the keys, thinking. Remembering from a documentary I once watched that the LDS community refers to certain buildings as temples. I decide to refine my search again, now specifically looking for a Church of Jesus Christ of Latter-day Saints. There's only one, and it's not very far from the high school, either, so I point at it with my free hand, making my way four blocks west.

I lean forward, watching as my fingers intersect on a residential street called Hickory Road. If Marcia's entries are accurate, then this should be the street where she grew up.

This should be the street where she disappeared, the very street where she was last seen.

I click over to the search bar, typing *1629 Hickory Road* before hitting Enter and watching as the map zeroes in on a house. Then I switch over to satellite as a picture materializes on the screen and I can tell, without a shred of doubt, that it's the same house from the article I just read. The siding has been painted, the stairs replaced, but it's the exact same one William and Jane stood in front of as they held that framed picture of their daughter in their hands.

I stare at the directions, the step-by-step turns, trying to wrap my mind around the fact that I could be there in less than three hours. I could jump in my car and show up on their doorstep, giving a family the answers no one else could. It's a dizzying notion, this level of power. The sense of responsibility I suddenly feel. Of course, I know it's possible the Rayburns don't actually live there anymore—it's possible they're not even *alive* anymore—but still, I lean back, exhaling slowly as I picture these strangers and their last four decades. All the nights they surely spent by that window, willing Marcia to find her way home. If they are still alive, they must have long ago accepted that their daughter is dead. There is no moving on from that, but I know better than anyone that there *is* moving forward. A slow, painful lurching in some tenuous direction, each day that passes providing a little more padding. A cushion to help soften the sharp edges of pain.

I open the desk drawer, eyeing the diary I had stuffed deep inside. I'd told myself I wouldn't read any more, that the details within were none of my business. That plunging into its pages each night was intrusive and wrong and I should leave it alone . . . but now this book feels like my only way to know for sure what to do. If Marcia left her parents on purpose, then giving up where she is feels like not only a massive betrayal but like taking a scalpel to those poor people's stitches, smearing salt in a wound that's still trying to heal.

But if she *didn't* leave on purpose, if she was somehow taken against her will, then her own words might be my only way to find out.

I grab it before I can change my mind, hoisting the diary up by its spine and revealing the picture tucked underneath. I forgot this was in here, the print I slipped in as I shuffled around that first morning, slowly unpacking all my things.

The picture of Natalie, here, in this same place.

I lower the diary onto my lap, lifting the picture from its home in the drawer and holding it between my still-slick fingers as I realize that *this* is the real reason I can't seem to stop digging. This is the thing that's been nagging at me, pulling at me to keep going like two fingers tugging at yarn, desperate to watch it all unravel and reveal the answers hidden beneath.

It's the fact that there are parallels between Marcia and my sister that I cannot even begin to explain. Their lives, their stories, despite them occurring two decades apart, seeming to be inexplicably linked.

I slide the picture into the journal before standing up from the chair and walking back to the bed, easing my body onto the sheets. Then I flip to the latest entry, hesitating for a second as I look at the date scrawled at the top of the page. It's just a few months before Marcia would go missing and something about this moment feels like a point of no return, a crossroads between two conflicting paths as I stand dead in the center, gazing into the darkness ahead.

I stare down at the text, Marcia's quaint cursive like a curling finger beckoning me in. Then I take a deep breath and continue to read.

CHAPTER 22

JANUARY 1984

She visited the Farm for the first time on a Tuesday.

It was Christmas break and Marcia had finally found a few weeks of freedom, her school shut down for over a month. Her father had been preoccupied at work, her mother preoccupied with all the things that weren't her, so she had managed to get away for a while. Lying about spending the day at the library, not wanting to fall behind at school.

She was getting good at that. Lying. Every falsity that came trickling out of her mouth easier to stomach than the one that came before.

She chewed on the side of her cuticle now as they bumped down a gravel roadway, Mitchell leading her farther from home and deeper into the wild unknown. She had no idea where they were going but instead of asking him outright, trying to pry out an answer she knew he wouldn't reveal, she simply slid off her shoes and propped her feet up on the dash, glancing out the window while they passed each road sign. Entering and exiting various small towns as winter's cool fingers brushed through her hair.

Her eyes darted down to the clock, half an hour gone since they had left.

"We're close," Mitchell said, reading her mind, so she turned toward the window again, skin prickling as a woman outside eyed their approach. She was older, back hunched as she shuffled out to her mailbox. Twin slits for eyes as they roared past.

Her gaze drifted to the rearview, watching as the woman continued to stare in their direction until her body was nothing more than a silhouette in the dust.

The car took a left, finally, a narrow ribbon of dirt adjacent to a small stream leading them into a field just ahead. Then she dropped her feet to the floor and leaned toward the windshield, searching for any indication of life. There was nothing around here—no neighborhoods or apartment buildings, nowhere a person could actually live—until she noticed a ramshackle house standing off in the distance, a collection of bodies lying out in the grass.

"Is this—?" she started, trying to choose her words with care. She didn't want to offend him, but at the same time, she couldn't imagine a person living like this.

"Home," Mitchell said simply. "This is home."

Marcia swallowed, her attention narrowing in on the house creeping closer . . . although she quickly realized it wasn't a house. Instead, it looked like a barn, weathered and worn. Spongy brown wood with holes like craters pocking the surface. The double doors were swung open wide and she watched as a woman appeared from inside, bare feet stopping in front of the entrance as she raised up a hand to shield the sun from her eyes.

"There's something I need to take care of," Mitchell said as the camper made its final approach, though Marcia was still trying to take it all in. The place was littered with junk: a small blue bicycle with a dislodged chain, an old mattress splotchy with mold. There was a dog loping around, ribs visible through matted fur. A couple cars clumped together beneath the bony arms of a sweetgum. "Go ahead and join the others. I want you to think of this as your home now, too."

She opened her mouth, the two other people lying in the meadow slowly perking up as they parked. Then she turned toward Mitchell, so many questions quivering on her lips, but he had already opened the door and was stepping outside, slamming it shut before she could respond.

She leaned back, exhaling slowly as he walked away. Picking at that phrase, *the others,* like a scab that was starting to itch. It was the same phrase he had used when they lay in his camper a few weeks ago, his fingers resting gently in the dip of her throat. She still didn't know what that meant, who they were, but now that she could see them, now that they were no longer some nebulous notion, she felt the words starting to squeeze at her chest. A coiling snake crushing the life from her lungs. After all, the existence of *others* implied that Mitchell was a part of a group, a piece of a whole. Something Marcia had never experienced before. Up until that point, she was under the impression that it was just them, just the *two* of them, and a small part of her resented the fact that there were now *others* thrown into the mix . . . but at the same time, she was drawn to the idea of belonging to something. Of no longer floating through life so alone.

She twisted her neck, observing as Mitchell made his way to the cars. At first, she had thought they were empty, but now she noticed the outline of a person in one of the driver's seats. The shadow of a man, twitchy and gaunt, his body slouched deep in the seat.

She watched as Mitchell opened the passenger door, sliding inside the occupied car. Then she turned back around and glanced out the windshield, the three other people present on the property now staring directly at her.

She sighed, forcing herself to get out of the camper before making her way across the field. The grass was calf-high, itchy against her exposed ankles. The entire place filled with weeds and wildflowers, vegetation in various states of bloom. Every single step felt heavy with effort as if her body itself was screaming in protest, warning her not to get too close . . . but at the same time, her mind kept replaying Mitchell's words from before, his command that she meet the others without him. The sound of his voice overriding everything else as the orders throbbed like a pulse, a rhythmic beating inside her mind that forced her feet to keep moving forward until they stopped next to the girl in front of the barn.

"Hi," Marcia said, a whiff of something strong wafting in her direction: the sour smell of body odor mixing with a scent that was herbal and damp. The girl was still squinting into the sun with that outstretched hand hovering over her brow and Marcia glanced at the other hand dangling down by her hip, a smoking roach clutched in her grip. Then her gaze traveled back up, carefully taking in the body before her. The girl was about Marcia's height, maybe a little bit shorter, dishwater hair twisted in knots and a constellation of pimples across her chin like a rash. She wore a linen dress, cream-colored and crinkled. Not even remotely close to the right size.

"I'm Marcia," she continued, cracking a shy smile, though the girl stayed silent, lifting the joint back to her lips. Her hands were dirty, what looked like dried blood caked into the corners of her nails. A collection of rings squeezed over each finger and eyes reminiscent of a summer storm.

The girl exhaled, finally gifting her with the smallest of smiles in return.

"Marcia," she repeated, a ribbon of smoke rolling off the curl of her tongue. "Welcome to the Farm."

The afternoon crawled by in a lazy haze, the first hour spent perusing the property as the girl took her on what felt like an official tour. There was hardly anything at all to show but Marcia watched as she gestured to various inanimate objects, a catch in her voice that sounded like pride.

"This is the willow," she said, sucking the last of the cigarette down before tossing it onto the ground, a mound of dark dirt that looked newly churned. "It's a good place to get some shade when it's hot. The firepit," she continued, gesturing next to an ashen pile of debris. "We cook our meals over the flames each night."

Marcia nodded politely, keeping her distance. The entire thing feeling like some strange dream.

"This is the bedroom," the girl said as they made their way into the barn, Marcia watching as she pointed to a heap of sleeping bags in the center; another mattress with a big yellow stain. "Of course, there's the camper, too," she continued, as if that were obvious. "We take turns, but that's where Mitch sleeps."

Marcia nodded like she understood, though she wasn't sure what *taking turns* meant.

"So, where did he find you?" she asked next, though Marcia was still glancing around, soaking it in. There were piles of food on the other side of the room, bags of potatoes sprouting spindly roots and a pyramid of pears dotted with flies. The place was musty, stale, smelled faintly of rot, and she felt herself swallow a sudden swell of nausea, the sharp taste of bile climbing its way up her throat. Still, there were things that made it feel oddly homey. Funny little details like a pink pillowcase nailed over a window, tied like a curtain with a piece of frayed string. A dining room table holding a vase of dead flowers, the water inside cloudy and green. There was a tall tower of books in the corner, pages stained yellow like nicotine teeth.

"Mitch," the girl pushed, and Marcia turned toward her, those curious eyes taking her in. "Where did he find you?"

"Oh," she said, feeling her spine straighten like a string that had been pulled too taut. Something about the question struck her as strange, though she wasn't exactly sure what it was. "We met at the theater," she replied, realizing it was that word, *find,* that made her uneasy. Like Marcia was some kind of odd collectible; something Mitchell had discovered and slipped into his pocket. Some lost, damaged thing in need of a home. "*Romeo and Juliet.*"

The girl smirked and Marcia felt herself flush like she had just been caught in a lie. It was the truth, technically, but she knew the way she said it had been misleading. Making it sound like more than what it actually was.

"I didn't know Mitch was into movies."

She swallowed, her throat dry as she unearthed the other thing that was making her edgy. It was the fact that this girl kept calling him *Mitch,* three times now, a nickname Marcia had never used herself but slipped out of this other mouth so easily it was obvious the girl said it often.

That her bond with Mitchell, with *Mitch,* was clearly deeper than Marcia's own.

"What about you?" she asked, a territorial stirring rising from the deepest depths of her chest. "Where did Mitch find you?"

The girl smiled again, as if she, too, could hear how wrong the name sounded on Marcia's own tongue. While this other girl said it so coolly, as fluid as the smoke that coiled out of her mouth, coming from Marcia it felt clunky and awkward like a foreign language she hadn't yet mastered. Her desperation so sour it left a lingering taste.

"Digging through a dumpster looking for lunch."

Marcia blinked, the unfiltered honesty catching her off guard.

"This is Annie," the girl said next, changing the topic quick as whiplash before turning around and walking back outside. Marcia jogged to keep up, suddenly remembering the two other people lying out there, and she watched as the second girl glanced up, smiling softly at the sound of her name. Her legs were stretched out in front of her; long blond hair spilling over her shoulders as her bare feet bounced back and forth in the grass.

"Montana," her host continued, gesturing now to the man beside Annie, who simply jerked his chin in their general direction.

"And . . . you?" Marcia asked, realizing the girl never gave her a name.

"Lillian," she said, reaching out to grab Marcia's hand. Then she looked down, ten frail fingers hugging tight at her wrists; the sweat from the girl's skin like a warm, wet kiss. "But everyone here just calls me Lily."

CHAPTER 23

My eyes are fixed to the inside of the desk, that single sentence scratched into the old, worn wood. Then I reach in my hand and rub my finger against it as if the motion itself will buff away all my questions and expose the answers hidden beneath. The etching is weathered, soft like hide, and even though I don't yet know what it means, it still feels like I've taken the smallest step forward, so I stare until the words are branded into my brain.

Lily was here.

It's morning now, another six A.M., muted pastels leaking into the sky as the cabin starts to grow warm in the sun. I'm running on only a few hours of sleep so I tilt my mug back and drain the rest of my extra-strong coffee. The much-needed caffeine making me shake.

I slide the drawer shut and push my chair back, shuffling over to the kitchen as I stare through the window. My senses blunted like my brain is stuffed full of gauze. Once again, I had stayed up too late reading, and although Marcia's diary is full, every single page filled with her words, I had made a sizable dent, making my way through almost two months. I could practically feel her nerves bleeding out of the ink, smelled the whispers of smoke still trapped in her lungs after she got home from that first day at the Farm. Imagined her crawling into bed with her diary in her lap, blue pen racing across every page as her mind stayed stuck on Mitchell and the others still out in that field; a bonfire burning hot between them and the sound of crickets as the sun set.

I want you to think of this as your home now, too.

I place my mug into the sink before rubbing my eyes with the heels of my hands, trying in vain to wake myself up. Then I hear a low growl and look down slowly, recognizing the hollow snarl of my stomach. I never ate dinner last night, I've hardly eaten anything in almost a day, so I open the fridge and grab a few eggs, breaking their shells on the edge of the counter and scrambling them in a small skillet on the stove.

I pour my breakfast onto a plate, steam twisting in the air as I pick at the pile.

I take a small bite, chewing slowly. My gaze trained on my laptop on the other side of the room as Marcia's memories play out like a movie in my mind. There's something that's been nagging at me, some strange sensation ducked just beneath the surface ever since I found that diary pushed into the vent, imagined Natalie's voice narrating the events on the page. Discovered that first article about Marcia going missing—the open window, the lost bag—all these little details between her and my sister that seem to be so much the same.

I walk to the desk and tap at my laptop, clicking into my search history and finding the article I first showed Ryan, the one about Natalie from back at the bar.

BOYFRIEND ARRESTED FOR MURDER OF MISSING GIRL

Then I read it again, more carefully this time.

An arrest has been made in the disappearance of Natalie Campbell, the eighteen-year-old girl who went missing from her bedroom on the evening of August 24, 2002. The suspect in question is Jeffrey Slater, a twenty-eight-year-old Claxton local who has been known to police for quite some time.

I take in the mug shot of Jeffrey now, a sting of sweat prickling under my arms. Then I clear my throat, force myself to keep going.

Detective Eric DiNello, the lead investigator in charge of the Campbell case, reports that eyewitness testimony, as well as a search of Slater's car, is what ultimately led to his swift arrest mere days after Natalie was reported missing by her mother.

"Jeffrey Slater is nothing more than a petty criminal who unfortunately graduated to taking a life," DiNello said during a recent press conference. "He has been in our system for years, charges ranging from drug possession and distribution to supplying alcohol to minors."

Although Campbell's body has yet to be found, several of her personal effects, including an article of clothing soaked in her blood, were discovered in Slater's possession, leading investigators to seek a murder charge.

I chew on the inside of my cheek, that niggling feeling still just out of reach until a tapping erupts from the other side of the room and I twist around in the direction of the sound. There's a face peering in through my window, the fogged-up glass blurry with dew, but I can tell it's Liam, a self-conscious smile snaked across his lips as he pushes his finger into the pane.

Are you ready? he mouths.

I glance back at the clock on the stove. It's starting to get late, the heat of the day rising fast, and despite how badly I want to keep going, all these unanswered questions continuing to climb, I know I'm only here because I was hired to work, so I reluctantly slap my laptop shut, forcing a smile as I make my way to the yard.

"Why New York?"

I look up, the sudden question cutting through the quiet.

"What do you mean?" I respond, glancing back down at my hands, the tips of my fingers tugging at the base of a grape. Liam and I picking in such a slow, silent rhythm, I almost forgot he was even here.

"It's just a big change from Claxton," he says. "There must be a reason you moved out there."

"Work, I guess," I say, feeling my nails plunge into something wet, the liquid insides of putrid fruit. Then I pull my hand back, taking in the leaves speckled with rot as Mitchell's voice worms its way into my mind.

If you neglect the crop, it'll die on the vine.

"You guess?" he repeats, turning to face me.

"I mean, I guess I could have gone anywhere," I say, wiping my fingers against my jeans before glancing up at the sky. I'm not sure what time it is, how long I've been ruminating on all these things that I've learned, though I would guess it's early afternoon, the midday sun still high up above. That, and I can feel the damp of my shirt stuck to my back, the slow dribble of sweat as it drips down my neck. "I just needed to go somewhere different. The city felt like a good place to start fresh."

Liam falls silent, no sounds between us but the rustling of leaves.

"I had never even been out of the state until I graduated high school," I continue, going back to the vines and continuing to pick.

"Can you imagine? Spending your entire life in one place? I honestly can't think of anything worse."

He stays quiet and I turn toward him now, the back of his neck red from the sun.

"Have you ever been?"

"New York?" he asks, his back still toward me. "No, can't say that I have."

"Never?" I ask, the word coming out harsh.

"I've never been up north."

"Wow," I say, wiping my forehead with the back of my hand before resting my wrists on the top of my hips. "Where's the farthest you've been?"

He twists around, a shy smile as he spreads his arms wide.

"Shit," I say, my stomach sinking as I think about what I just said, the condescension of my earlier words. I should have known better, the urban bubble I've called home for the last fifteen years making me forget where, exactly, I am. "Liam, I'm sorry. I didn't mean—"

"It's fine," he says, laughing. "Really, don't sweat it."

"It's a great place," I offer, trying to backpedal, though there's been a tangible shift in the air, a tension I hadn't felt before. "Pretty much everyone I know has never left here, either. My mom, my—"

I stop, the word *sister* hanging limp from my lips, and I can't believe I almost said that out loud. Like Natalie actually had a choice in the matter; like her life wasn't cut short in the very place it began.

Liam is quiet, eyebrows lifting as he waits for me to continue.

"My dad," I say, averting my eyes. "My point is, there's no shame in staying put if you're happy. The small-town life just wasn't for me."

We go back to picking, a heavy silence between us that feels awkward and strained.

"What were you doing before you started at Galloway?" I ask, trying to revive the conversation. Then I take a few steps forward, searching his expression for any lingering offense. "Did you always know you wanted to—"

My brain stops mid-thought as a scream erupts from my throat, the sudden sensation searing through my body leaving me blinded by white-hot pain.

"*Fuck!*" I yell, watching as Liam whips around fast, big, blue eyes stretched wide in surprise. Then I look down just in time to catch a glimpse of a golden-brown body slithering into the brush, the flick of a tail before it melts into the shade. "I think—I think I just—"

"That looked like a copperhead," he interrupts, unstrapping his bucket as he makes his way toward me. I remember, too late, what he warned me of earlier—all the creatures that like to hide from the sun—and I glance down at my ankle, to the place I just felt a sharp bite as two pinprick punctures start to seep blood.

"It's okay," he says. "Just try to relax."

"*Relax?*" I ask, the skin on my leg already starting to burn. "How am I supposed to relax? I just got bit by a *snake*."

"Because the faster your heart beats, the faster the venom will spread."

I drop down to the dirt, extending my leg straight out in front as I will my body to somehow stay calm.

"That was a little one," he says, kneeling by my side as he inspects the wound. "Plus, copperhead bites are rarely fatal."

"Very reassuring," I say, wincing as he grabs my leg in his hands.

"Thought I heard a scream."

We twist to the side, to the sound of a new voice cutting through the quiet, and I watch as Mitchell makes his way over before coming to a stop just above.

"Snakebite," he adds, hands on his hips as he assesses the scene.

"I should probably get to a hospital," I say, looking back at my ankle as the skin starts to swell. "Is there even one on the island?"

"It's about an hour away, but that won't be necessary," Mitchell says as he cranes his neck. "We've got everything we need right here."

I turn toward him, not sure if he's kidding.

"Of course, I'd be happy to take you, but antivenom is expensive. You have insurance?"

My heart sinks as I think about how I lost my coverage right after I quit. How I kept telling myself I'd get it soon, later. Maybe once I sold a few stories. My lack of a paycheck making it impossible to stomach the monthly cost.

"No," I say at last. "I don't."

"Uninsured, you're looking at ten grand a vial. Minimum. Plus, they'll make you stay overnight, maybe multiple nights. That, and lab work. Pain medication."

I close my eyes and tip my head back, feeling the familiar panic flare up.

"Or I can treat you right here, for free."

I open them again, the searing heat starting to sneak up my leg as I stare at this stranger standing before me, my mind winding around all the unusual things that I've learned as I try to decide if I should trust him.

As I wonder if I even have a choice.

CHAPTER 24

I'm in the main house ten minutes later, my body collapsed onto a chair in the living room and my leg propped up on an old stool. Liam is dabbing at the wound with warm, soapy water, my teeth clenched tight as I stomach the pain.

"You'll be okay," he says, not bothering to look up. He's concentrating hard, a tenderness to his touch that's at odds with the calloused skin of his hands. "Mitchell knows what he's doing."

I exhale as I look around. There's no sign of Marcia. She must be upstairs, tucked away somewhere else in the house, and while Mitchell went outside earlier to gather supplies, I hear him walk in a few seconds later and I twist my neck as he enters the room, a bunch of green leaves clutched in his hand.

"What is that?" I ask, noticing the plant with blatant suspicion.

"Broadleaf plantain."

He picks a few leaves from the stem before popping them into his mouth, gnawing hard with his back molars.

•

"And that'll work?" I ask, suddenly skeptical. Wondering if I should just drive myself to the hospital now and deal with the outrageous medical bills later.

"Nature's antivenom," he says. "Just as good as anything you'll get from a doctor."

He kneels down before me, spitting the paste into his palm before slathering it onto the bite.

"The leaves neutralize and draw out the venom," he explains as he works, dabbing at the puncture marks with his fingers. He's being gentle, but still, I wince—from the pain, the stinging heat continuing to crawl up my leg, but also from the fact that this stuff on my skin was just in his mouth. "Antiseptic properties to soothe the area, clear out any lingering bacteria."

He gets up and walks into the kitchen as Liam starts to wrap my ankle in gauze.

"Drink this," he says as he returns, reentering the living room with a mug in his hand.

"And what is *that*?"

"Just a little something to take the edge off."

I grab it, bringing the cup to my lips until I'm hit with another memory, this entire experience calling to mind the very first night I sat in this chair, nursing the exact same mug of hot tea.

I lower it slowly, suddenly uneasy about this whole thing.

"You don't just have a painkiller or something?"

"That is the painkiller," Mitchell says, shrugging when I stay quiet like he couldn't care less if I drank it or not. "Of course, it's your choice, but you'll feel a hell of a lot better with that in your system."

I look over at Liam again, eyes diverted as he continues to wrap. My leg is still throbbing, a mounting heat as the venom seeps in, so I finally give in, returning the mug to my mouth and taking a long drink. It goes down easy, herbal and fresh, and after a few minutes,

I feel my eyes start to close. My body relaxing into the chair as the pain slowly subsides.

I wake up with a dull headache, the muffled thump of my heart in my ears, and a tacky film coating my tongue like glue. Then I sit up slow and rub at my temples, the remnants of reverie skimming the back of my brain.

I had the dream again, the dream where my sister's face replaces my own, but instead of it ending the way it usually does, her body wafting away before I wake up, this time, the visions continued to change.

I pinch my eyes shut, an attempt to memorize the details before I can forget as I visualize myself standing in front of the mirror, my head twisting in a slow circle as Natalie's reflection did the same. Then she had turned around, her body retreating down the long hall before gliding into her bedroom; my dream-self studying her every move as she opened her window and glanced over one shoulder before hoisting both her legs out. Once she was gone, I had peered out, too, expecting to find her climbing into Jeffrey's car . . . but instead, she slid into a camper and slipped off her shoes, propped her bare feet up on the dash as her eyes found mine in the rearview mirror. Our gaze locked in a weighty silence until, at last, it drove away.

I open my eyes again, though it doesn't make much of a difference. It's practically pitch-black in here, though the glow of the moon reflecting off the water is giving me the faintest hint of light and I finally realize I'm back in the guesthouse.

I look to the side and flip on the lamp. Then I tap at my phone resting on the side table, the illuminated screen reading four in the morning.

I have no idea how long I've been out—and not only that, but I have no idea how I got here.

I glance around the cabin again, trying to adjust to the sudden bright light as yesterday comes to me like a mosaic, a dozen little shards haphazardly placed to form a picture that's disjointed and strange: sitting in the main house, Liam wrapping my ankle in gauze as Mitchell brought me that tea from the kitchen. Taking a slow, tentative sip before feeling the hot liquid gush down my throat. My limbs growing heavy as the conversation around me morphed into static until, at last, it all went dark.

I lean against the headboard, eyes on the ceiling as I think back to the first night I got here; how Marcia had been asleep in that chair as Mitchell handed me a mug then, too. The way I drank it so quickly, not wanting to be rude, before stumbling into the cabin and collapsing onto the sheets. Then I blink a few times, the room getting sharper as I recall some of Marcia's earliest entries: meeting Mitchell in the back of that alley, a roach in his grip as he filled her heart with hope and her lungs with smoke. Waking up in his camper without remembering how she first fell asleep; her brain bubble-wrapped and her mind moving slow. My own mind starts to move faster now, though it still feels sluggish, like I'm attempting to sprint through mud. Still, I unleash my memory, letting it curl around every odd thing that's happened since the second I stepped into this place. How Marcia often looks so groggy, so ill, and how Mitchell never wants to leave us alone. My headache that first morning, heavy like a hangover, and feeling like I could have slept for days. Back then, I thought it had just been exhaustion, the remnants of a terrible two months followed by a long twelve-hour drive . . . but now, I'm not so sure.

"Is he *drugging* you?" I whisper, imagining Marcia's frail body as I realize: he might be drugging me, too.

I fling off the covers and look down at my legs, more muddled memories trying to make themselves known. Liam helping me out of that chair, walking me slowly across the yard before easing my body into this bed. I'm still fully clothed, still in my dirt-streaked shirt and shorts from before, and I eye the gauze wound tight around my ankle before sitting up further, my fingers shaking as I start to unwrap. The fabric is stuck to my skin, sweat and pus making it gummy and wet, though when I finally get the whole thing off, I can see the green leaves inside have turned putrid and black and already, the bite looks so much better.

The swelling has subsided, the searing pain from before muted into a throb.

I exhale, pushing my fingers through my hair as I wonder why Mitchell would actually help me if he had any intention of causing me harm. It doesn't make sense, none of it does, and I turn to the side, trying to decide what I should do, when I notice the diary peering out from beneath the damp sheets.

I pick it up, my fingers flipping through the remaining pages.

I'm about halfway done, maybe a few more hours until I reach the end.

I exhale, returning to the last page I left off. I'm still so tired, my brain bleary from whatever it is that I drank. I want to keep sleeping, slip back into oblivion and get some real rest, but it feels like I have to keep going if I have any hope of uncovering the truth, so I force myself to stare at the words, the age-stained pages and cobalt pen.

Fighting the murk still floating around in my mind as I attempt to focus, to slither back in.

CHAPTER 25

MARCH 1984

"Lily of the valley."

Marcia turned to the side, a pinch in her scalp as Lily braided her hair. They were sitting out by the barn, their usual spot, bare legs crossed in the grass as a sleepy breeze carried in the stink from the river.

"What?" she asked, only half listening as Lily held out a spray of white flowers, delicate petals drooped into a bell.

"They're why Mitch gave me my name."

Marcia swallowed her response, that familiar flood of envy starting to swell in her chest.

"They're dainty but tough," Lily continued, pushing a stem into the braid. "Invasive, under the right conditions. They can make the most hostile environments home."

Marcia glanced down at her leg, a red ant crawling its way up her thigh. Then she moved to flick it off, send it sailing safely away, but instead, she found herself pushing her finger down hard, flattening its body against her slick skin.

A sound from behind made them both turn around, the screech of old brakes as a car pulled up beneath the shade of the sweetgum. It was the same car Marcia had noticed her first day at the Farm, the one with that man sitting uncertainly inside. After Lily had introduced her to the others, Marcia had next asked about him, though her answer had provided more questions than answers.

Oh, that's one of our regulars, Lily had said with a shrug. *Some rich guy who just inherited a fortune and doesn't know how else to spend it.*

"You know, you don't *have* to leave."

Marcia blinked back to the present, to Lily's voice in her ear. Then she glanced to the side, staring at the streams of hushed light through the trees. The sun was starting to make its descent, which meant it was getting late, close to dinner. Around the time she had to get home.

"You could stay here with us."

Marcia kept quiet, not sure what to say. At that point, she had been going to the Farm a couple times each week: after class, over the weekends. Her initial discomfort about the state of the place bleeding away like the slow drip of a faucet, an oozing wound. Sometimes she would walk to school in the mornings to find Mitchell parked behind the building, burnt-orange camper idling in the lot. In the beginning, there was always a moment of hesitation, a single second when she thought about pretending she didn't see him at all, but every single time, she felt her body move toward him as if it had commandeered all control.

Then she would simply open the door and slide inside, skipping class completely as the day slipped away in a lazy haze.

"I wish I could," she responded, surprised to find she actually meant it.

"What's stopping you?" Lily asked, and Marcia could feel the warm breath on her neck as she thought about the inner workings of the Farm, this little community that they had built. They each had their own duties: cooking, cleaning. Every few days, Montana would drive one of the girls into town and they would come back with arms full of supplies. Most of it was strictly functional, things like food and soap and tampons for the girls, but every now and then, Marcia would catch a glimpse of something strange like an antique pitcher with a chipped lip, a small oil painting Lily would hang on the wall. A quiet hum as she decorated the barn with their bounty, each item adding its own personal touch.

"My family," Marcia said, suddenly embarrassed at how childish it sounded. She knew she was the only one who actually left this place, that all the others stayed even after the sun set, and she hated that she wasn't around for that. For the things that unfolded when the stars snuck out.

"Hm," Lily grunted, continuing to braid.

Marcia pictured them now, her family back home: her father reclined in that chair by the fire and her mother in the kitchen, dutifully doing her chores. She knew they were starting to suspect something, some shift in her behavior they couldn't quite place, but so far, they hadn't pushed it. They hadn't actually caught her breaking any of their rules, so they simply eyed her each night as she crept into her bedroom, probably counting down the days until the school year would come to a close. She was eighteen now, set to graduate in just a few months. College was off the table, which meant she would be expected to settle down soon, and the thought of that made her sick with dread. The idea of her life ending the second she was starting to feel so alive.

"What about yours?" she asked quietly, suddenly grateful they weren't facing each other. She and Lily seemed to be about the same age and Marcia always wondered how she got away with it all, spending every second here at the Farm. She wasn't sure how to question it, though. She didn't want to be rude, but now that the opportunity had presented itself, now that Lily had opened the door, she decided she had to see where it went.

"My what?" Lily asked, the words hard and flat in her throat.

"Your family."

"Oh, I don't have one."

"Come on," she nudged. "Everyone has a family."

"Well, I don't," she replied. "I grew up in foster care. Aged out a year ago, so here I am. This is my family. The only family I need."

"What about Montana?"

"He moved here from Missoula a few months back."

"And he lives here, too?"

"Comes and goes. He's still in school."

"How about Annie?" she asked, realizing, somehow for the first time, that she hadn't actually seen Annie in weeks. She used to be here every time Marcia came by, floating through the field and mostly keeping to herself. She was unassuming, rarely said a thing, but she was a quiet constant. A familiar presence that blended into their surroundings as perfectly as the wildflowers that grew along the river, the subtle smell that occasionally wafted over with the wind the only reminder they were even there at all.

"Orphan," Lily responded, continuing to braid. "But don't worry about Annie. She won't be coming around anymore."

"Why not?" Marcia asked, her head yanking back with too much force.

"She wasn't committed."

"Committed," Marcia repeated, a familiar heat rising into her cheeks as she felt Lily tie off the ends of her hair. Then a strained silence settled over them both until she heard the girl mutter something under her breath, her voice so low she could barely make out the words.

"To the family," Lily said, fingers lingering against Marcia's smooth skin as she felt her pulse begin to mount in her neck. "To us."

CHAPTER 26

I turn the page to be ripped from the memory, some strange acronym scribbled in the corner drawing my attention away from the scene.

I lean in closer, my nose practically touching the paper as I take in the silver ink, an odd collection of letters and numbers that looks blatantly out of place. Whatever this is, it was clearly written at a different time than the rest of the entry, but before I can work out what it could mean I hear a noise from outside, the sound of footsteps making me flinch.

I turn to the side, the window still open to let in a breeze as the silhouette of a body approaches the guesthouse just as the first hint of light starts to show.

I shut the book quickly, sliding it back into the sheets before standing up and making my way to the door, opening it before Liam's fist can connect.

"Good morning," I say, my mind still trying to process all that has happened.

"Good morning to you," he responds as I look down at the two mugs clutched in his hands. "It's just coffee," he says when he senses me staring, thrusting one in my direction before bringing the other to his lips and taking a sip. "Promise."

I stare at him, not sure if that's his attempt at a joke.

"What was that yesterday?" I ask at last, crossing my arms instead of inviting him in.

"What was what?"

"That drink Mitchell gave me."

"Oh, he's into herbal remedies, things like that. Not a big fan of modern medicine . . . or anything modern, for that matter."

I think back to one of our first conversations, my questions about Mitchell as we worked in the vineyard and Liam's blunt answer. *He's good with plants.*

"He drugged me," I state, my voice flat as I continue to stare.

"I don't know about *that*," Liam responds. "He told you he was giving you a painkiller."

"I can barely remember a thing."

"Well, it worked, didn't it?"

I think of unwrapping that gauze, the venom in my leg clearly diminished and the plantain leaves juicy and black.

"It's really no different than an oxycodone or something," he continues, and I look down at my ankle next. That searing pain that's all but gone, the flesh returned to its natural state. "Or any of that synthetic crap they prescribe."

We're both silent, a mounting discomfort as Liam stands in the doorway, neither of us sure what to say next.

"Anyway, I was just coming to check on you," he says, his body shifting like he's suddenly embarrassed. "I figured I'd bring you some coffee, but I can leave you alone."

"No, I'm sorry," I say, reaching out to touch his arm. My mind is muddled with new information because now I realize that Liam is right—Mitchell *did* tell me what he was giving me, I had the option of turning it down—so I lift my hand and take the mug from his grip, feeling the pinch of warmth on my palms. "I'm still just a little rattled, I guess."

"Can't blame you for that. Those things can be scary."

"I just need a few minutes to get ready," I say, glancing at the clock on the counter as a new wave of exhaustion works its way through. Not only is this physical work, hours on my feet in the unbearable heat, but I'm now acutely aware of how little sleep I've been getting. My nights consumed by the diary, that dream. The deprivation starting to seep in like a stain.

"No need," Liam says. "You should rest more, take the day off."

"Are you sure?" I ask, looking over his shoulder at the vineyard in the distance. All that work I've been hired to complete. We've barely made a dent, my second day cut short after I got that bite, but Liam is already shaking his head.

"Positive," he says, turning around before making his way toward the direction of the vines. "I'll just be out there if you need me."

I linger in the doorway as Liam walks away; then I turn around and head straight toward the kitchen, pouring my untouched coffee down the sink.

It's tempting to stay in here all day, the cool of the air-conditioning and the rest of the diary beckoning me back, but at the same time, I need to think through how to make the most of this time. I have the entire day to myself, a luxury I'm not sure I'll get again, and while the diary is tempting, this forbidden glimpse I'm getting into the past, its contents have so far led to more questions than answers and I'm starting to wonder if it's time to take action, time to take matters into my own hands.

I walk to the bed, the outline of the book rippling the sheets as I think back to the moment I found it; dust and cobwebs covering it completely like it had been lost for a long, long time. It would be logical to assume that whoever hid it like that hadn't wanted it to be found—but now I wonder if it might be the opposite.

I think back to my first morning here, Liam leading me around the grounds as I inquired about their workers, surprised to learn it was only him.

We used to hire a handful of seasonals, he said had. *Give 'em each a couple hours a week, but now, with only one, we can put them up in the guesthouse.*

I know I've only been at Galloway for a few days, but I realize now that I've never once seen Marcia leave the property . . . and I get the feeling she never does. I've never even seen her leave the house; the farthest she's ventured is out onto the porch, but even then, she's still watched by Mitchell. Her movements monitored like he doesn't trust her at all in his absence. This place is secluded, completely cut off, and I wonder now if she put her diary in here in hopes that someone would someday find it. If she knew there would be a person living in the guesthouse each summer and she thought that maybe this was her chance: that someone would read it, put the pieces together themselves.

Maybe this diary is her scream for help.

It's almost unthinkable: the idea of a woman being held captive for forty-one years, stuck under the spell of a man so strong she feels as though she can't move, she can't speak. She can only sit there, silent, waiting to be rescued . . . but then I think of Mitchell's truck parked each day in their driveway, the key ring dangling from the loop in his jeans. I think of the fact that she has access to the internet, that this place used to be teeming with people. A litany of chances to plan her escape. She isn't young and vulnerable anymore. It's not as if he has her chained up, locked in a basement and unable to leave— but of course, I know there are so many ways to trap a person.

There are so many ways to exert control.

I think of all the stories I've covered, the countless women who are toyed with and traumatized. I know it's hard for people to understand if they haven't actually experienced it themselves but it happens more often than one would think: trauma bonding and Stockholm syndrome. The idea of a person forming feelings for their captor; finding themselves simply unable to leave. Just last year, Ryan reported a piece about a child who used to accompany his kidnapper every time he went to run errands, the entire town thinking they were father and son. It was so hard to imagine the two of them walking around a crowded store together, eating breakfast each weekend at the same diner. The boy never once running or screaming for help. It's tempting to want to shake them from their stupor, tell them their freedom is so close within reach, but that kind of behavior takes *years* of conditioning. A methodical grooming until the person in question is no longer a person.

Instead, they're a pet, obedient and broken. Cowering in the corner to keep from being kicked.

I blink out of the memory, the burn of fresh tears welling up in my eyes as I think about the summer Natalie went missing and all the things I should have done back then, all the disclosures I should have made. The regret following me around for the last twenty-two years making it impossible to truly move on—but now, though, now that I'm here, it feels like I'm getting a second chance. Like I've been given an opportunity to make things right, because even though Marcia isn't my sister, I know she's not, she's someone *like* my sister. Someone who slipped into the grip of the wrong person.

Someone who made one simple mistake—getting into the wrong man's car—and had her whole life severed as a result.

I glance out the window, my eyes resting on the main house in the distance. Then I stand up and start to get dressed, a new resolve digging into my chest as a semblance of a plan begins to take shape.

CHAPTER 27

"I thought you were taking the day off."

Liam is kneeling in the dirt, harvest bucket already strapped to his chest as I make my slow approach.

"I'm just stretching my legs," I say, glancing over to Marcia and Mitchell sitting on the porch, twin mugs clutched in both of their hands.

"I'm not sure that's a good idea."

I turn back toward Liam, cocking my head as he squints into the sun.

"You're supposed to keep that leg elevated," he says, gesturing to my ankle. "Avoid unnecessary movement."

"I'll keep it short," I say, already making my way toward the water. "That cabin gets stuffy. I need some fresh air."

I stick close to the marsh, keeping my eyes trained on the distance, though I have a feeling that I'm being watched. Still, I pretend not to notice, biding my time as I trail my fingers across various plants—until I pause, recognizing the leaves now grazing my skin as the same ones Mitchell had applied last night. I grab them gently, fingers stroking the rubbery veins as I remember him popping them into his mouth, chewing until they became a thick paste.

I lower the plant, recalling my first day on the side of the house; Liam and me snapping those flowers and sucking the honey straight from the stem.

Just don't go blindly eating stuff around here, he had said after I stuck that blue berry into my mouth. I had teased him about it, but still, he'd insisted. *Marshland grows all kinds of things.*

I twist back around, my eyes darting between the vineyard and porch. Liam has gone back to the harvest and Marcia and Mitchell have gone back inside so I turn toward the plant again and remove my phone from my back pocket, checking the service in the corner of the screen. I'm still close enough to the main house to have a single blinking bar so I navigate to the camera as I think about a trick Ryan once taught me, one of those iPhone features nobody knows that they have. Then I snap a picture of the plant and click on the image, swiping up to find an icon of a leaf at the bottom of the screen.

I tap on that next, my phone giving me the option to look up what it is.

Plantago major, also known as broadleaf plantain, is an herbaceous, perennial plant. The young, tender leaves can be eaten raw, and the older, stringier leaves can be boiled in stews.

I look down at the picture on my screen, identical to the plant that was just in my hand.

Commonly used in folk medicine for wounds, sores, and insect stings, broadleaf plantain leaves are known to reduce inflammation, block bacterial growth, extract venom, and relieve pain.

I chew on the inside of my cheek, wondering if this is all an overreaction. After all, the description on my screen right now is the exact same as the one Mitchell gave me last night, which means he really was only trying to help . . . but then again, I still don't know what was in that tea he gave me. I don't know what Marcia is constantly drinking, whatever it is making her so lethargic and slow, so I swipe back to my camera and take a picture of the next plant I can find, skimming the article before moving on to another. There are all kinds of things growing out here: needlegrass and nettles, cordgrass and cattails. I eye a cluster of scorpion grass next, the pale blue petals huddled together making some faraway memory itch. Everything seems to be perfectly benign and I'm about to keep walking until I come across a vertical collection of lush green leaves, the description on the screen making me stop in my tracks.

Convallaria majalis, commonly known as lily of the valley, is a garden flower that is both sweetly scented and highly poisonous. All parts of the plant are toxic, including the berries, leaves, roots, and stems.

I stop reading, glancing back at the plant as Marcia's last entry writhes around in my mind.

Its compounds attack all parts of the body, most notably the heart and nervous system. Upon consumption, initial symptoms of lily of the valley poisoning include a slow and irregular heartbeat, nausea, vomiting, confusion, drowsiness, weakness, and blurry vision.
If left untreated, symptoms will progress to cardiac arrest and, eventually, death.

I look back at the plant, remembering the fox I saw by the marsh. Its copper fur blowing gently in the breeze. Then I hear the screen door slap and I twist around fast, watching as Mitchell makes his way toward the shed. I stand still as he walks, his body disappearing inside before coming back out a few seconds later with yesterday's harvest all bagged and stickered and ready to sell. Then he loads it all into his truck along with crates of produce and cartons of eggs before sliding into the driver's seat and slamming the door shut behind him.

I watch as he reverses fast down the drive, a tornado of dust erupting from his tires. Then I turn back toward Liam, still picking in the vineyard, as the first part of my plan kicks into motion.

"I'm going back in to grab a nap," I call out, pushing my phone into my pocket as Liam looks up, squinty eyes trailing me across the yard. "You were right, all this walking is wearing me out."

He lifts his hand in a friendly salute as I make my way toward the guesthouse. After a few yards, I chance a glance around, making sure he isn't paying attention.

Only then do I reverse course, jogging up the steps of the main house and rapping my fist hard on the door.

"Marcia?" I call out after a few seconds, shielding the sun from my eyes as I peer through the windows. "Marcia, it's Claire."

I knock again, turning back around as the first trickle of nerves work their way up my spine. Liam is still in the vineyard, his back to me while he picks, but I don't want him to glance back around and find me standing on the porch instead of in my own house. I'm sure I could come up with an excuse, some simple reason to explain it away, but more than that, it's the prospect of Mitchell returning that's making me nervous. He's going into town, like he does every day, and while I haven't been here long enough to keep a precise log of his movements, based on the distance between here and there, I figure I have about an hour until he comes back.

If I'm going to talk to Marcia, steal these precious few moments of her being alone, I need to talk to her *now*.

I wait another few seconds before finally deciding to try the knob, surprised to find it twists easily in my hand. The door pushes open as if on its own and at first, it seems strange that they would keep it unlocked, given how private they seem to be—but then I realize that living their lives in seclusion like this means they don't have to worry about strangers breaking in the way other people do. They don't have a security system; no hidden cameras or alarms on their doors.

Mitchell doesn't seem all that concerned about keeping people out; instead, he seems to dedicate his time to keeping them *in*.

"Marcia?" I call again, stepping gingerly over the threshold and closing the door quietly behind me. "Marcia, it's Claire. Can I talk to you for a second?"

I tiptoe deeper into the house, the memories washing over me as I remember more snippets from when I was in here last night. My plan is still shaky, still starting to form, but as of right now, my intention is to just come clean. I figure there's no point in trying to be coy, not when I only have this hour-long window to get to the truth. Because of that, I'm going to tell Marcia I found her diary and that I've read enough of it to be concerned.

I'm going to offer her the opportunity to explain, and if I don't like the things that I hear, I'm going to leave and I'm going to get help.

"Marcia," I say again, a little louder this time. "It's me, Claire—"

I enter the living room, stopping dead in my tracks as I find Marcia's body lying limp in a chair. I feel a pang of something shoot through my chest—panic, fear, the sight of her unconscious body like this making me practically choke back a scream—but then I notice her breathing, the rhythmic rise and fall of her chest.

She's asleep, *deeply* asleep, like the very first night I came into this house.

I creep closer, thinking about how my voice didn't rouse her awake. Even through my knocking, my yelling, she didn't seem to hear me at all . . . and that's when I register the mug by her side, the same one she was sipping out of this morning.

The same one she has almost every time I see her. A clean, simple, ceramic white.

I peer inside, finding it empty except for some leafy residue caked to the bottom. Then I pick it up, my theory about Mitchell continuing to grow as I push the pad of my finger into the base, feeling a few leaves stick to the surface of my skin.

I pull my hand out, bringing it slowly up to my nose. There's a hint of something herbal, a concoction of smells I can't recognize. Then I bring my fingers to Marcia's neck as I check for a pulse.

It feels strong and steady, albeit somewhat slow, but still, she's breathing. She's breathing fine.

I put the mug down, trying to think through what to do next. Talking to Marcia clearly isn't an option, but now I realize I might have something better.

Now, I have free rein to search their home.

I pull out my phone and glance at the clock—ten minutes have passed since Mitchell left—and decide to poke around a bit, see if there's anything here that might help. I start in the kitchen, opening the fridge and scanning the contents. Finding all the right things in all the right places, nothing jumping out as out of place. Then I move toward the cabinets, opening the doors to find a bunch of canisters of dried herbs. I sniff a few, not sure what they are, before I make my way back into the foyer, trailing my fingers across the banister.

I lean back, checking to make sure that Marcia's still asleep. I can just barely see her from down the hall but I can tell that her eyes are still closed, her breathing steady, so I take the stairs two at a time, making my way to the second floor and cringing as the old wood creaks. Once I hit the landing, I find one long hallway with three closed doors—two on one end, one on the other—and it makes me blink for a second, my mind suddenly back on our hallway at home. The layouts of the houses are practically identical and I picture our two rooms now, the way Natalie's and mine were situated side by side.

How I would lie in bed and hold my breath, listening for traces of life through the walls before I heard her leave and slipped in behind her, snooping through her stuff like I'm doing right now.

I shake my head, ignoring the hammering of my heart in my ears, and decide to start with the door on the left.

I approach the knob, twisting it gently and peering inside. It seems to be a guest room with a full bed in the center and two small tables on either side, a large wooden dresser pushed flush to the wall. The bed is made, a checkered blue quilt folded tight across each corner, and I think about stepping in farther, looking around, when I realize twenty minutes have probably passed. There isn't much evidence of life in here. The walls are sparse, all the lights off, and if it is just a guest room, I'd be better off using my remaining minutes in Mitchell's room instead.

The room where he probably spends most of his time, the room he's most likely to stash his secrets.

I close the door and peek inside the second door beside it, finding a small bathroom that's immaculately clean. I do a cursory scan of the cabinet, sneak a peek behind the shower curtain, before I close the door and make my way back down the hall. My eyes trained on the last room left.

I grip the knob, my breath held in my throat as it turns.

The room behind this door is the primary bedroom, unmistakably, and I step inside, keeping it open to ensure I can hear any noises from downstairs. The first thing I spot are two windows facing the front of the property and I walk toward them quickly, glancing outside. The driveway is still empty, nothing but tire tracks where Mitchell's truck is typically parked. Liam is sitting in the shade of a live oak, eating his lunch, so I turn around and start my scan of the bedroom, pulling open various drawers as I search.

I find a tube of hand cream and a wad of thin tissues, a couple torn bookmarks and crumpled receipts. Then I close the drawers again, sighing as I survey the rest of the room. There are some clothes scattered across the ground, balled-up socks and a stray pair of sweatpants peeking out from beneath the bed . . . and then I notice a patch of the floor that looks different than the rest, the boards slightly lighter than the ones that surround it.

I drop to my knees, running my hands along the edge of the boards. The lighter ones are slightly loose like they were ripped out once, the wood worn down from being repeatedly handled, and I dig my fingers under one of the planks, surprised to find it comes up easily. It isn't nailed down; instead, there's a hollow spot beneath it with some kind of fabric stuffed deep inside, so I keep lifting the others, removing two more until there's a distinct hole in the floor.

I peer in, a knife in my chest when I see what's there.

It's a bag, charcoal black and covered in dust, and I feel my fingers shake as I think back to August of 2002, somehow just yesterday and a whole lifetime ago. Then I take a deep breath, imagining myself listening as Natalie opened her window, grabbing a bag from deep in her closet before climbing her way down that old tree.

A bag that looked just like the one I'm staring at right now.

A bag that disappeared the same night she did.

CHAPTER 28

My hands are shaking as I reach my arms out, lifting the duffel from its hollowed spot in the floor.

There are clumps of gray grime clinging to the fabric, the musty smell making me stifle a sneeze. Then I pull it onto my lap, the tips of my fingers grazing the surface before reaching for the zipper and yanking it open. I'm terrified to learn what might be in here, bracing myself to find more of Natalie's things—clothes I might recognize or, God forbid, the remains of her body that have yet to be found—but instead, the word BERKELEY appears from between the two lips and I twist my head, eyeing an old sweatshirt folded on top.

I touch the fabric, faded blue cotton with the collegiate name stitched in white thread. Then I feel a shiver travel down the length of my spine as I think back to one of Marcia's earliest entries.

This is the sweatshirt she found in the camper, the one she wrapped around her shoulders as she and Mitchell lay in the dark.

I pick it up now, rubbing the cotton between my fingers. The strangest feeling washing over me like I had actually been in there with them, like I had physically been in that car. It feels suddenly surreal, the idea of Marcia's words on the page actually existing in real life; this thing in my hands being the exact same thing she held forty-one years ago. The same thing I read about my first night here. It's like a part of me hadn't been convinced of the diary's truth before, those pages a portal to some strange, separate world, but just like finding Lily's name scratched in the desk, discovering the location of Marcia's childhood home, this old sweatshirt now clutched in my hands feels like more irrefutable proof that her recollections are actually real.

That the events in those pages really did happen.

I drape the sweatshirt across my lap and unfold it slowly, the cloth smelling like dust and decay. Then I think of the diary again, Marcia describing the way she tried to stitch Mitchell together piece by piece.

Not all that different from what I'm doing right now.

I run my fingers across the fabric again, thin as tissue, and notice a tag sticking out from the inside. It has the logo of a university bookstore—but there's something else there, too. Some kind of bleeding black ink staining the satin.

I flip the tag over to find a set of initials written in Sharpie on the back.

KAP.

I stare at the letters, little black veins branching off from where the pen bled, as I try to figure out what they could mean. I don't recognize them from anywhere, I don't recall seeing them anywhere in the diary, so I reach for my pocket, grabbing my phone and opening the camera before taking a picture of the tag and deciding I'll have to dig into it later.

I place the sweatshirt off to the side, directing my attention back to the bag as I eye the other things nestled inside. There's an old leather wallet, a white towel, and a thick brown folder stuffed full of files. It's an odd collection of items, but I decide to start with the folder first, so I pull it out and flip the flap open, eyeing the papers tucked neatly inside. Immediately, I recognize it as the deed to the property, the address I now know to be Galloway Farm . . . but after skimming the first few pages, I realize I can't find Mitchell's name anywhere.

Instead, it appears to be the deed from *before* it came into Mitchell's hands. The deed between the previous owners.

I stare at the document, trying to come up with an explanation that never arrives. Then I place the folder to the side and reach next for the wallet. The leather is smooth and soft and I flip it open to find an old driver's license tucked inside. The ink is faded, the card expired back in the eighties, but then I notice the name printed at the top.

A name I came across when I first started my search, ignorant to where it all would lead.

A name I just saw on the deed a few seconds ago.

This license belongs to Steven Montague, the man who sold the land to Mitchell. The last owner of Galloway Farm.

I stare at the man's picture, trying to work out if I recognize him at all. He looks young in his license, fair-haired and fragile. Probably somewhere in his late twenties and hovering around 130 pounds.

I grab my phone again, snapping a picture of the license before setting it to the side. Then I reach for the towel, finally, the very last item. Wondering if this will somehow provide any clarity but not feeling confident it actually will. So far, everything I've found has only led to more questions, but still, I lift it from the bag and am immediately thrown off by its unexpected weight. It feels like I'm holding at least five pounds, way too heavy for something like this . . . and then I realize the towel isn't folded up like the sweatshirt was. A neat, perfect, tidy little square.

Instead, it's crumpled into a ball like there's something inside it. Something heavy and hard, wrapped like a present.

Something I'm suddenly not sure I want to open.

I look down at the wad in my hands, forcing myself to take a long breath before I start to slowly unwind. It feels like undoing a bandage covering some deep, deadly wound. My stomach clenched tight as I prepare myself for the horrors that could be hidden beneath.

I remove the last layer and exhale slowly, silently studying the gun in my lap.

I don't feel much at first, an eerie numbness as I register the feeling of cold steel on my thigh. For a few seconds, I simply stare at the weapon, not sure what to do, when a noise from outside grabs my attention. It's a subtle sound, the high-pitched whistle of rusted brakes, and I twist around fast, snapped from my trance as my eyes rush to the window. My palms suddenly slick with sweat.

I place the gun on the ground before standing up slowly, trying to keep low as I make my way to the glass. Then I peer outside, that familiar feeling of fear burrowing into my chest when I see Mitchell's truck parked just below.

CHAPTER 29

I sprint back toward the bed, suddenly aware of how heavy my steps sound as I hear the front door creak open downstairs, the bones of the house shaking as it shuts.

I stare down at the gun on the floor, my mind pulled in too many directions. There isn't enough time to think through my options so I just start throwing things back into the bag, attempting to put it all back where I found it. I stuff the folder in first, followed by the wallet, then the sweatshirt. I grab the towel next, ready to fold it around the gun . . . but then I stop, looking back down at the weapon on the floor. Listening to Mitchell walking around downstairs and suddenly feeling so exposed.

I know I shouldn't do it, I shouldn't even be in this house at all, but at the same time, I suddenly can't stomach the thought of being on this property completely defenseless, especially considering what I just found.

I think of Liam's words again, that very first day as we sat beneath the trees.

I guess you can say they're protective of their privacy.

I wonder now, for the very first time, what exactly it is Mitchell is trying to protect—and how far he might go to protect it.

I decide, in a flash, that I need a way to protect myself, too, so before I can bother to think through the consequences, to fully comprehend what exactly I'm doing, I wrap up the towel and toss it back in the bag before shoving the gun in my back pocket.

Then I rezip the bag, stuffing it into the floor and silently sliding the boards back into place.

I stand up and glance around the room now, everything appearing just as I found it. Then I creep into the hallway, closing the bedroom door behind me as the weight of the gun sits heavy on my hip. I slink over to the top of the stairs, listening intently as I recognize the rush of a running faucet. The opening of a cabinet, the clinking of glass. It sounds like Mitchell is in the kitchen getting himself water so I take the opportunity to descend the stairs slowly, trying to remember the squeaky boards from my climb up and hoping I don't step on one now.

Halfway down, I chance a glance over the railing, peering into the hallway and craning my neck to look into the living room. Marcia is still asleep in her chair and I start to lower myself further, my eyes darting between the hall and door as I attempt to gauge both distance and time.

I'm five stairsteps away, only a handful of feet. I could make it outside in less than ten seconds if I bolted out now . . . but Mitchell could come out of the kitchen at any time. He could round the corner to see me in his home, my hand reaching fast for the knob.

He would know I was upstairs, rooting through his things while he was away.

I'm still trying to work up the nerve to move when the groan of old wood erupts from the hallway as Mitchell comes ambling out of the kitchen, mere feet below where I now stand. I recoil, pressing my body against the wall and grateful I hadn't chosen that moment to run. He doesn't look my way; instead, I listen as he heads into the living room before chancing a glance over the railing again. He's hovering over Marcia now, his fingers reaching for her braid and twisting a few strands of her hair in his hands. She looks so small like that, her fragile body crumpled beneath him like a sapling crushed beneath the sole of a shoe, and I wonder what he's about to do next until he seems to notice something on her neck, his eyes squinting as he twists his head.

He drops the braid, now reaching for a spot beneath her jaw. Then he holds his finger there like he's looking for a pulse before removing it and bringing his hand to his nose.

I continue to stare, not understanding what he's doing until I feel a twist of something in my chest—comprehension, fear—as I look down at my own hand, the leafy residue from when I brushed my fingers into the base of her mug. I had touched Marcia's neck immediately after and I wonder now if some of it had rubbed off on her skin, lingering little scraps that Mitchell now sees.

He's probably wondering where they came from, how they got there when Marcia was asleep the entire time he was gone.

I push myself back against the wall and pinch my eyes shut, my heart hammering hard in my throat. Mitchell could start searching the house now, turn the corner into the hall to find me hiding on the middle of the stairs. I wonder if I could make it into the guest room, conceal myself in the closet or something, and I'm about to turn around and attempt to hide when my phone starts to vibrate in my pocket, the sound of it deafening in the silence of the house.

I reach for it quickly, pulling it out and jamming the silencer on the side. Ryan is calling and I cuss under my breath as I remember what Liam said about the modem in the main house.

I have plenty of signal in here, enough for a call to actually come through, and now I can hear Mitchell start toward the stairs and I know he must have heard it, too.

I squeeze my eyes shut, preparing myself for him to round the corner when a new sound emerges on the porch. It's footsteps, unmistakably, and I open my eyes just as the front door bursts open beneath me.

"Hey, it's getting ready to storm."

It's Liam's voice, urgent and strong, and I flatten myself harder against the wall as if the force alone could make me disappear. I can't see him from here, his body hidden by the stairwell wall, but that doesn't mean he can't see me: my long shadow spilling down the steps, the sound of my breath suddenly so loud in my ears.

"Looks like a big one," he continues as I hear him take a few steps into the foyer. Then I glance out the window, noticing the marbled clouds in the distance. The sky was so clear only an hour ago, but now it's dark, practically black, and I can smell the metallic threat of rain through the door.

"I need some help securing everything," he adds. "Wind's already starting to pick up."

A thick silence settles over the house as I imagine the two of them in a stiff standoff, Mitchell staring at Liam from a few feet away.

"Where's Claire?" Mitchell asks at last as I feel a spasm in my chest at the sound of my name. Just a few days ago, it had almost been *soothing* listening to him say it from the top of the porch, his voice a salve easing the sting of these last few months. It had felt like he knew me, somehow. Like he understood me. Like I could actually see my problems floating away with a simple snap of his fingers, dandelion seeds getting swept up in the breeze—but now it just sounds *wrong*, coming from him, and I have the sudden urge to crawl out of my skin. Burrow under the covers to keep myself safe.

"Sleeping," Liam says. "She's still recovering from yesterday. Be-sides, it'll be faster if you help. She doesn't know where anything is."

A sigh erupts from Mitchell's direction followed by the clink of glass as he puts his cup down. Then I track his footsteps as he makes his way down the hall before he and Liam retreat to the porch, slamming the door hard behind them.

CHAPTER 30

My hair is dripping by the time I get back.

Once I was sure Mitchell and Liam were gone, I finally allowed myself to let out a breath while simultaneously scolding myself for how close I just got to getting caught. Then I had waited a few seconds before tiptoeing down the rest of the stairs and peering out the front-door windows.

I could see their two bodies making their way to the shed, presumably to grab supplies for the storm. Then Mitchell went in first as Liam glanced back at the house, hesitating for a second before he took a deep breath and stepped in after.

Only then did I bolt to the door, twist the knob, and fling myself out and into the rain.

In the few seconds it took for me to get between the two houses, the skies opened up with a strength that was startling. The pelting drops sharp as nails as I jogged across the yard and into the relative safety of my room. I know this kind of weather isn't unusual in

July—I'm familiar with these microbursts that come out of no-where, violent little spurts that appear and disappear in the blink of an eye—but right now, despite my soggy clothes and rain-drenched hair, I'm just thankful for the distraction. For the opportunity to get out of that house, away from Mitchell.

The excuse to hole up in here and plan my next move instead of having to act like everything is fine.

I attempt to dry off as soon as I step inside, twisting my hair into a towel before my attention returns to my phone. It's vibrating in my pocket again and I pull it out, Ryan's face and name appearing on the screen.

"Claire," he says as soon as I answer. "Where have you been? I've been trying to get ahold of you all morning."

I look down at the display to find a smattering of texts. They must have gotten stuck in the ether while I was walking around the property, the spotty service going in and out keeping them from getting through.

"Sorry," I say, trying to keep my voice steady and light, though even I can hear the shake in my throat. The adrenaline pushing its way out after those tense few minutes as I hid on the stairs. "I've been . . . busy."

"Doing what?" he asks, and I feel myself flinch at his brusque tone—still, it's a fair question. Ryan thinks I'm back at home, back with my mom. I've led him to believe I have nothing at all going on in my life, nothing stealing my attention for hours at a time, so of course he's curious about where I've been disappearing to, day after day.

Why I'm suddenly unable to pick up the phone.

"Claire, you're starting to worry me," he says when I don't answer, his voice softening into concern. "It sounds like you're out of breath."

"I'm fine," I say, though it's painfully obvious that I'm not.

"I picked up your mail," he continues. "You got a letter from your mom."

I freeze, a lump lodging itself in my throat, because whatever it was I was expecting Ryan to say, I know for a fact it wasn't that.

"How do you—?"

"Her name was on the envelope along with a Claxton return address."

"What does it say?"

"I don't know," he says. "I didn't read it, but why is your mom sending you mail if you're staying with her in her house right now?"

I sigh, running my fingers through my wet hair.

"Claire, what is going on?" he asks as I glance out the window, the rain lashing hard on the glass. The storm is picking up quickly now and I can practically feel the chill in the air, the temperature dropping as the sky grows dark. The wall of gray clouds gathering in the distance offering no glimpse of imminent relief.

"I'm not at home, okay?" I say at last, finally deciding to just come clean. I'm too tired of the secrets, the lies—and besides, it's starting to feel like I'm in way over my head here. It feels like I should tell Ryan about these things that I've found so maybe he can somehow help. He's a journalist, too, after all. The two of us working together could get to the bottom of this, whatever *this* is, in half the time. "I left right after I got there. After my first night back."

"Then where are you?" he asks, his voice suddenly sounding afraid. "You're not back in the city, are you? Where have you been living?"

"No," I say, pulling the gun from my pocket before looking around, trying to decide where to put it. Then I walk over to the desk and place it inside the drawer, staring down silently like I'm afraid it might spring to life on its own. "I'm not in the city."

The line is quiet as I try to decide how I should start, until I eventually start at the beginning: turning into my neighborhood that very first night, all the odd feelings that reared up in my chest the second I stepped into my childhood home. The memories bashing me like a tidal wave, dragging me down, and the nightmare I had that scared me away. I tell him about the pictures of the vineyard I found in the shoebox, reminiscing about Natalie's summer job. Overhearing my mother and the snap decision to come to Galloway before learning about their guesthouse, the two thousand dollars. The way it felt like a solution to all my problems until I found that diary pushed deep in the vent.

I tell him about how it's consumed me slowly, a secret obsession I can't understand. Marcia's words like a parasite chewing away at my brain, keeping me awake well into the night.

"There's something going on here," I say when I'm finally finished, Ryan's breath heavy on the other side of the line. Then I plop down in the chair, sliding the drawer shut as my pants drip water onto the hardwood floor. "I've been thinking it from the second I found all those articles, but just now, I snuck into their house—"

"Wait, wait, wait," he says at last, stopping me mid-sentence. "You snuck into their *house*?"

"I went inside to talk to Marcia, but she was asleep, so I started looking around."

"Jesus, Claire."

"I found a bag," I continue, ignoring his tone. "A bag stuffed beneath the floorboards of their bedroom. It looks *just* like the bag Natalie took the night she disappeared."

Ryan is quiet on the other side of the line, the silence stretching on for so long I look down at the phone, wondering if I lost him.

"What did it look like?" he asks at last, the weight of the information hanging over us both.

"It's just a black duffel bag."

"Did it have her name on it? Any identifying proof?"

"No," I say, rubbing the back of my neck. "I'm not even sure if it's hers, to be honest—I mean, I can't remember *exactly* what hers looked like—but the cops always thought Natalie left with a bag."

"Claire—"

"A *black duffel bag.*"

"Everyone has a black duffel bag," he argues. "*I* have a black duffel bag."

"Hidden beneath the floorboards of your bedroom?"

"No," he admits. "But what makes you think it could be Natalie's? It could be anyone's."

I fall silent, thinking of the article that reported on Marcia's disappearance; the fact that she went missing with a bag then, too. Now I'm suddenly doubting myself, realizing that Ryan is probably right.

The bag could be anyone's.

"Maybe they're the kind of people who hide money in their mattress or something and that spot is like a makeshift safe. What else did you find in there?"

"The deed to their property," I say, Liam's voice emerging in the back of my mind as he talked about Mitchell and all of his quirks. He does seem like the kind of person who would distrust a bank, instead opting to keep his valuables hidden at home.

Not a big fan of modern medicine . . . or anything modern, for that matter.

"Okay," Ryan says. "Seems like the kind of thing they'd want to keep safe. What else?"

"A wallet," I say, and I can just see Ryan nodding, his theory cementing itself even further. "But the wallet had someone else's license in it."

"All right," he continues, though I can hear a subtle shift in his voice. "There could still be an explanation for that. Anything else?"

"A gun," I say, my eyes darting to the desk next, trying to

decide if I should mention I took it. "Why would they have a gun hidden in their floor?"

"Because you're in the middle of nowhere in South Carolina," he says with a laugh. "Everyone around there has a gun."

"Okay," I concede, though my frustration is starting to mount, the fact that he clearly isn't taking this seriously. "I get your point, but I'm telling you, Ryan. There's something not *right* here. I'm worried about Marcia. I'm worried she's being held against her will or something—"

"Claire," he says, cutting me off, and I bite down hard on the inside of my cheek as he lets a small sigh slip through. "You realize what's happening here, right?"

I stay silent, not sure what he's getting at.

"This story in the city, the one from the bar. You said it was similar to what happened to your sister. That it dredged up a bunch of bad memories."

I begin to ruminate on my last two months in New York, that case on the news consuming me slowly as I stayed up late, pored over evidence. The past and present beginning to blur.

"Do you think maybe you're doing the same thing here?" he continues as I think next about how I've been draping Natalie's voice on top of Marcia's words; seeing glimmers of my sister in the most mundane details and that dream slowly morphing until she and Marcia were one and the same.

"But the bag," I argue, trying to steady my voice. "The tea, and the articles—"

"All of that stuff is entirely circumstantial," Ryan continues. "You're worried about this woman because, what, she sleeps a lot? Maybe she's sick. Maybe she's battling some kind of disease that's none of your business."

"It's more than that."

"Okay, then is it because they live in solitude? Maybe they enjoy their privacy—which, by the way, you're completely disrespecting, snooping around their house like that."

I swallow, embarrassed by the pitch of his voice. Ryan has never talked to me like this. He's never scolded me like a child, doubted the validity of the things I've told him.

"Is it because she ran away with him when she was eighteen?" he pushes, talking faster now. "Because if so, she was *eighteen,* Claire. That's perfectly legal. He didn't kidnap her. She wasn't a kid."

"Natalie was eighteen," I counter, immediately regretting it.

"See, this is what I'm talking about!" he barks, his voice growing louder, more desperate. "They're not the same! This woman and your sister are not the same. What happened to Natalie was terrible, Claire, and I understand the desire to equate the two, but not every older man is a murderer, you know."

"Then what about the deed," I push, grasping at anything I can possibly find. "The deed didn't have Mitchell's name on it. It was the deed between the previous owners."

"Okay . . ." Ryan says, not sure what I'm getting at.

"Why would he have the property deed from before it even belonged to him?"

"I don't know," Ryan concedes. "But there could be plenty of reasons. Maybe they're family with different last names and he inherited the place after they died."

"But Liam said it's not family land."

"Who is Liam?" he asks, sounding exhausted, and I feel a sudden spasm deep in my chest. A strange hesitation as I struggle to respond.

"My point is, you don't know these people," Ryan continues when I don't answer. "You don't know anything about them."

I nod, swallow, finally realizing he's right. Other than the diary and the few cursory details I found online, I don't know anything about them at all.

"You're making up a story based on a diary written by a kid," he says. "A diary that's over forty years old."

"I thought you just said Marcia wasn't a kid," I mutter, unable to help myself. A fierce protection for this girl I don't even know flaring up like someone struck a match in my chest. I can't even explain why I'm doing it, either; why I have a burning desire to defend her like this. I suppose it's because my sister was discounted, too. Because I spent my childhood listening to people make up excuses to explain what happened, biting my tongue as the cops called her difficult, troubled. Impossible to control. As if that somehow meant she deserved what she got.

"Claire," Ryan says, and I look down at the pity in his tone, my eyes drilling into my damp jeans. "I think you're jumping to conclusions because you still haven't come to terms with what happened back then. That you're turning this woman into your sister, and now you're trying to *save* her because you feel like you couldn't save Natalie."

The sharp sting of tears pricks at my eyes, nothing but sheets of rain on the roof and the low growl of thunder masking my breathing.

"That dream," he continues. "The one you had on your first night home. I think it's pretty obvious what it means."

"Please don't psychoanalyze me, Ryan—"

"Your hands were holding the pillowcase," he continues, trudging along, despite my reluctance. "In that dream, you were killing her, Claire. You feel responsible for your sister's death, for whatever reason, but you need to know it wasn't your fault."

I feel a catch of something in my throat now, a sharp intake of breath at hearing those words. *It wasn't your fault.*

Nobody has ever said that to me before.

"There's nothing you could have done," he continues, but I'm shaking my head now, back and forth, because I know that just isn't true.

There are so many things I could have done, *should* have done, had I been brave enough to speak up.

"I think that's what's driving all of this," he says. "Some un-resolved sense of duty to your sister. But once you accept it wasn't your fault, you can drop this and start to move on."

"But it was my fault," I whisper, suddenly unsure if I'm still talking to Ryan or just needing to get the words out myself.

"No, it wasn't," he argues. "You were eleven years old. How could it have possibly been your fault?"

I sigh, pushing my fingers into my eyes. Then I open my mouth and start to talk, the memory of that night seeping out like the slow bleed of a reopened wound.

CHAPTER 31

It was dark, I remember. The kind of dark that swallows everything, my own hand lost in front of my face as I tried to find
silhouettes in the murk: the canopy above me, cast wide like a net.
My closet in the corner stretching like an inkblot or bleeding black
hole.

"Claire, what are you talking about?" Ryan asks as I feel my
body tucked deep in my childhood sheets, the smothering silence
like cotton in my ears.

"She was always sneaking out," I say, thinking about how I
heard Natalie's window slide open; the scrape of her jeans over the
ledge and the crank of a car before it rolled down the drive. "I knew
she was, because I could hear it through the wall."

I imagine myself getting up slowly, slinking my way into the
hall before creeping into her bedroom behind her. Yet another long
night spent reading her books, wearing her clothes. Painting my
face with her makeup as midnight stretched into morning, as I tried
to understand what it might be like to be her.

"I was by myself a lot as a kid," I continue, that familiar shame climbing the length of my spine as I picture Bethany sitting in the kitchen, the pity in her eyes as I stood there alone. "I didn't have many friends, but especially that summer, with my parents' divorce—"

I stop, trying to work out how to explain.

"Those nights in her bedroom, they were an escape for me," I say at last. "They were a few hours where I could pretend to be someone else for a little. Someone who seemed to have all the things that I wanted. Who was pretty and popular, outgoing and brave."

Ryan stays silent on the other side of the line and I take it as my cue to keep talking, to purge the guilt I've been carrying for the last twenty-two years.

"That night, I fell asleep," I say, reminiscing on how I woke up in Natalie's bed with a start. I was still wearing her sweatshirt, all those unfamiliar smells wrapping me tight like a hug, before I sat up quick, bleary eyes blinking while I turned to the side. The clock on her nightstand reading five A.M. "Normally, I would see her headlights shining in through the window. I would leave just as she was getting back home."

I remember perusing her room in a lazy haze, vaguely wondering where she could be before slipping out of bed and making my way into the bathroom we shared. Bare feet cold on the slick white tile as I stared at my face in the moonlit mirror; streaks of her lipstick staining my skin as I longed for her reflection instead of my own.

"But then, she never came home," I continue. "I knew from the second I woke up that something was different, but I didn't say anything. I just went into my room and went back to bed."

"Claire," Ryan says. "That doesn't mean anything."

"Yes, it does," I say, louder now as I think about my mom and me at the table that morning; her scream from upstairs and her mug on the ground.

The way I sat there silently, already knowing my sister was gone.

"Even when the police came, I still didn't speak up. I didn't want to get into trouble."

I drop my head in my hands now, imagining the cops picking over our house as Detective DiNello leaned on the table, looked my mother square in the eye.

She probably spent the night at a friend's house or something. You know how girls can be.

"They told us everything was probably fine," I say, shaking my head as the tears stream out faster. "That she took a bag and she'd be back soon, so I never mentioned how she'd been sneaking out for weeks at that point. That I thought she was seeing someone because I could smell it on her clothes."

"*Claire,*" Ryan says again. "None of that is your fault."

"But what if I could have helped her?" I yell, the sentence coming out with a wet choke. "What if I had told someone sooner? My mom was so distracted that summer she never even realized what Natalie was doing, but maybe if I just *told* her she would have grounded her or something. She would have stopped her from leaving."

"You don't know that. You have no way of knowing that."

"But instead, I kept it a secret because I liked going in there. I was selfish," I say, the weight lifting from my shoulders as I confess it all for the very first time. "And I was scared, Ryan. A few days later, the police found Jeffrey's car, that shirt with her blood, and it felt like the truth didn't even matter. More than that, it felt like my fault."

Ryan is quiet as I think back to those first few days, the slow realization of what my silence had done. My sister losing her life in

the very moment I was trying it on, twirling around in her mirror to admire the fit. Soon, I could no longer stand to be in her
bedroom. The constant reminder of all the ways I had failed her
haunting me quietly, driving me away.

"I think you should come back," Ryan says at last, bringing my
attention back to the phone. "Going out there might have been a
mistake. And I'm sorry, I know I said it would help, but I can see
now I didn't know the full story."

"I'm staying," I say, my newfound resolve settled in deep. "I
have a bad feeling, Ryan, and I'm not going to ignore it. Not again.
I'm not going to spend the rest of my life wondering if I could have
made a difference had I done something different."

The line stays silent for a few more seconds until a thrash of rain
rails on the roof. Then I turn toward the window, a bright strike of
lightning illuminating the sky as the wind whips through the trees,
invisible gusts making them bend.

I open my mouth, ready to tell Ryan I'm sorry, that I know he
doesn't agree but this is just something I have to do, when another
crack of thunder cuts through the silence. It sounds like a gunshot,
furious and loud, and my hand shoots to my chest as the lights blink
out, my little house now shrouded in black.

"God, that *scared* me," I say, wondering if Ryan heard it, too.
He's still silent on the other side of the line and it dawns on me
suddenly as I wait for a response.

If the power is out, then the internet is, too.

I lower my phone, the call dropped as I stare at the exclamation
point in the place of where the signal once was. Then I turn toward
my laptop, sighing as I realize I won't be able to use that, either.

That this gift of a free day is suddenly gone.

I glance back at the bed, the rumple of covers like a shadow in
the dark. With no other options, I peel off my wet clothes and slide

into the sheets, gliding my hand through the blankets until I come across the diary, patiently waiting for me to make my return.

I pull it out, resting it against my propped-up knees and squinting as I take in the cover. It's too dark to read without the bedside lamp or light of the sun streaming in through the windows . . . but then I look down at my phone again, realizing it still has a use without a signal.

I tap at the screen, navigating to the flashlight and turning it on. The battery is drained after taking those pictures, my conversation with Ryan, and constant search for a signal, so I figure I only have about an hour until it dies for good.

I perch the phone on my chest before opening the diary, the flashlight aimed at my next page. Then I lick my finger, rubbing it gently against Marcia's words and watching in silence as the blue ink smears. The smudge is subtle, but it's definitely there, and I realize with a sense of acute exhilaration that I altered it, this thing that was written over four decades ago. I changed history, left my own mark, and there's something about that that gives me hope. The idea of *then* and *now* coalescing.

The present tenderly dipping its toe in the past like a grape seed in water, dozens of ripples made by one small change.

CHAPTER 32

APRIL 1984

Marcia twisted the knob on the shower wall, a spray of goose bumps erupting across her arms the second the water trickled to a stop. Then she closed her eyes and tipped her head back, the wet from her hair dripping down her neck before trailing down the length of her spine.

She felt cleaner than she had in weeks, almost like her old self again if she ignored the bouquet of pimples blooming across her back, the start of a wart itching the bottom of her foot. Her nails dirty, a perpetual yellow. The back of her hair matted with knots. A shower felt like a luxury at this point; lately, she had been washing in the river, pumps of pink hand soap lathered beneath her arms, between her legs. Artificial peony that clung to her for days and sheets of toilet paper tearing across her skin whenever she attempted to blot herself dry.

She whipped back the curtain, stepping out of this stranger's tub before placing two wet feet on the mat. Then she glanced at

the mirror, the words *Lily was here* written with a tip of a finger in
the fog.

"*Lily*," she yelled, slightly unsettled at the thought of her friend
creeping in unannounced. She wondered how long she had been in
there, hovering on the opposite side of the plastic as the white noise
from the shower masked her movements.

Marcia hadn't even heard her open the door.

A laugh erupted from somewhere down the hall and Marcia
watched as the steam dissipated before her, the words on the mirror fading away as she stared at her own reflection. It was a bit
jarring, the face that stared back. All the changes etched into her
skin; the contours of her body so foreign and strange. She had lost
weight, definitely, her hips protruding into two sharp right angles,
her arms even bonier than they were before, though her stomach
seemed bloated in that malnourished sort of way. Her legs like stilts,
long and skinny and awkward under her gaze. It had barely been
a month since she had come home that last night, Lily's suggestion
that she could stay with them festering like an infection as she sat
in the camper with her hand on the handle, her eyes trained on her
house in the distance and her mind on her parents just inside. She
had been thinking about the routine that awaited her the second
she stepped through the front door, the reliable tedium of her
everyday life, and the fact that Mitchell would soon drop her off
for the very last time.

The truth—a truth she had been doing her best to avoid—was
that she would be graduating soon, in less than six weeks, and once
that happened, that would be it. Her small semblance of freedom
would come to a close. She wouldn't be able to get away with it
anymore. She would lose the only real life she had ever actually
known and the thought of having to give it all up was suddenly so
suffocating it felt like lopping off a limb, an amputation so severe she
might not survive it. So, she made up her mind, creeping through

the house after her parents went to sleep, adrenaline twitching the tips of her fingers as she tossed a few items into a bag.

A spare dress, a sweater. The diary she kept tucked in the back of her dresser, every single detail of the last few months written about with meticulous care. Her father would find it, no doubt about that. He would find it and he would read it so she had taken that, too, stuffing it into the bottom of her duffel before slipping out the window for the very last time.

She blinked, the memory fading like the fog on the mirror as her pupils traced the borders of her naked frame. Then she leaned forward, rifling through cabinets as she looked for a towel.

She dried herself off, combing through her hair with her nails before getting dressed and stepping into the hall.

"Why do you do that?" she asked once she found Lily in the kitchen. She was sitting on a counter, legs absentmindedly kicking the cabinets.

"Do what?" she asked as Marcia stared at her silently, this girl with whom she now shared so much. She was fascinated by her, terrified of her. Envious of the way she carried herself; a liquidity to her movements like she had long ago stopped caring how she came across.

"You know what."

Marcia walked deeper into the room, too comfortable in a home that wasn't her own. Ever since she had moved onto the Farm, she had quickly come to learn that any time they left for supplies, they weren't shopping in any real store; instead, they were shopping in houses, Montana waiting in the car outside as Lily perused through people's belongings like she had broken into her own personal mall. At first, Marcia had been jumpy whenever she tagged along. She was in disbelief about how easy it was to get inside; that most people left their doors unlocked, others kept keys in the most obvious of places. Beneath doormats or inside of fake rocks, on the ledges of windows that were well within reach. Over time, though, she had learned to relax. People were at work, or in school, and they always hopped between towns, careful not to hit the same spot twice.

Still, there was something strange about the way Lily meandered around, flipping through closets and slipping rings on her fingers. Sauntering around in fur slippers two sizes too big. Not only that, but she went out of her way to move things slightly out of place in the process: a carton of milk left to spoil on the counter, the TV turned on when it had been off when they arrived. And she always scrawled her name somewhere—*Lily was here*—in the surface of a countertop, written in lipstick on a hallway mirror.

Now, staring at the girl as she sat on the counter, Marcia wondered if it had to do with her upbringing. The fact that she spent her life getting moved from place to place, never welcome for long enough to leave any real mark.

"Look what I found," Lily responded, once again not bothering with a real answer.

Marcia cocked her head, watching as Lily dug her teeth into an apple, a drip of juice quivering on the curve of her chin.

"The fridge," Lily directed, jerking her neck to the appliance beside her. Marcia walked toward it, reaching for the handle, when Lily's voice rang out again. "On it, not in it."

She stopped, hand hovering in the air as she took in all the magnets stuck to the surface. There were Polaroids and postcards, a short grocery list scribbled in pen—and then she caught sight of a familiar face, a face she hadn't seen in almost two months.

"It's Annie," she said, grabbing the picture stuck to the center as she stared at this girl she so briefly knew. She looked more put together than she ever had at the Farm: split ends trimmed and grazing the bones of her shoulders, a new weight settled into her cheeks. "Did you know?" she added as she looked back up. "That this is her house?"

Lily just smiled, the rhythmic smack of her heels on the cabinets matching the pulse of Marcia's heart in her ears.

She thought back to that day by the river, a strange sensation slipping through her stomach as she picked over the moment Lily declared the girl gone.

She wasn't committed, she had whispered. *To the family, to us.*

At the time, the way Lily said it had made Marcia assume that wasn't necessarily by choice—but now, now that she could see that Annie was okay, she found herself wondering why she had never even questioned the suggestion that she had been harmed. Instead, she had simply swallowed her guilt like she had always done, pushed it into the depths of her chest the same way she had when she snuck out her old window, slid her way into the back of that theater. Left her parents without so much as a note and settled into her new life at the Farm, every small step shedding a layer of the person she used to be like a serpent molting a too-small skin.

She stared at Lily, watching as the girl hopped off the counter before dropping her chewed-up core into the sink.

"Come on," she said at last, plucking the picture from between Marcia's grip before making her way toward the front door. "Montana's waiting."

CHAPTER 33

My flashlight clicks off, the room around me dreary and dim. There's been a tangible shift in the air, another stretch of lost time I can't account for as I let myself get wrapped up in Marcia's old memories. Tales of her past devouring my present with an inexplicable strength.

I look down at my phone, the screen dead and the battery drained. Then I flip the book closed, dropping it onto the mattress before glancing out the window to find the rain still falling. Water coming down in vicious sheets I'm sure are flooding the marsh.

I slip out of bed, gooseflesh erupting across the skin of my legs as I pad my way to the other side of the room before tapping impatiently at the keys on my laptop. The power is still off. I'm not connected, I know I'm not, but my fingers are practically itching to pick back up on my search.

To try and make sense of these pieces that seem so disconnected, so impossibly hard to grasp.

I slap the lid closed, sliding open the desk drawer instead and staring at the gun stashed inside next to that sentence crudely etched in the dark. Then I hear a low rumble and glance out the window. There's a figure making its way across the lawn, barely visible beneath the bloated gray clouds.

It's hunched over, attempting to hide from the sideways rain. Beelining its way straight toward me.

I look down, realizing I'm still barely clothed, so I slide the drawer shut and walk toward the dresser before pulling on a pair of shorts and a sweatshirt, making my way to the other side of the house. Then I run my nails through my still-damp hair before twisting the lock on the door and swinging it open.

"Nasty weather," Liam says by way of a greeting, eyes peeking out from beneath his hood. "Mind if I come in?"

"Of course not," I say, gesturing for him to step inside. He brushes past me and I shut the door fast; fat, wet drops slipping their way in as he flaps out the moisture clinging to the shell of his coat.

He looks up at me now, the two of us standing just a few feet apart.

"Looks like this might hang around for a while," he says before pulling off his hood to reveal a mop of wet hair. "Did you get caught in it?"

The moment feels intimate, how dark it is. The air between us still and stale after the last hour with the power shut off. There's water running down the bridge of his nose, dripping onto the hardwood floor, and I realize now that he's looking at me so strangely: head tilted to the side like he's trying to work through some problem he can't understand.

"I thought you came inside before it started," he adds.

I look down, two twin spots of damp on my shirt where the ends of my wet hair are resting on the fabric. Then I open my mouth, ready to croak out a lie about taking a shower when I see

Liam's eyes dart down to my legs before glancing at the clothes crumpled up by my bed.

The clothes he saw me wearing earlier, the ones that got soaked during my run across the yard now pooling water onto the floor.

"I went back out," I say instead, looking next at my ankles, the smears of dried mud caked to my skin. My mind is racing to come up with something new, something plausible. Something he might actually believe. "I couldn't sleep, so I went back out, but then the skies opened up and you weren't in the vineyard. I thought I saw you walk into the shed?"

"Yeah," he says, still eyeing me like he doesn't actually believe the things that I'm saying. "When the wind picks up like this, we try to secure things the best we can."

"I'm assuming this means we're done for the day."

"Probably tomorrow, too," he says, nodding as he takes another step inside. "Soil's gonna be too wet to be walking around."

I smile, relieved he's not pushing it, but I also can't tell if he's just being polite.

"Two days off," he adds. "Lucky you."

"When do you think we'll get the power back?" I ask, twisting around as my eyes land on the diary sitting in plain view on the bed. I didn't hide it this time, Liam's unexpected arrival catching me off guard, and I position my body between him and the mattress, trying my best to obscure his view.

"Hard to say," he says. "Maybe tomorrow, but you just never know."

"Do you think it's out everywhere?"

"I'm really not sure," he replies, turning to the side as he surveys the kitchen. My dirty cookware and dishes, dried eggs peeling from the skillet in the sink. "The center of town is a bit more connected, but when the lines are down out here, they're usually down all over."

I nod, chewing over the fact that I'm now completely cut off.

I watch as Liam turns back in my direction, squinting again like he's digging through his mind for some explanation that refuses to make itself known.

"Was there anything else?" I ask, not wanting to be rude but suddenly uncomfortable under his gaze. I'm practically sitting on top of the diary now, my body backing up slowly as the two of us talk, and while I doubt he knows what it is, I doubt a simple glimpse at the cover would give anything away, I can't risk him finding it and looking inside.

I can't risk him flipping it open and reading that first line—*I guess I'll start with my name, Marcia*—suddenly realizing the reason behind all my questions, a probing curiosity I can't contain.

He opens his mouth, then closes it again, like he's trying to work up his nerve. He's wearing the same uneasy expression as when he was about to step into the shed behind Mitchell, glancing back at the house before taking a breath, and I feel a faint tingle somewhere in my chest as I wonder if he somehow knew I was there.

I clench my fists, waiting for him to ask me outright, but instead, he hoists up a bottle I hadn't noticed he was holding.

"You want a drink?" he asks, a small smile peeking through as he wiggles the glass neck in the air. "I figured, since the day is a wash, we might as well have a little fun."

I look down, realizing the bottle must have been tucked inside the flap of his jacket. Then I glance at the digital clock on the stove, nothing but a black box where the little green numbers would normally be. I have no idea what time it is, probably sometime in the late afternoon, and while it feels a little too early for a drink, there's really not much else we can do.

"Why not," I say as he places the bottle on the counter before stripping off his jacket, turning around to hang it up on the wall.

I take the few seconds with his back turned to grab the sheets and whip them over the diary, obscuring it from view before he turns back around.

"What are we having?" I ask as he takes a couple mugs from the cabinet next, twisting the cap off the bottle with a crack.

"Muscadine wine," he says, glugging a healthy pour into them both. "Made it myself."

"A man of many talents."

"I always keep some grapes at the end of each harvest," he explains, walking across the cabin to join me on the bed. Then he hands me a mug and I look down at the liquid, eyeing it with a sudden sense of unease. "It's sweet, but good," he adds, maybe mistaking my reluctance for an aversion to the taste. "Don't knock it until you try it, you'll be pleasantly surprised."

I nod, trying to bide my time, because the truth is, I'm still on edge about accepting that tea in the main house. I don't really want to drink this until Liam does first, and as if on cue, I watch as he takes a long sip himself.

Only then do I lift my own mug to my lips, a syrupy sweetness coating my throat.

"It *is* good."

I look back up to find Liam still watching, his eyes on mine in a steadfast stare.

"What?" I ask, feeling progressively more uncomfortable under his gaze. "What is it?"

"Sorry, it's nothing," he says, glancing away like he just realized what he was doing. "There's just so much I want to know about you. You're not exactly an open book."

"I could say the same for you."

"Touché," he says, raising his mug to take a long drink.

"A question for a question?" I ask, wondering if I can use this moment to my advantage, get Liam a little tipsy and convince him to talk. I still don't know how much he knows about Mitchell, if he can shed any light on my concerns, but at the same time, I at least get the sense that he knows more than he's letting on—and that he's somehow on my side.

"Fair enough."

"All right," I say, pulling my feet up beneath me before leaning my back onto the headboard. "You go first."

He sighs, twisting his neck. Eyes on the ceiling like he's searching for a question somewhere up above. Then he turns toward me, finally, his expression solemn in the barely there light.

"Why are you here?"

The query catches me off guard, the frankness of it, and I have no idea how to respond. Instead, I look down at my mug, the finger of liquid still sitting at the bottom, and drain it completely before reaching for the bottle and pouring some more.

"I mean, why are you *really* here?" he adds, almost like he knows I'm searching my mind for a lie.

I sigh, chewing on my cheek as I weigh all my options. Thinking back to earlier as I hid on the stairs, Liam bursting in at just the right time. It was just like that first night when he swooped in from the kitchen, always aware of when I need to be saved, and I start to wonder now if those moments weren't really a coincidence.

If maybe Liam has been looking out for me on purpose, keeping an eye out to help me stay safe.

"I came here as a kid," I say at last, deciding to try on a version of the truth. "To visit my sister."

I look up at him now, his expression empty as he waits for me to go on.

"She worked here one summer, back in 2002, and then she died shortly thereafter."

"What was her name?" he asks, his voice soft and still.

"Natalie Campbell," I say, realizing I can't even remember the last time I said it out loud. "I came here because I was curious, I guess. I had no intention of staying, but then, I don't know. It was almost like I could *feel* her here and I was trying to hold on to that. The sensation of being close to her again."

I pick at my nail, not really sure why I'm being so honest. Maybe it's the lack of light, sitting here in the dark, and the fact that it feels like I'm talking to myself. Or maybe it's the alcohol already coursing its way through my veins, the low growl of thunder like static in my ears. Whatever it is, though, I'm suddenly certain that Liam can help me—and that if I expect to pry any information from him, I first need to give him some of my own.

"I'm so sorry," he says, and I can tell he genuinely means it.

"It's fine," I say, feeling the sting of impending tears. I reach my hand up, wipe them away before they can escape. "I mean, it's *not* fine, but you know. I've been trying to make it fine."

"What happened?" he asks, and I look up at him again, his face twisted in pity.

"This is more than one question." I smile.

"I'll give you more in return."

I sigh, leaning farther against the pillows. Turning the mug around in my hands.

"She was dating an older guy," I say. "A twenty-eight-year-old named Jeffrey Slater."

I think back to the article I reread yesterday morning, the few details about him the police had shared.

"I guess he was known to hang around younger girls," I continue, Liam's gaze on the side of my face as he clings to my every word. "He would buy them beer, go to their parties. He had a few misdemeanors, a short stint in jail, and I guess Natalie thought that was cool. Instead of, you know, realizing how creepy it was."

"Kids are so vulnerable at that age," Liam responds, and I find myself nodding. The fact that my sister probably never even considered someone like that might cause her harm. "They think they're invincible. Like the concept of mortality doesn't even apply."

"Yeah," I say, the word getting lost as a rumble of thunder cuts between us, the sound strong enough to rattle the house. Then I watch as Liam grabs the bottle, pouring another splash into each of our cups.

"To Natalie," he says as he holds out his arm, his mug suspended up in the air. Then I clear my throat, an attempt to swallow the sob climbing its way up.

"To Natalie," I repeat as a total silence settles around us, broken only by the soft *clink* of our mugs in the dark.

CHAPTER 34

I open my eyes to a startling light, the sun outside blindingly bright.

The rain must have stopped while I was asleep and I spend a few seconds listening to the birds chirping in the trees, the cicadas singing their song in the distance. The kind of slow, serene morning that seems somehow jarring after the violence of the storm that came before it.

I fling off the covers, the sweat coating my arms alerting me to the fact that the power is still out.

I glance over at the sink, the two sticky mugs sitting in the bottom prompting my memories of last night. Liam had stayed for at least a few hours, the two of us polishing off the bottle as my eyelids grew progressively heavier, my body sinking deeper into the sheets. Our conversation trickling into some semblance of small talk after the weight of that first question melted away.

"So, be honest," I had said, finally getting around to talk of our hosts as our bodies tilted together in the dark. "There's something a little *off* about them, right?"

"Off?" he had asked, studying me from above the lip of his mug. He had gotten more comfortable, too, resting easily against the headboard. Our outstretched legs lying side by side.

"Their relationship," I continued. "Marcia and Mitchell. I mean, it's a little strange."

"How so?" he had asked, giving me nothing in return.

"Just the dynamics of it," I pressed, trying to figure out how to word it all carefully. Despite my earlier bout of honesty, I still wasn't ready to admit to finding that diary, the illicit things I've been doing behind all their backs. "The way they interact. She barely talks at all, especially when he's around."

"Not all the time," he argued. "Besides, things were different back when they met."

"You mean, you think it's just a gender role thing? Like Mitchell is the alpha and Marcia is expected to slide into place?"

"That's not all that uncommon for people their age." Liam shrugged, looking down at his lap. "Doesn't mean I agree with it."

"So, you don't think he's too controlling or something?"

He had sighed then, rolling his neck like he was quickly getting sick of the conversation.

"And she doesn't seem, I don't know, *sick* to you?" I continued, knowing my time was running out. "It's never struck you as odd before?"

"Odd, sure," he had said, draining the last of his wine before standing up, a silent cue that our evening was over. "Everything about their lifestyle is a little odd. But like I said, they're private people. They do things their own way."

"So, you're not worried about her," I pushed, still not ready to let it go. "You really don't think there's anything wrong."

"No, I'm not worried," he replied, placing his mug in the

sink before walking to the door and turning around, tired eyes landing on mine in the dark. "And I really don't think you should be, either."

I slide out of bed now and tap at my phone lying dead on the table. I know I won't be able to charge it in here, the lack of power rendering it useless, so I pick it up and walk to the desk before slipping it into my bag. Then I tuck in my notebook and laptop along with the diary before getting dressed, pulling my hair into a bun, and grabbing my keys from their spot on the counter.

I step out of the cabin, making sure to lock the door behind me. My surroundings still as I walk to my car.

I recognize the soft *squish* of mud beneath my shoes, the buzz of mosquitos in the damp air. There was a full moon last night, the marsh already rising long before the skies saturated it further, and as a result, the whole place is flooded. Salt water seeping into the yard as the river laps against waterlogged grass.

I reach my car and twist around, my eyes landing back on the main house behind me. Mitchell's red truck still parked in its spot. My plan is to make my way into town today, maybe find a restaurant with Wi-Fi—a place where I can charge my phone and laptop and finally pick back up on my search—but then I hesitate, wondering if I should let my hosts know where I'm going. Despite the weirdness of this last week, I still feel ingrained with that strange sense of duty. A programmed politeness that inherently comes with being a woman in this world. It somehow feels wrong, just leaving like this . . . but at the same time, I know I have an excuse. Liam told me we weren't working today.

Besides, even though it sometimes feels like it, it's not like I'm *actually* forbidden to leave.

I unlock my car, easing into the driver's seat. Then I twist the key, listening as the engine sputters to life, a tingle of nerves beginning to emerge the second I begin the slow crawl down the drive.

It's almost like I'm expecting Mitchell to come running out onto the porch, slamming his hands down hard on my hood and dragging me back, not letting me leave. Still, I move forward, one eye on the house in the rearview and the other scanning the woods on either side of the road. The place feels empty, oddly serene in the silence, and I exhale only once I reach the end of the drive, my car gliding to a stop at that old wooden sign.

I take a left off the property, my foot heavy on the gas and my knuckles white on the wheel. Then I look into the mirror one last time, watching as the sign grows small in the distance, the words GALLOWAY FARM fading away.

CHAPTER 35

Ladmadaw's Main Street is practically deserted and I park my car into a spot across from the only restaurant I can find. The place is sleepy, only a handful of people slinking their way down the walk, and I slam my door shut before jogging across the street, a little bell ringing as I open the door.

"Order at the counter," a voice says, and I look up to see a woman behind the cash register busying herself with some out-of-sight task. "Take a seat wherever you want."

I glance around, the place empty with the exception of two patrons hunched over heaps of coagulated eggs. There's a smattering of tables in the center of the room, a couple booths in the corners with ripped leather seats, and I pick one at random, placing my bag onto a chair before making my way to the counter to order.

I eye a pastry display full of muffins and bagels, a collection of ground coffees and teas by the bag. Then the woman looks up, a subtle bulge in her eyes as she takes me in.

"I'll take a blueberry muffin and a black coffee," I say. "Do you have Wi-Fi?"

"Sure," she says, her eyes flipping across my every feature as if she's attempting to drink it all in. They're pretty, a light hazel with flecks of green. "Password is written on the card on the table."

"Thank you," I say, reaching into my pocket to grab some cash. "Glad to see you guys have power."

The woman cocks her head, like she isn't sure what I mean.

"The storm last night."

"Oh," she says. "Yeah, well, it takes a lot more than that to down these lines."

"But just down the road—" I start, pointing toward the door, the direction of Galloway . . . but then I stop, feeling the cogs turn in my head. A slow, silent lurching as my mind starts to march in another direction.

The only other direction that makes any sense.

"We're built for hurricanes around here," she continues as I nod, feeling a bit dazed as I think about how I had crept down the stairs, watching as Mitchell touched Marcia's neck. The way he had noticed those leaves stuck to her skin before my vibrating phone cleaved through the quiet. "This island can handle a lot more than some rain."

I look down at the counter, my mind picking up speed as I imagine myself bolting out of the house and wondering what Mitchell did once he got back inside. I wonder if he walked into his bedroom, started changing out of his soaking clothes before looking down at that lightened spot on the floor.

If he lifted those boards and pulled out that bag, peering inside to find everything tucked in the right place . . . except, of course, for the gun that was supposed to be wrapped in that towel.

The gun that's currently back in my guesthouse, waiting patiently in the drawer of that desk.

I chew on the inside of my cheek, realizing that the storm could have just been a convenient excuse. That something *else* could have cut off the power—or, more accurately, some*one* else. Someone who knew I had been digging around.

Someone who wanted to stop me from finding out more.

"You don't recognize me, do you?"

I blink back to the present, the woman at the register biting her lip. Then I squint, drawing a blank as I take in her jet-black hair that doesn't look natural, the silver stud in her nose and the long sleeve of tattoos winding its way up her arm.

"You look just like her," she muses. "Natalie, I mean."

"You knew my sister?" I ask, tilting my head.

"Yeah." She smiles, although it seems sad. "It's like I'm looking right at her after all these years."

I swallow, scrutinizing her more carefully now. The woman blinks a few times, like she's getting uncomfortable under my gaze, and that's when it hits me.

It's the eyes, *her* eyes. That light, milky brown with flecks of green. The only thing about her that hasn't changed.

I drop my hands to my sides, staring at the woman as I remember all the days she came by after school, backpack slung off in that spot by the door. The picture of her I found in that shoebox, bottles of beer littered in the distance, as my mom's watering eyes drank it all in.

I think she got a little strange. Started getting tattoos.

"Bethany," I say, thinking of her long blond hair that's no longer there; her old air of innocence now totally gone. I feel guilty for not recognizing her, but at the same time, people change after so many years. She hardly even looks like the same person anymore. "Of course. You're Bethany Wheeler."

CHAPTER 36

In the weeks following Natalie's disappearance, my mom and I entertained a slow trickle of visitors until, one day, they all dried up. At a certain point, I learned that people simply run out of words. The condolences grow stale, the flowers die.

All that to say: I haven't seen Bethany since 2002, this once-solid presence of my past vanishing as completely as my sister did.

"God, how have you been?" I ask her now, leaning my arms against the counter as I think about how she was always there in the beginning, bringing us dinner she reheated in the kitchen. Lingering like she wasn't quite ready to leave. She sat in our row at the funeral, an empty casket at the head of the church and Natalie's senior-year picture perched in a gold frame. It wasn't abrupt, though. Her eventual departure from our lives. Instead, she faded away slowly like a ghost simply dissolving into the background until a year passed and I realized with a jolt that I couldn't actually remember the last time she came by.

"Oh, you know," she says, gesturing to the little room around her like she's embarrassed about where she wound up.

I look at her now, her clear discomfort, and wonder if she feels bad about disappearing like that, abandoning my mom and me when we needed her most. Even back then, I couldn't blame her. I knew she did all that she could. She spoke to the police and gave her statement, so once Jeffrey was arrested and the case was closed, she decided to do the next natural thing.

She simply decided to move on with her life.

"How have *you* been?" she asks, flinging a rag over her shoulder as I wonder next when she dyed her hair, when she got that sleeve of tattoos.

As I wonder, strangely, if Natalie's name is etched on there somewhere. A permanent memento inked into her skin.

"Fine," I say. "Living in New York, working as a journalist."

"Good for you," she says, sounding like she genuinely means it. "Are you in town visiting your mom?"

"Just for a few weeks."

"What are you doing all the way out on Ladmadaw?" she asks, shifting her weight from one leg to the other. "I mean, there are a lot of other places to grab a coffee. Seems a little out of the way."

"I'm actually staying out here, spending some time on Galloway Farm."

I watch as Bethany's face falls, her lips morphing into a thin, straight line.

"Have you ever been?" I ask. "Natalie worked there that summer."

"Oh, I remember."

I sense a venom in her voice now, a disdain for the place dripping from her lips.

"What?" I ask, leaning forward, not understanding the sudden shift in her mood. "What is it?"

"I guess I'm just surprised you'd want to go out there."

"Why is that?"

"You know," she continues, sounding a little hesitant now. "Since Natalie got a little obsessed with that place."

I stare at her, my voice clotted in my throat as Bethany looks down at the counter, clearly trying to decide what to say next.

"What do you mean, *obsessed*?" I ask at last.

"I mean, she was there *all* the time."

"Well, she worked there—" I start to argue, but then I think about that day we visited, my parents sitting us down shortly there-after. Breaking the news about their divorce. Natalie quit just a few days later, that rebellious streak gaining momentum and speed like a runaway train that would soon burst into flames. I always assumed the fact that she quit therefore meant she also stopped going . . . but now I realize that's not necessarily the case.

"Yeah, for barely a month," Bethany says, reading my mind. "But she kept going even after that."

"Why?" I ask. "What was she doing?"

Bethany just shrugs, averting her eyes like she's suddenly ashamed.

"She snuck me into their woods once. It was a good place to party at night."

I swallow, my mind on those trees surrounding the vineyard; Liam's words, *fifty acres,* bouncing around in the back of my brain.

I think of those pictures I found in the shoebox, the one of Beth-any and Natalie surrounded by brush. There were so many shots of Galloway in there, stills of my sister deep in the vines, and I realize now that the ones in the woods might have come from the same roll.

If those pictures were still in any kind of order, they might have been taken on the exact same day.

"Did anyone else go with you?" I ask, remembering the one of Jeffrey now, the way his arm hung around Natalie's neck like a noose, a cigarette dangling limp from her fingers.

"A couple other people," she says. "I think they were mostly her coworkers."

I nod as she pulls out a muffin before pushing it in my direction with one gloved hand.

"Anyway, it was good to see you," she adds, an apology in her eyes for all this talk of the past. "I'll have that coffee out in a minute."

I make my way to the table now, my mind spinning from what I just learned but still not sure what it all means. Then I plug in all the things from my bag and wait impatiently for them to turn on, my phone buzzing back to life before a trickle of texts start to come through.

> Claire, are you okay? What just happened there?

> I'm sorry if any of that came out harsh, I'm just really worried about you.

I sigh, remembering the way Ryan and I ended our call. That conversation cut short by the strengthening storm. I know I should probably check in with him soon, reassure him that everything is fine, but at the same time, I'm still angry at how he hadn't believed me. Dismissing my concerns as nothing more than hysteria, like I'm somehow imagining these signs that something's not right.

I ignore him for now, instead opening my laptop and tapping at the keys, my mind chewing over our conversation again. As much as I hate to admit it, he was right when he claimed I don't know much about Marcia and Mitchell; that I might be jumping to con-clusions solely based on the things that I've read. I've learned a little about Marcia through all of her entries, those articles I found once I searched her name, but Mitchell is still an enigma to me. A mystery I've barely begun to crack.

I launch a new browser window, deciding I'm going to focus on him next. I don't have much to go on—the last time I tried searching his name had revealed nothing significant at all—but then I think of some of the diary's earliest pages when Marcia was on her mission to piece him together herself.

What did you study at Berkeley? she had asked, wrapping that sweatshirt around her bare shoulders.

People, he said. *I studied people.*

I pull up the Berkeley website, navigating to the alumni directory and finding a phone number at the bottom of the screen. Then I grab my phone, punching in the number and hitting Call, my foot tapping hard on the floor as I listen to the endless ringing. Realizing it's still early out in California, doubtful anyone will even pick up.

"University of Berkeley Alumni Association."

"Hi," I say, sitting up straight once I hear an older woman's voice on the line. "Hi, yes, I was wondering if you could help me confirm the graduation date of one of your alumni."

"Do you have their member number?"

"No," I say, my foot bouncing harder now. "But his name is Mitchell Galloway, and I think he might have graduated around or before 1983."

The line stays quiet for a beat too long.

"I'm sorry, but we're not supposed to give out alumni information without a member number."

"Please," I say. "I'm a friend, and I'm throwing him a surprise retirement party. I just want to make sure I have the right year."

The woman is silent and I feel my hopes start to deflate.

"I know he majored in psychology," I add. "Maybe that could possibly help?"

"Well, if he majored in psychology, then he didn't graduate before 1983."

A faint tapping erupts on the other side of the line as the woman starts typing, the phone suddenly slick in my hand.

"Berkeley didn't offer that as a major until 1988," she adds.

I think back to the diary, those dates I know for a fact are correct. Mitchell met Marcia in 1983. Galloway was founded in 1984, which means Mitchell was far away from both Berkeley and the entire state of California the only time he could have gone to school.

"Are you sure?" I ask, even though the answer is so obvious now. Mitchell was never a student at Berkeley, though he wasn't lying when he said he studied people—only, instead of in class, instead of with books, he studied by watching, observing. Scrutinizing the things that made them tick and tucking them away for his own gain.

I think of those early entries again, the way he had eyed Marcia in the back of that alley. Saying all the right things to pick away at her armor; homing in on her insecurities like they were scribbled all over her face.

"Positive," the woman says, drawing me back. "You either have your dates wrong or he was enrolled somewhere else."

"Okay," I say, getting ready to thank her and hang up when she starts to speak again.

"Of course, '83 was a hard year for the college, so it is possible he graduated late."

"What do you mean a *hard year*?" I ask.

"We had a student disappear that year. The investigation took a toll, as I'm sure you can imagine. Quite a few kids took some time off."

"A student disappeared," I repeat.

"Sadly, yes. Right after finals. I remember it like it was yesterday."

"What happened?" I ask, leaning forward as my hands start to shake.

"Unfortunately, she was never found."

I exhale, feeling like the wind was just punched from my lungs as I think back to that sweatshirt I found in their bedroom, buried like a body in the depths of the floor.

"What was her name?" I ask as I lower my phone, swiping to my pictures and opening one of the very last ones that I took.

The one of the tag with the university logo, those initials—*KAP*—written in bleeding black ink.

"Katherine," the woman says, her voice suddenly muffled by the rushing blood in my ears. "Katherine Ann Prichard. To this day, her case is still unsolved."

CHAPTER 37

"Here's your coffee."

I jump at the sudden presence of Bethany beside me, her body too close as she holds a mug by my side.

"Sorry," I say, lowering my phone and taking it from her with trembling hands. "Sorry, thanks."

"Cream or sugar?"

"No," I say. "I drink it black."

"All right," she says, turning around to walk back to the counter until she stops, tilting her head. "Are you okay, Claire? You seem sort of jumpy."

"Yeah, I'm fine," I lie, pushing the pad of my finger into a drip I spilled on the table, a feeble attempt at keeping them still. "It's just this story I've been working on. I guess it's got me a little on edge."

"What's it about?" she asks, and I look down at my phone, those initials still pulled up on the screen.

"I'm not really sure," I say, the most honest answer I can currently come up with as I think about how it started as nothing more than a hunch, a nosy curiosity inspired by boredom and a simple desire to understand this couple who had graciously welcomed me into their home. But then, slowly, it became so much more. A nagging feeling that something wasn't quite right; finding that article and learning Marcia was missing. All the little details that seemed so familiar and the sense of duty I felt to figure it out, a responsibility to see it all through . . . but whatever it was I was searching for, whatever it was I had been expecting to find, I know for a fact it wasn't *this*.

"Okay," Bethany says slowly, eyeing me curiously from across the table as I think about these names that keep popping up. All these young, missing girls who seem to have only one thing in common.

That they all wandered into Mitchell's vast web.

"Well, I'll just be back there if you need me," Bethany adds and I nod, attempting a smile before I twist back around, grabbing my notebook from inside my bag and flipping it open to where I left off.

I look down at the page, *Steven Montague* written at the top, and then I start to create a list. Adding all the other names I have underneath it.

Marcia.

Lily.

Katherine.

Natalie?

I turn back toward my laptop, my fingers furiously tapping away at the keys as I search *Katherine Ann Prichard, Berkeley, 1983*. Almost immediately, a flood of archived articles appear on the screen and I click on the first one I can find.

Berkeley freshman Katherine Ann Prichard was reported missing by her parents on Saturday, June 2, 1983, after her roommate, Denise

*Johnson, alerted them to the fact that she hadn't been home in several
days. According to her parents, Prichard had recently bought a car, a
1978 GMC camper she purchased with the intention of traveling in
the summer after her freshman year.*

I stop reading, my mind back on the diary again. Marcia's description of Mitchell's camper and the way it would idle in front of
her house, a prowler silently stalking its prey.

*Investigators have issued a BOLO for the vehicle, which, at the time
of this publication, is also missing.*

There's a picture printed beneath the paragraph, grainy and old
like the one of the Rayburns I saw the other day, though the one on
the screen now depicts a large car with a teenaged girl standing beside it, skinny hip leaning against the bumper. She's smiling wide,
hair blown out in Farrah Fawcett curls. The same lust for life I had
identified in the image of Marcia framed in her parents' hands, the
one of Natalie at Galloway grinning with that grape.

I lean in closer, skin prickling as I take in the girl's outfit. She's
wearing a pair of baggy blue jeans and an oversized sweatshirt with
the sleeves rolled up to the elbows, the word BERKELEY peeking out
from behind crossed arms.

I tip back in my chair, lifting my hands to my head and massaging my temples before glancing down at my phone on the table.
Then I pick it up, wondering if I should call the police . . . but at
the same time, I know I don't have enough. Not nearly enough.
Like Ryan said earlier, all this evidence is entirely circumstantial. I
have no real proof linking Mitchell to any of this, and I turn around
now, staring at Bethany behind the counter as I think about all the
things she just told me, the fact that it seemed like she knew more
than she had wanted to let on.

I stand up quickly, making my way toward the front of the diner as my eyes scan my surroundings for an excuse to approach— and then I notice those tins stuffed full of teabags on the counter, the same ones I saw when I first walked in, so I grab one at random and push it toward the register.

"I'll take one of these," I say, smiling as Bethany looks in my direction. She grabs the tin and I wait a few seconds while she rings me up before I keep talking, twisting my tone into something breezy and light. "Hey, did you ever tell the police what you told me earlier? About Natalie going to Galloway even after she quit?"

"Yeah, of course," she says, the cash drawer popping out with a *bang*. The sound makes me flinch but I try to ignore it, digging into my pocket to pull out a five. "I told them everything I knew."

"Like what, exactly? What did you say when they brought you in?"

"That I was pretty sure Natalie was seeing someone," she says. "That she could have been with him the night she disappeared."

"You were *pretty sure*," I repeat. "But you didn't actually know."

"I mean, she did talk about sneaking out to see someone, but it was in such vague terms. Like she didn't want me to know who he was."

I nod, thinking of how Natalie had kept Jeffrey a secret from us, too.

"So, what *did* she tell you?"

"That he wasn't in school," Bethany says with a sigh, like she's still disappointed after all these years, "so, of course, I figured he was older. That they used to hang out a lot in his car."

I keep nodding, my head starting to swim as I imagine my sister's hair being pulled from the root, the single strand they found stuck in the seat.

"Then they asked me about Jeffrey and I remembered seeing Natalie in his car one time," she adds as I think of the fingerprints she left as she grasped for the handle, blood-soaked shirt crumpled into a wad. "People would go in there during parties to smoke."

"Okay," I say. "What else?"

"That was it."

"That's really all she told you about him?" I press, my desperation to keep digging making me pushy and frank. "I thought you guys were best friends."

"We were."

"I thought you were together all the time—"

"We *were*," she snaps, cutting me off, and I can't help but clock the subtle hurt in her tone. It still sounds so raw after all these years and I think back to that summer now, my assumption that Bethany was always around, and realize I might have been wrong about that, too. "But then she started working at Galloway and everything changed. She got all distant."

"The divorce—" I start, thinking about how Natalie distanced herself from me, too, but Bethany is already shaking her head.

"It was before that," she says. "That's why I was surprised to hear you've been hanging around there. That place did something to her."

"*Did something*," I repeat, a quiet discomfort starting to slip up my neck at Bethany talking about Galloway as if it's somehow alive.

"It changed her," she adds, finally grabbing the bill from my hand. Then I watch as she slips it into the register, the drawer snapping shut like lockjawed teeth. "It devoured her."

CHAPTER 38

I crash into my car before cranking it on, immediately reaching for the air and turning it up as high as it will go. Then I lower my face to the vent, a new sickness settling into my stomach. A rolling nausea like I just consumed something foul.

I force myself to take a deep breath, willing the cool air to travel in and out of my lungs. Then I close my eyes, attempting to fight the blinding light now funneling into my vision; the bright white spots in the corners of my eyes. I feel like I'm about to pass out. My head is spinning, my body numb, as I try to make sense of all these things I just learned.

I think back to that summer, the way Natalie had been acting so different, so strange. Screaming at my mother and sneaking out every night; spending all that time alone in her bedroom before slipping through the window and disappearing in the dark. Then I feel my phone start to vibrate in my pocket and I pull it out quicky, finding an unknown number on the display. I ignore it, not wanting to break my concentration as I keep racking my mind for more details.

For every single thing I now know about Galloway, every last thing I've come to learn.

I picture Liam walking me around on my very first day; spouting out facts as we picked in the vineyard and the picnic we shared beneath the shade of a tree.

Places like this don't exactly do things by the book, he had said, an attempt to get me to open up, share a few details about my own life. *We've employed plenty of people with shady pasts.*

My mind goes still as I look to the side, Natalie's shoebox still propped up on the seat. Then I lean over and open it, sifting through pictures until I come across the one of her and Jeffrey, Bethany's words still whirling around as all these different currents pull me in too many directions.

Did anyone else go with you? I had asked, this very same picture at the forefront of my mind.

A couple other people. I think they were mostly her coworkers.

I blink a few times, a new clarity uncurling as I realize that Jeffrey and Natalie must have been coworkers. He must have worked at Galloway, too. That must have been how the two of them met and I pick up my phone again, tapping on the map before typing in an address.

Then I crank my car into reverse, backing out of my spot before speeding my way off the island. Heading in the direction of my hometown.

The Claxton Police Department is a tiny red building of chipped brick, as small and unremarkable as the town itself. It took me close to an hour to make the drive here and I ease into a parking spot outside the front door, turning off the engine before taking a deep, steadying breath.

I force myself to step out of the car, my legs walking me into the lobby as if they've developed a will of their own.

"Hi," I say, approaching a receptionist tapping away at a key-board, a series of closed doors in the hallway behind her. "I have some information regarding an old case and I was wondering if there was a detective available that I can speak with."

The woman looks up, chewing gum gnashing between her back teeth.

"Chief DiNello is taking lunch at the moment. Do you have an appointment?"

I pause, surprised to learn that not only is Detective DiNello still here, but also that he's *Chief* DiNello now . . . but then again, once I stop to think about it, that doesn't actually come as a shock. People tend to stay put in a town like Claxton. He had seemed young when I met him, probably somewhere in his thirties when he first worked Natalie's case. He must have spent the last twenty-two years climbing the ranks, his small role in Jeffrey Slater's arrest the most scandalous thing our town had yet seen.

"No," I say, though I now realize this might actually work to my advantage. "But I only need a few minutes of his time."

The woman glances back at her computer, apparently not in-clined to let me in.

"My name is Claire Campbell," I add, willingly offering up my full name for the first time since I can remember, knowing it's likely my only way in. "I'm Natalie Campbell's sister."

Five minutes later, I'm sitting in Eric DiNello's office staring at a collection of plaques on the wall. There are newspaper clippings of various cases he's worked, a matted diploma in the center of it all, and some pictures on the periphery flaunting his various stages of life: an official headshot in a navy-blue suit, shiny bronze badge pinned to the lapel. One of him on a horse with rolling hills in the distance, another of him shaking hands with the mayor.

"Claire Campbell," he says, almost like he can't even believe I exist. I turn my head, my attention directed at him on the opposite side of the desk. I knew he wouldn't be able to resist seeing me, talking to me, considering the last time he's actually seen me in person was when we both sat in my kitchen the day my sister disappeared. "Look at you, all grown up."

I take him in slowly. I can tell he's quite tall, even when seated, long arms resting on the top of the desk and a neck as thick and sturdy as a trunk. His hair is brown, cut short on the sides, and I glance at the wall again, the steady progression of his career, as I wonder if anything even mildly interesting has happened over the last two decades or if Natalie's case was his professional peak. I would bet on the latter; Claxton, South Carolina, doesn't get much murder. Our violence is petty crime–related, drug-related, and rarely ever involving a child . . . although, as everyone liked to remind us, Natalie was, at eighteen, technically an adult.

"What brings you in today?" he asks when I don't respond, threading his fingers on top of some papers. "Does your mother know you're in town?"

"She knows," I say, not exactly the truth, considering she thinks I'm back in New York. "But I'm actually here because I have some new information pertaining to my sister's case."

"New information," he repeats, eyebrows lifting in surprise.

"I just ran into Bethany Wheeler. Do you remember interviewing her? She was Natalie's best friend back then."

"I remember Bethany," he says, nodding. "Sweet girl, very helpful."

"She told me something I didn't know before. She told me Natalie had been spending a lot of time over at Galloway Farm."

I watch as Chief DiNello narrows his eyes, his silence a cue for me to go on.

"Are you familiar with Galloway?" I ask. "The muscadine vineyard on Ladmadaw Island?"

"I am, yes."

"She worked out there for a few weeks," I say. "She quit some-time early that summer, but Bethany just told me she kept going back, even after she was no longer employed."

"Okay . . ." he says, the word trailing off like he isn't sure where this is going.

"I guess I was just wondering how you found Jeffrey," I say. "I mean, what led you to do that search of his car?"

"Bethany did," Chief DiNello responds as he leans back in his chair. "She was the one who told us Slater was seeing your sister."

"But she just told *me* she didn't know who Natalie was seeing. Only that it was someone older. Someone with a car."

"Right," he says. "And we found your sister's blood in Jeffrey Slater's car. We found her prints, and her hair—"

"Did you ever look into Jeffrey's employment records?" I inter-rupt, his terseness starting to prick at my nerves. "Did he work at Galloway, too?"

"That never came up, no," DiNello says, and I feel myself de-flate until I remember again what Liam had said, how they don't exactly do things *by the book*.

"It's possible there was no record of it, that he was paid under the table—"

"Claire," Chief DiNello cuts in, a skeptical expression like he's having a hard time following my train of thought. "I'm sorry, but what exactly is this? Your sister's case is closed. Slater's in jail."

"I know," I say, growing increasingly more frustrated at how I'm sure this is starting to sound. This man probably thinks I'm delusional, still in denial all these years later despite the evidence staring me straight in the face. "But Jeffrey never confessed. He never brought us to her body—"

"Of course he never confessed!" DiNello barks, his expression now shifting into one of amusement. "This state has the death penalty. The only reason he got the sentence he did was *because* we never found her body."

I stay silent, refusing to acknowledge his point.

"That asshole got lucky," he adds. "If it were up to me, he would be dead already."

"But Mitchell Galloway," I continue, slogging along, despite his reaction. "The owner of the vineyard. He has a history."

"A history," he repeats, his voice dull and flat, and I get the sense he's only humoring me now.

"I can link him to cases of other missing girls. *Multiple* girls. That seems like a coincidence we shouldn't ignore."

Chief DiNello is silent, his teeth gnawing on the inside of his cheek.

"Which cases?" he asks at last, his attention piqued for the very first time.

"A girl out in California named Katherine Ann Prichard," I say, talking too fast but suddenly eager to get it all out. "And his wife, Marcia Rayburn, was reported missing in the eighties. I think there's someone else named Lily, though I don't know her last name—"

"This is one hell of an accusation," he says, cutting me off as he leans in close. "A serious accusation. You have proof of all this?"

"Well, no," I say, reddening slightly as I watch him shrink. "Not definitive proof. Not yet, anyway. But I've read all these articles—"

"Claire," he says again, holding up his hand as he stops me mid-thought. "There's a principle you should understand called Occam's razor."

"I know what Occam's razor is," I spit.

"Okay, what is it?"

I stare at him, put off by his blatant patronization until I finally decide to just play along.

"The most logical explanation is likely the one that's also the simplest."

"Right," he says, nodding gently. His tone now softened into one of concern. "We were told by Natalie's best friend that your sister was seeing an older man and that they spent a lot of time in his car. Jeffrey Slater is an older man, and your sister's blood was found in his car."

I stay silent, the bluntness of his statement catching me off guard.

"Jeffrey Slater was a criminal," he continues. "He sold drugs. He spent time with minors. He is the simplest, most logical explanation. We got our guy. Justice was served."

"But Bethany was acting like there was something about *Galloway* that drew in my sister," I continue. "I'm wondering if maybe she met Jeffrey there—"

"I do remember her being a bit jealous," he says, as if he just realized it himself. "Before she learned what happened, that is."

"Jealous," I repeat, tilting my head.

"That Natalie was outgrowing her," he explains. "That, all of a sudden, her best friend was spending all this time with someone who wasn't her."

I bite my lip, familiar with the feeling. After all, that was the way I felt when I saw Natalie and Bethany together, envious of the bond the two of them shared.

"So, was Bethany resentful of the place? Yeah, maybe," Chief DiNello continues, a lump lodging itself in my throat as I remember when I first noticed Natalie took off my necklace, when she started to ignore me when we passed each other in the hall. "Did Natalie meet Jeffrey there at some party, then all of a sudden, she started spending less time with her friend and more time with him? Sure, it's possible. But I seriously doubt it's anything more than that."

We sit in silence for a few more seconds until he sighs, his eyes flicking down to the desk below him like he's suddenly eager to get back to work.

"Is there anything else I can help you with?"

He stacks a few papers, my mind churning at how I can reel him back in before it becomes abundantly clear that I've already lost him. Natalie's case is over two decades old; not only that, but it's the case that built the foundation of this man's entire career. Of course he's not going to consider reopening it with nothing more than a hunch.

I need proof. Real, solid, concrete proof.

"No, that's all," I say, standing up before making my way back to the door. "Thanks for your time."

"Not a problem," he says as I extend my hand to reach for the handle, his voice cutting through the quiet one last time. "And tell Annie I said hello, would you?"

I freeze, fingertips hovering over the knob.

"Annie," I repeat, turning around as my skin bristles like the prickling of hair just before lighting strikes.

"Yeah," he says, glancing up at me before his expression falls. "Oh, that's right. I forgot she doesn't go by that name anymore."

"I don't know who you're talking about . . ."

"Your mother," he says, a scarlet flush creeping into his cheeks like he's suddenly embarrassed, like he hadn't actually meant to say that out loud. "It was what people called her around here, back when we were kids."

I stare at him blankly, all these loose pieces slipping into place as Eric DiNello stares uncomfortably in my direction, fidgeting his fingers on the top of his desk.

"Truth be told, it was a terrible nickname," he continues. "Given, you know. That both her parents died young."

"People called my mother Annie," I repeat, my mind conjuring up an image of Marcia sitting out in that field, Lily playing dreamily with her long hair.

And Annie? she had asked, looking around once she realized she hadn't seen the other girl in weeks. The shy, quiet girl who kept to herself.

"I didn't come up with it," DiNello adds, hands in the air as he comes to his own defense. "And she was a good sport about it, didn't actually seem to mind . . ."

He waits for me to say something, to rescue him from his own mistake, but still, I stay silent. That scene from the diary swirling around like a fat cloud of translucent smoke as I imagine Lily sliding a flower into Marcia's thick braid. Long fingers trailing their way down her spine.

Orphan, she had said. *But don't worry about Annie. She won't be coming around anymore.*

CHAPTER 39

It feels like I'm floating as I make my way through the building, sweat prickling my neck once I step into the sun. Then I glide across the parking lot, unlocking my car before sliding into the driver's seat, immediately reaching for the box by my side.

I open the lid, fingers shaking as I grab all the pictures and flip my way through each one until I come across that print of my parents.

The print I had first seen at the top of this stack, the one of the two of them standing on our porch. Their expressions so blissful, so young and in love.

I turn it around, eyeing the inscription written in pencil.

Alan and Annaliese, March 1984.

I drop the image onto my lap, my mind spinning as I stare at the date. Then I reach into my bag and grab Marcia's diary, flipping to the very last entry I read. It's dated in April, only a month after this picture was taken, and I close my eyes now, imagining Marcia stepping out of the shower before rummaging around in the bathroom cabinets. Walking into the kitchen to find Lily perched on a counter, that picture of Annie stuck to the fridge.

I open my eyes again, realizing that wasn't just any house they broke into.

It was *our* house. Marcia and Lily had been in our house.

I take a deep breath as I attempt to wrap my mind around Marcia washing off in our guest bathroom downstairs; Lily scouring around in our pantry, plucking an apple from the back of the fridge and dropping her core into the bottom of the sink. Of course, all this happened long before I existed, before Natalie and I were even born, but it's still the same house my parents bought before they got married, the very same house where Natalie and I grew up, and the thought of them wandering through all our rooms, sloughing their cells all over the floor, is enough to make my skin clammy with fear.

I lean back in my seat, trying to map it all out in my mind. Marcia had written about how they used to hop between towns, choosing houses at random so they wouldn't get caught, and I wonder now, just as Marcia had, if Lily had known my mom was from Claxton, if it came up in passing during their time at the Farm, or if hitting our house had been nothing more than a fluke. If she had simply been shutting the fridge door and saw that picture of my parents stuck to the surface, my mother's blond hair uncharacteristically combed and my father's arms wound around her waist. The boy she had been with since she was sixteen.

She wasn't committed, Lily had said. *To the family, to us.*

I slide the diary back into my bag, thinking about how my mother's face fell the second she saw that picture of Natalie surrounded by vines; that choke in her throat as she muttered *Galloway Farm.* She knows Mitchell, which means she must also know more about what happened back then, so much more than she's been letting on, and I grab my phone before tapping on her number, listening to the ringing before it abruptly ends.

"*Hi, you've reached Annaliese Campbell. I can't come to the phone right now . . .*"

I wait impatiently for the recording to stop, launching into a message as soon as it beeps.

"Mom, it's Claire," I say, a quiet anger radiating through the phone. "Look, I'm still here, I'm still in town. I've been staying over at Galloway and there are clearly some things you need to tell me."

I fall silent, my leg bouncing up and down as I think.

"Call me back as soon as you get this."

I end the call, lowering the phone into my cup holder before glancing back down, the picture of my parents still on my lap. I pick it up, moving to slip it back into the box when the new image on top catches my eye.

I lean to the side again, plucking the photo between my fingers. It's the one of Natalie and Bethany out in those woods, the one I've thought of so many times, but now my eyes zero in on a detail I barely noticed before. It's that car in the background, a flash of metal hidden in the trees. I had seen it the first time I looked at this picture but back then, back in the living room as I sat with my mother, I just assumed the car belonged to one of the kids at the party—but now, I think about the article outlining Katherine's disappearance.

Her missing camper, the one I'm now sure Mitchell was driving around.

I pull it in closer, squinting as I notice the car's orange tint. The license plate is still there, still attached to the back, but the image isn't clear enough to make anything out.

I lower the picture as my mind starts to churn. Thinking about what Chief DiNello just asked me, if I have any proof of these various crimes.

This would be proof.

If Katherine's camper is still out there, if the plate matches the BOLO issued in 1983, then this would be irrefutable proof that Mitchell was somehow involved. The police would be forced to search his whole property.

They would insist on talking to Marcia, hearing the whole story straight from her lips.

I toss both pictures into the box, ready to crank the engine and make my way back, when my phone starts to vibrate again, the loud clatter in the cup holder making me jump.

I reach out and grab it, swiping at the screen before even bothering to check who it is.

"Mom," I say, my voice sharp as I push the receiver into my ear. "We need to talk."

"Ah, no, sorry," the voice says, and I pull my hand back, eyeing an unknown number on the screen. The same number that tried calling after I left the diner. "Is this Claire Campbell?"

"It is," I say, attempting to place the voice on the other side of the line. I don't recognize the number, I have no idea who this could be, though this person does sound familiar. A middle-aged man I know I've somehow met.

"Hi, Ms. Campbell, this is Bill from Lowcountry Electronics just letting you know your prints are ready."

I stay silent, still not exactly sure who this is or what he's referring to, until it hits me like a slap, the recollection of the film at the bottom of that box.

The film I dropped off almost a week ago now. The film I had forgotten all about.

"Sorry for the back-to-back calls," he continues. "Just trying to reach you before we close."

"The prints," I say, my heartbeat starting to pick up speed as I realize *this* could be the thing that's still missing, the hidden piece that might finally form the full picture. "You were able to develop them?"

"Sure was," he says, a hint of pride in his voice. "The film held up surprisingly well. You said it got lost in some clutter?"

"A shoebox," I say, a new thrill starting to work its way through my chest. "In the bottom of a drawer."

"That makes sense. They probably turned out so well because it was kept in the dark."

"Wow," I say. "Wow, okay. Thank you so much. I can be there in twenty."

"Sounds good," he says. "I'm here 'til five."

I arrive at the store just before they close, peeling into the same spot as before. Then I jump out of my car and jog inside, recognizing the same man behind the counter. Wire-rimmed glasses on the tip of his nose.

"Hey there," he says, reaching to the side and grabbing a white envelope. He slides it across the counter as I reach into my purse, fingers trembling as I pull out my wallet. "I think you'll enjoy looking through these old memories. There's a lot of really good stuff in there."

"I'm sure I will," I say, my foot tapping as he runs my card. He pushes a receipt across the counter and I sign it quickly before grabbing the envelope and whipping around, gliding my finger beneath the seal. I'm too impatient to wait until I'm back in the car so I dump the prints into my palm, acutely aware of Bill's eyes on my back as I take a few more steps toward the door . . . but then I stop, staring at the image resting on top.

An image of a woman I don't recognize.

I lean in closer, trying to make sense of what I'm seeing. The woman looks to be in her forties, maybe. Auburn hair and dark brown eyes. She's sitting at a picnic table with a beer in her hand

and I flip to the next one, a shot of the same woman posing at the base of a redwood.

"Excuse me," I say, flicking through a couple more before I turn around to find Bill still staring from behind the counter. "I think you gave me the wrong envelope."

"No," he says, shaking his head. "That one is yours."

"But I don't—" I stop, looking down again at the woman holding a hiking stick, her leg perched on a rock as she stares into the sun. "I don't know who this person is."

He stays silent, a prickly expression taking over his face.

"These can't be right," I continue, remembering the hesitation I had felt when I first dropped off the roll; the clutter of this place and the fear that Natalie's last moments might somehow get lost. "This woman is a complete stranger to me."

"I'm sorry," Bill says, shoulders tense as his tone turns defensive. "But I don't know what to tell you. Those pictures are from the roll you dropped off."

I flip through a few more, though they're all the same. Various shots from a stranger's vacation I can't even begin to comprehend.

"The roll I gave you belonged to my sister," I press, an anger starting to settle in deep as I think about how close I was to the truth, to finally having this all figured out, only for it to slip straight through my grip. "I *know* these don't belong to my sister."

"Look," he says as he folds his arms in front of his chest, "I just developed the film you gave me. I can't control what winds up being on it."

I sigh, looking down at the stack before slipping the pictures into the envelope, not even bothering to look through the rest. Then I make my way back to the car, a deep disappointment sitting on my chest as I slide onto the seat.

I stare down at the envelope still in my hand, wondering if I should throw it away before deciding to toss it into the bag by my side. Maybe the film belonged to my parents or something. Maybe Natalie found it in a box of old memories, the same place she found that picture of them, so I crank the engine, looking at the digital clock on the dash. It's five o'clock now, and on the one hand, given all that I've learned, I'm not actually sure if I should go back to Galloway . . . but on the other hand, if Katherine Prichard's camper is still out there, if it's still sitting abandoned in the middle of the woods, then finding it feels like my last shred of hope.

I make the drive in silence, my mind blank and my body on autopilot until I approach that same wooden sign, the arrow begging for me to come back in. Then I feel my car roll to a stop, my fingers drumming against the wheel as I let myself imagine simply turning around, driving back in the direction of town. Running from my problems the way I always have ever since that day in the kitchen when I decided it would be easier, safer, to simply sit back and do nothing at all.

Instead, I take a deep breath and turn down the dirt road, bumping my way toward the house in the distance for what, I hope, will be the very last time.

CHAPTER 40

I ease my car into its regular spot, clocking Mitchell's truck parked in his, too. Then I lean to the side, grabbing my phone from the cup holder and my bag and the shoebox from the passenger seat, suddenly wary of letting it out of my sight.

I slide my way out, the ground slick beneath the soles of my shoes as I glance down at my phone still clutched in my hand. There's a little exclamation point back in the place of where my service once was, the sight of it driving home the fact that I'm all on my own.

I lower my phone, suddenly useless, before slipping it into my pocket and starting to walk back to the guesthouse. The grass is spongy beneath my feet, the smell of pluff mud permeating the air. I've been gone for the whole day at this point but the property is still as stagnant as it was this morning like those tense few minutes in the eye of a storm.

Like the air itself is holding its breath, patiently waiting for the violence to return.

I'm attempting to think through my options as I make the short walk, ultimately deciding to head into the woods once the sun sets and use the cloak of night to mask my movements. After all, Mitchell has been watching me so intently, his eyes trailing me around as he rocks on the porch, I can't risk him seeing me go out there. Following me as I creep into the trees and making sure I don't return.

I approach my front door before turning around and glancing back at the main house, imagining Marcia and Mitchell sitting inside. I don't see any lights on, meaning the power on the property is probably still out, and I find myself wondering what they're doing in there.

I think about Mitchell concocting those drinks in the kitchen, Marcia sitting silently in her regular seat as she waits for him to bring her a mug of hot tea, and I suddenly feel guilty at the thought of leaving her behind. I know the smart thing to do would be to come back for her later—to bring my evidence to the police and only return with reinforcements in tow—but the fact is, there is so much about this plan that might not work. I don't even know if that *is* Katherine's camper in the back of that picture . . . and even if it is, it's been so long since that photo was taken. These woods are massive, I may never find it. Mitchell could have moved it or the license plate could have corroded away.

If my search turns up empty, if I drive away tonight with nothing helpful at all, I wouldn't be able to live with myself if I left Marcia to fend for herself.

I dig into my purse for my key to the cabin, that tin of tea I bought at the diner peeking out from the inside. Then I pop the lid open, eyeing all the bags lined up side by side as a new seed of a plan begins to take root.

"Mind if I join you?"

I ascend the steps as the sky starts to dim, two hours gone since I got back. I've spent all that time packing up the guesthouse, folding my clothes into my duffels and leaving them zipped and ready at the door. My keys are on the counter, all my things waiting to be grabbed as soon as I'm back from the woods—and then I had waited, glancing out the windows at the main house in the distance. Biding my time until Marcia made herself known.

She looks at me now, not bothering to respond as I think about how I watched her walk out onto the porch, lowering herself into a chair as she held a mug tight in her hand. I'm holding my own mug, too, and I settle into the chair next to hers before lifting it slowly up to my lips.

"I'll never get over these sunsets," I say, rocking back and forth as the sky starts to bleed. Then I glance to the side, clocking Marcia's mug sitting untouched on the table. Steam pouring from the surface as she waits for it to cool. "It's no wonder you never leave."

She turns her head slowly, eyes on mine as I stare straight back. Then I place my cup next to hers, our two drinks sitting side by side. The mugs are identical, ceramic and white, from the exact same set, and when I can tell she's paying attention, almost like she knows what I'm about to do, I reach my arm out, grabbing her cup instead of my own.

I stay silent, pulling her mug onto my lap as I think about the last time I tried to get Marcia to talk, her blatant unease once Mitchell came out and the way her hands squeezed at the armrests. Eyes boring hard into the boards of the porch. I don't want to get her in trouble again. I don't want to scare her away. I can't be too pushy, I know that now; besides, now that Mitchell has likely heard my arrival, seen my car parked outside, I figure I only have a few minutes until he joins us, too.

Marcia stares at me for a few more seconds before she picks up the handle of the mug I set down. There's a squeeze in my chest as she takes a slow sip, as I wonder if she noticed I made the switch. Surely, she did. She was looking right at me, but especially now, after tasting the difference—that tea I bought back at the diner completely different than whatever Mitchell makes—she must know what I'm trying to do.

Still, I can feel my pulse mount in my neck as I wait to see what she's going to do next.

Her mouth opens, finally, but just as it seems like she's about to speak, the screen door slaps open and I turn to the side to find Mitchell making his way toward us, an amused look stuck to his face.

"Welcome back," he says, pushing his fists deep into his pockets. "I was starting to think you left us for good."

I force myself to smile, wrapping my palms around the mug I just swapped like I'm expecting him to wrestle it out of my grip.

"Where did you run off to?" he asks as I wonder if he saw me make the switch through the window, if he somehow knows what I'm planning to do.

"Just popped into town," I say. "Liam said the soil needed time to dry."

"That's right." He nods. "That's right. How's the ankle?"

"Better," I say, looking down at my leg. Those pinprick punctures that are practically gone. "Thanks again for treating it for me."

"My pleasure," he says, his expression giving nothing away.

I look back at Marcia, my replacement mug still clutched in her grip. I had realized earlier, back when I eyed that tin at the bottom of my bag, that she seems to drink this concoction twice each day—once in the morning, before Mitchell leaves for town around noon, and once in the evening, before they go to bed—so my hope is, by swapping out her drink tonight, she might be lucid enough to meet me outside after Mitchell falls asleep.

That she might leave with me when I return from the woods, let me drive her straight to the station and tell her story to the cops herself.

"Well, I'm off to bed," I say, eager to get off of this porch now that Mitchell is here. Then I stand up and make my way toward the stairs, turning around once I reach the top step.

"This was nice," I add, talking directly to Marcia now as she stares in my direction, those liquid gray eyes trained on mine. "We should meet out here again in the morning."

I barrel back into the guesthouse, the gush of hot air like an impenetrable wall the second I step through the front door. Then I close it behind me, my heart hammering hard in my chest as the singe of Mitchell's gaze burns the back of my neck like two cigarettes pressed into the skin.

My head rests against the door as I glance around the room, this home of mine for only a week. Then I look down at the mug still in my hands before taking a few steps to the sink, pouring the tea straight down the drain.

I turn on the faucet, letting the water run for a while before glancing back at my bag on the floor, Marcia's diary still slipped into the pocket. I have a few more hours until it's dark enough to venture back out so I walk to my briefcase and grab the diary before making my way to the bed and picking up my phone from where it rests on the table. I check the battery—still half full from when I charged it in town, the time on the screen reading half past eight—and climb on top of the sheets before opening the book's covers, thumbing my way through the last hundred or so pages.

I can practically taste the end of it, Marcia's recollections coming to a close, and I take a deep breath as I turn on the flashlight, helping myself to her memories one last time.

CHAPTER 41

Marcia stared down at the strip in her hand, the little blue square staring straight back.

She didn't know what to do, what to think, other than sit on the edge of the water-stained tub as she held the thing between her slick fingers. Her head felt detached from the rest of her body, her limbs tingling like they did every time she sucked from one of Mitchell's thin joints, sipped from a mug of his homemade tea. In truth, she didn't even know this kind of technology *existed*. She had simply been doing the same thing she'd been doing for weeks: rooting around in a stranger's cabinets as she and Lily hit a house a few miles from the Farm. They were closer to home than what they normally liked but they only needed a few things this time: toilet paper and towels, some food for dinner. Lily was on the hunt for a dress, beelining straight to the bedroom closet, so Marcia had come into the bathroom on her own, combing through cupboards until her fingers grazed against a box wedged in the back. Big blue words screaming at her in the dark.

ADVANCE PREGNANCY TEST: Accurate Results in 30 Minutes!

Then she had leaned back on her legs, a queasy feeling sliding through her stomach as she ticked off the last few months in her head. Her parents had never really bothered to teach her these things, though she knew the basics from health class at school, and she suddenly thought it strange that she couldn't actually remember when she had her last period.

It had been a few months, at least.

"Marcia!"

She twisted to the side at the sound of her name, Lily's voice echoing from the other side of the door.

"What are you doing in there? It's been forever."

She turned back around, staring down at the strip in her hand. Blinking a few times as if the blue box was nothing more than a mirage and a simple flip of her lids might make it dissolve back to white. Of course, she hadn't actually been expecting it to be positive. She took the test out of pure curiosity, closing the door with a quiet *click* and that creeping heat rising into her cheeks only once the color started to change. Then she began to tally all the evidence she had simply shrugged off: the fact that her stomach had started to look so subtly swollen, those waves of nausea she sometimes felt when she caught a whiff of something strong on the Farm. Up until that point, she had attributed those things to all the changes that had taken place in her life. Her diet was different. She didn't eat much anymore, all their food in such scarce supply, but the things she *did* eat were often rotten, leaving her feeling bloated and ill.

"Marcia!" Lily called again, sounding impatient, so she tucked

the strip into her pocket as she tried to think through what to do next.

"What?" she asked, emerging from the bathroom to find Lily sprawled across a king-sized bed. She was wearing a coat of faux white fur, something bulky and black in her hand. Then Marcia saw a bright light, a mechanical whining as Lily laughed out loud.

"Say cheese," she said, giggling as Marcia blinked away the black spots.

"What are you *doing*," she snapped, her vision swimming as the room slowly started to come back into view.

"Relax," Lily said, lowering the camera as she climbed off the mattress. "It's just a picture."

"I don't want my face on there."

Marcia stared at the girl, realizing the magnitude of what she'd just done: the flash preserving her image in ink, proof of their presence in this place where they didn't belong.

"Take it out," she hissed, gesturing down to the camera before her eyes darted to something strange on the headboard, that familiar sentence etched into the surface and the coiled wood shavings dusted across the duvet.

Lily was here.

"I'm serious," Marcia pressed, suddenly seething at the hubris of it all. The way Lily was flaunting their crimes as if it were all a big game. "Take it out."

"Fine," Lily muttered, popping open the camera and dumping the film onto the bed. "What is *with* you today."

Marcia stalked into the closet, not even bothering with a response. Then she started flipping through hangers, opening drawers. The test hot in her pocket as the reality of her situation settled in like a sickness, the last handful of minutes since she learned she was pregnant enough for her to have experienced a small mental shift. She felt a new kind of clarity as she looked at her life, the plates in her mind clicking into place to reveal the full picture of what it had become. In the beginning, those early days at the Farm had felt like an escape. She had been dipping her toes into forbidden waters, getting a taste of a life she had spent so much time watching from afar. A life of brazen independence, of wild free will. The exact opposite of the life she had at home . . . but slowly, silently, she had started to realize it was all just pretend.

Like sneaking into that theater at night, losing herself in some faraway dream, it was an illusion, a fantasy.

She was playing a part in a film that wasn't even her own.

"Are you okay?"

She turned around to find Lily standing in the entrance of the closet, her expression twisted in genuine concern.

"I'm fine," Marcia lied, turning back around as her mind continued to spin. In truth, it was the picture of Annie that had started all this: plucking it from the fridge that day and glancing at the girl with another man by her side, a look of love scribbled all over his face. It made Marcia realize that Mitchell had never looked at her that way; whatever he felt for her, it wasn't *that*. Instead, he looked at her the way a wolf looks at a flock of lost sheep, zeroing in on the runt of them all before separating it slowly from the rest of the herd.

"I don't believe you."

Marcia ignored her, kept opening drawers as she thought back to that day in Annie's kitchen. How Lily had grabbed the picture from between her slick fingers before they both went back to the Farm. Lily had brought it with them, eager to show Mitchell what she had found—but then, Marcia took it, slipping it into the spine of her diary so she could glance at it whenever she was alone. She didn't know what it was about the picture that gave her such a small semblance of hope. Maybe it was how Annie looked so healthy, so strong, all that new weight back on her body that wasn't there just a few months before. Maybe it was the fact that she had a home of her own—a *real* home, not a mattress in a barn or a camper she shared with so many others—and that served as a quiet reminder that perhaps one day, Marcia could still have those things, too.

She felt Lily slide up beside her just as she opened the very last drawer—and then she froze, a knot in her throat when she saw what was there.

It was a handgun, shiny black metal resting on top of a few folded-up shirts.

She reached out to touch it, the air between them silent and still as Marcia's fingers lingered a foot from the trigger, this simple escape so close within reach.

"Marcia . . ."

She dropped her hand, suddenly terrified of the dark thoughts that had seeped their way in. Then she dug into her pocket, fingers brushing against the blue strip. She wasn't yet sure if she wanted Lily to know—but at the same time, she didn't know what else to do. If her math was correct, she should be about four months along. Soon, it would be obvious, and by the end of the summer, a baby would be here . . . but Mitchell didn't believe in doctors, in hospitals. They barely had enough food to survive. Some mornings, she'd wake up in the barn with little red welts peppering her ankles, the sting of fleabites that itched so bad she'd feel the skin rip beneath her nails as she scratched. It was no place to live, let alone raise a child, so she pulled it out quickly, handing the test over before she could change her mind.

Lily looked down in silence, an inscrutable expression emerging on her face.

"Is this—?"

Marcia nodded, guilt and shame creeping into her cheeks.

"You have to help me," she whispered. "I have to leave."

The two girls stayed silent, both of them staring at the strip in her hand, until a new voice cut through the quiet.

"Who the fuck are you?"

They whipped around fast, startled to see a woman standing a few feet away. She was small and slight, brown hair slicked back in a tight bun.

"What are you doing in my house?"

Marcia stared straight ahead, the realization of what was happening dawning on her like the slow parting of clouds. She had been so wrapped up in her own thoughts, her own problems, that she hadn't even heard the door open downstairs.

She hadn't registered the sound of footsteps as they ascended the staircase, made their way into the bedroom from down the long hall.

"We were just leaving," Marcia said, holding up her hands as if in surrender. Then she watched as the woman blinked, eyes widening as she stared at them both.

"Oh my God," she muttered. "You're Marcia Rayburn."

Marcia turned to the side, wondering how the woman could possibly know who she was, though Lily's expression was just as vacant. Her mouth cut into a thin, straight line.

"You're missing," the woman continued, taking a step closer. "Your parents are looking for you."

She didn't want to react at the mention of her parents, though she could already feel the sharp sting of tears. That word, *missing,* like a knife through the heart. She had tried not to think about them over these last few months, but they often weaseled their way into her mind uninvited whenever she found herself wondering what they would do if she ever went back.

She imagined the flick of her father's eyes as he opened the door, his gaze trailing down the length of her stomach as he muttered those words—*Neither can filthiness or anything which is unclean be received into the kingdom of God*—before turning around and closing it again.

"Your picture was in the paper a few weeks ago."

Marcia blinked, watching as the woman gestured to a stack of newspapers on the top of a chair. Then she took a tentative step toward them before reaching out, shuffling through a few sections and holding out a page from the back.

"They miss you."

Marcia looked down, the image on the front of her and her family. The headline shrieking at her from the top of the page.

DRAPER, SOUTH CAROLINA, TEEN GOES MISSING
RAYBURN FAMILY DESPERATE FOR ANSWERS

"Are you girls living with that man by the river?" she continued, a softness in her voice that made Marcia want to cry. "He is not a good person," she said. "We all know what he's been doing and he's not going to get away with it much longer."

Marcia swallowed as she remembered the older woman she saw during her first drive to the Farm, glaring eyes on the camper as they roared past.

"I'm a cop," she continued as Marcia's eyes darted back to the gun in the drawer. "My name is Carmen, and I can help you."

"We don't need help," Lily snapped as Marcia felt herself flinch, turning to look at her friend by her side. In the midst of the moment, the memories of her parents winding around her, she had somehow forgotten Lily was even here.

"Yes, you do," the woman pressed as Marcia felt her fingers twitch, a sudden desire to run toward this stranger starting to work its way up her legs. "Whether you were taken against your will or you think you went there on your own accord, I can help you. I can bring you both home."

Marcia tried to talk, though the words got stuck somewhere deep in her throat. Just a croak coming out when she parted her lips.

"*No one* will blame you," the woman continued like she was somehow reading her mind. "All your families want is for you to come home."

Marcia found herself nodding, tears streaming down her cheeks as her hand hovered over her stomach. Then she opened her mouth wider, finally ready to speak, when a loud crack from the corner made her let out a scream.

She turned to the side, the gun from the drawer now in Lily's right hand and pointed at the woman on the other side of the room. Then Marcia spun back around to watch the woman's wide eyes look down at her chest, the slow bloom of blood unfurling like a flower just before her body crumpled onto the floor.

CHAPTER 42

The sound of chimes pulls me back to the room.

I look down at the phone on my chest, the alarm I set earlier blaring in the dark. Then I let out a breath, pushing the snoozer on the side as I try to process what I just read.

I glance down at the diary again, only a few pages left until I reach the end, though that last entry was scrawled in such a messy, frantic script it almost felt like it came from someone else entirely. Gone was Marcia's careful cursive, those swooping blue strokes I've quickly come to know. Instead, it feels like she scratched down that memory in a desperate attempt to keep it alive, what was once a dreamy reminiscence of how a young girl had been spending her days morphing overnight into something more like a ledger.

A recollection like she was intentionally leaving a trail.

I try to imagine Marcia lying awake that night, slipping away once everyone else was asleep as she filed away this horrible story in preparation for the day she might somehow escape. Because she *had* wanted to escape, that much is now obvious. I could practically feel her fear saturating each page as she recalled the moment she learned she was pregnant, a protectiveness for her child settling into her stomach along with a desire to somehow make her life right. Marcia was smart, I can tell, and that last entry felt like she was collecting evidence. Organizing her thoughts into something cohesive so someone, someday, could revisit them later and put the pieces together themselves.

My mind is still replaying the events I just read when I feel my body shoot up quick, an abrupt realization jerking me from bed before I run to my bag on the floor.

I dig through the pockets, pulling out the envelope I picked up earlier as I think about the man back at the store, the way he tugged at the film when I first dropped it off.

This is old, he had said, admiring the canister like it was something fragile and sacred. *Really old.*

I had assumed, back when he said that, that the pictures were taken in 2002. That when he said the film was old, he was referring to twenty-two years. Just another camera Natalie took when she was out with her friends—but now, I realize it's so much older than that. It isn't from two decades ago, like I had originally thought. It's from *four* decades ago.

That film was from 1984.

I dump the prints out as my hands start to shake, my fingers lining them up on the desk before I swoop the flashlight across them all. Then I stare at the woman again, the woman on vacation who I didn't recognize, though I now understand that this is the woman from that very last entry. This is the woman who owned the camera.

This is Carmen, the cop who came home to find Marcia and Lily rooting around in her closet. Who had tried to help them only to lay dying on her bedroom floor.

I scan my way across the stack until I come across the very last shot, a picture I hadn't seen before as I tossed the envelope into my bag, not even bothering to reach the end. I pick it up now, eyeing a young Marcia like a deer in headlights as she looks unwittingly into the lens. There's a bathroom behind her, the door cracked open like she just walked out, and she looks slightly startled, maybe even afraid. Her mind surely still stuck on the test in her pocket, her entire life changing just a few moments before.

I lift it up closer, a pinch in my chest like I know her so intimately along with a strange sensation uncoiling in my stomach, a nagging feeling I can't quite place. Then I turn the print around, something I never even thought to do before. The time stamp on the back reading May 15, 1984.

I flip it back over, racking my mind for some answer that's attempting to make itself known when the alarm erupts from my phone again.

I look down, ten minutes passed since I silenced it before. There's barely any charge left, the battery drained to 20 percent, and I realize that if I'm going to search those woods, use the light from my phone before it dies for good, then I need to do it now.

I step outside, the air around me heavy and wet like trying to breathe through a damp towel. It's too dark to see much, though the glow from the moon reflecting off the water is giving me the faintest hint of light. Still, I don't want to turn my flashlight on. I don't want to draw attention to myself, risk Mitchell seeing the beam if he's still awake, so instead, I attempt to position myself based solely on the sounds.

There's a lapping of waves off to the left, the gentle churn of the water against the dock. That means the tree line is off to my right.

I twist around, squinting as I lock the guesthouse door before pushing my phone and the key into my pocket and walking toward the woods in the distance. Fifty acres is a massive amount of land to cover, and I know I won't be able to search it all. Still, some of that is the vineyard. Even more is the marsh itself. The trees probably make up half the property, so my plan is to start with the section closest to the vines.

After all, if Mitchell drove the camper into those woods, then he must have come from this general direction . . . and if *Natalie* was near the camper during one of those parties, then I doubt they had to go far to find it.

I can feel the crunch of brush beneath my feet as I walk, the soft soil of the vineyard morphing into twigs and dead leaves. The forest is thick, and as soon as I enter, it immediately starts to feel darker out here: the moon blotted out of the sky, long shadows casting shapes in the night. I try my best to stay in a straight line, tapping on my flashlight as soon as I've ventured in a few yards.

Then I shine the light in a slow circle, the silhouettes of the trees staring straight back.

I take a deep breath, forcing myself to keep moving forward; swallowing my fear and counting my steps as I walk. It would be so easy to get lost out here, disoriented in the bitter black, so I figure keeping track of my distance is the best way to avoid getting too turned around. I go for twenty minutes, over one thousand steps, sweeping the light back and forth across the dense forest floor as tiny gnat teeth nip at my ankles, sticky wet leaves adhere to my jeans.

Another thirty minutes pass and I look down at my phone, the battery drained to 10 percent.

I let out a sigh, stopping in place as I begin to wonder if this might have been a mistake. It's creeping close to two in the morning and I could have easily underestimated the sheer size of this place, the time it would take to scour the grounds. Covering the whole property could realistically take me all the way to dawn and I don't want to be stuck out here after my phone dies.

More than that, I don't want to still be here when Mitchell wakes up.

I twist around, my eyes still struggling to adjust to the dark. I *think* I'm looking in the direction of the house, the way I need to go to make my way back, but at the same time, I can't really be sure. Every inch of these woods is practically identical, so I take my best guess and start to walk back, my gait going faster as I start passing things I can't remember passing before: a stump that looks different, the mangled limbs of a tree I don't recognize, though I can't tell if I'm actually lost or if my mind is just starting to play tricks.

I take another breath, a flimsy attempt at keeping myself calm, though I can feel my throat quiver as I start to pick up speed, sticks snapping like bones beneath my feet as I run. My flashlight is bouncing across the ground now, the blacks and greens and browns of the forest like an abyss that's threatening to open beneath me and swallow me down—and then I lurch forward, my legs getting twisted in some kind of root, and I feel myself trip before coming down hard on my hands.

I lie still for a moment, catching my breath before standing up slowly, my skin stinging in pain as a flood of wet blood starts to gush from my palms. I can see my phone resting on the ground a few feet ahead, the light shining like a beacon into the sky, and I walk forward to grab it, looking down at the dirt smeared on my jeans, the liquid red glistening on both of my hands . . . but then I freeze, the sudden cushion of color obscuring my feet looking strangely out of place. I'm no longer standing on twigs or dead leaves; instead, I'm surrounded by a bed of wildflowers, delicate petals spreading out in each direction as I sweep my flashlight across a sea of light blue. They're absolutely everywhere, a hidden meadow in the midst of all this black, and I raise my gaze slowly. My eyes following the light until it lands on something a few feet ahead: a mound of rusted metal atop an altar of flowers like a lost tombstone or private shrine.

CHAPTER 43

My pulse picks up speed as my feet carry me forward, closing the final few feet in less than a minute. Then I lift my light higher, my phone illuminating this strange thing before me.

Yet another relic from Marcia's memories, the most concrete proof I currently have.

It's a car, unmistakably, and I take a few seconds to study the long aluminum body; the four deflated wheels and burnt-brown stripe. It's almost completely obscured by vines and leaves, creepers crawling across the surface like the forest is a snake that unhinged its jaw and swallowed it whole, but I can still tell it's the camper Marcia described in her journal. The same camper from that picture in the article about Katherine.

There's not a single doubt in my mind.

I walk in a wide radius around it, the windows tinged green with pollen and mold. Then I turn off my light and start snapping pictures, the flash from my phone illuminating the woods for one, single, sickly second before my world is plunged back into black.

I blink a few times, the bright white orbs dotting my eyes making it even harder to see. Then I turn the flashlight on again and make my way toward the back of the car before sweeping the beam across the bumper. There's a license plate there, caked in green, and I reach my hand out, buffing away the years of grime to uncover the collection of numbers printed beneath.

It's from California, a golden sun rising at the top of the plate, and I take some more pictures, disbelief flooding my chest when I realize I actually got what I came for.

I can leave now, slide into my car and drive away fast. Never to see this place again.

I walk around to the front, fingers running along the rough side as I imagine barging back into the station, dropping my phone with these pictures onto Chief DiNello's desk. Then I'll show him the article about Katherine's disappearance, the BOLO issued for this exact car. I'll make him read all the entries in Marcia's diary, bring him onto the property myself before forcing him to talk to her directly. Leading him straight to that bag buried deep in the floor.

I exhale, a strange sense of delirium taking over until my hand brushes against the camper's handle.

I stop, my fingers curling around the lever. I know I already got what I came for, I don't actually need to go inside, but now my curiosity is suddenly too big to contain as I imagine Marcia and Mitchell as they lay in the dark. I've read so much about this camper, that diary like a projector casting movies in my mind. I've envisioned it trundling down all those old roads, Marcia's dainty ankles propped up on the dash before they eased to a stop beneath the limbs of that tree.

I look down at my phone again, now at 8 percent, deciding I can take a quick look.

I grip the handle harder, giving it a yank. I have to pull a few times, years of disuse lodging it stuck, but when the rusty hinges eventually fly open a slap of must hits me like a solid wall. I climb the steps carefully, one at a time. Flashlight lifting as I eye the old steering wheel, the radio and knobs. Then I shine the light to the left, illuminating the living space of the car. It's exactly the way Marcia described it, down to the yellow plaid couch and brown shag carpet; the small dining table off to the right and the queen-sized mattress still stuck in the back. It's like the interior is a time capsule and I snap some more pictures once I'm fully inside, the flash from my camera feeling like a strobe light.

I look down at the waterlogged floor, dark like tar. The brown fabric ripping across the ceiling and the cobwebs collecting in every last corner, a single spider dangling just a few feet ahead.

I glance again at my phone—6 percent—and pick up my pace as I move along the inside, my eyes brushing across every surface I can find.

I enter the kitchen and open the fridge, taking in a few cloudy bottles of beer. There's a chipped dish in the sink like someone was just in here, washing away the remnants of a late-night meal, and I make my way to the back next, sweeping my flashlight across the old mattress until the beam catches on something reflective, a quick flash of the light bouncing right back.

I freeze, wondering what it could be. A shard of glass, maybe. A piece of a mirror. Then I walk closer, forcing myself to crawl on top of the bed. Years of damp soaking into the knees of my jeans and the slippery sensation of mold on my palm. At last, I lean forward, as far as my body will go, and I reach out to grab it, my fingers curling around some kind of cold string . . . but then I realize it isn't a string, my skin recognizing the faint ripples of chain.

It's a necklace. I'm holding a necklace—but then the needles of fear start to prick at my neck as I eye the little gem attached to the center, the lime green cloudy from two decades in the dark.

CHAPTER 44

I stumble out of the camper, the necklace still clutched tight in my hand. Then I whip my head back and forth, an attempt to orient myself in the dark. The woods seem to be shrinking around me, a yawning mouth swallowing me down, and I look at my phone again—5 percent—before trying to figure out how to find my way back.

I take a deep breath, closing my eyes as I try to stay calm, letting Galloway emerge in the back of my mind.

I imagine that large white house with its big band of porch, twin rockers swaying with every hint of a breeze. Then I see those curled ribbons of vines stretching out in the distance, the long dock reaching out toward the water. Orange sun spilling over the marsh every morning a camouflage for the poison the place really is.

My eyes shoot open, fingers shaking as I swipe at my phone. Then I navigate to the compass app, watching as the digital needle points north. I know the sun rises in the east and I look around now, twisting in a circle as I find my bearings before taking off in the direction of the water. Flashlight bouncing as I sprint through the woods.

My charge is at 2 percent once I finally emerge, the light of the moon ricocheting off of the water silhouetting the guesthouse in the distance. I'm practically panting from exertion, my skin soaked in a cold sweat, and I pocket my phone, clocking the time at just past three before creeping my way through the rest of the yard.

I approach my door, finally, hands shaking so hard I can barely get a grip on the knob until at last, I grasp it, twisting it hard and letting myself in.

I run to the bed first, making my way to the side table and grabbing the diary from where I left it. Then I flip it open, this time not interested in the remaining pages but instead looking for that picture of Natalie I had stuck in the spine. I finally find it and pull it out, that shot of her messing around with that grape; then I dig my phone out of my pocket, tapping it on for what I'm sure will be the very last time as I use these final few seconds of charge—and there, *right there*, is the exact same necklace nestled into the dip of her throat. A thin gold chain with a verdant peridot the same color as the vines behind her.

I run my fingers across her face, my chest constricting as I think about how she wore this for years until, that summer, she suddenly stopped. I always thought she took it off, that she outgrew it the same way she outgrew me . . . but now I know that wasn't the case.

Now I know she *lost* it that summer, the cheap clasp breaking as she lay in that camper, the chain swallowed up in those dirty old sheets.

I exhale, a wave of relief coursing through my veins once I realize she didn't remove it on purpose—but then I think of the alternative, the reason why she might have been in that bed in the first place. All along, the police thought Jeffrey had been the older boyfriend who Natalie kept secret, but now a new surge of revulsion swells up in my stomach as I think about Marcia and Lily, Katherine and my mother. All those young girls who Mitchell had groomed, meeting them in their most vulnerable moments. Girls with domineering parents or distant parents; girls without any parents at all or who were away from their parents for the very first time. The thought makes me sick, but I know now that I have to consider it. Mitchell would have been in his forties back in 2002; Natalie left shortly after she turned eighteen. That's the same age as the others when they suddenly stumbled into his grip, and while it's hard for me to imagine a world where my sister would have fallen for someone like him, someone who was over twice her age, there was also so much she kept from me. I barely even knew her that summer, so defiant and difficult and hard to pin down.

Maybe Mitchell learned about our dad leaving and somehow made her feel special, zeroing in on another lost, lonely girl.

I blink away a tear, focusing on my sister's smiling face in an attempt to wash down the nausea clawing its way up my throat . . . but then I notice something else in the picture—or, rather, some*one* else. There are a few other people in this one, the faces of coworkers I never paid attention to. I had simply blurred them all out, my admiration for Natalie overpowering them all, but now I zero in on a person off to the right, the edge of his profile barely in the shot, though his adolescent face is suddenly so familiar I have no idea how I didn't see it before.

I drop the picture, turning around before dashing to the desk. Then I grab the knob and open the drawer, looking for the gun I have hidden inside—but as soon as the light lands I see that it's empty before my flashlight blinks out, my phone dying for good.

I stand still in the dark, my breath clotted in my throat as I realize the door wasn't locked when I came back in. I locked it when I left, I *know* I locked it, and now I remember the day I returned from the vineyard to find that basket of supplies already inside. There's another key to this guesthouse, someone else has been able to let themselves in, and I glance down at the desk in the dark, its surface cluttered with all the evidence I've found.

"I'm sorry, Claire."

I close my eyes, the cold tip of the gun pushing into my back as Liam's soft voice cuts through the night.

CHAPTER 45

We start the slow march across the property, the gun still wedged between my shoulders as Liam leads me beneath the glow of the moon.

"You knew her," I say, thinking of his face in the back of that photo. He looked so young, maybe only eighteen, but that was definitely Liam standing behind Natalie. Blue eyes trained on the side of her face. "You knew my sister."

He stays silent, the squelch of mud beneath our feet as he walks me across the yard.

"And you knew who I was, too," I continue, thinking of how he looked at me the first day I pulled into this place, head cocked to the side when I rolled down my window. The recollection seeping out of his eyes like he was trying to place me, like he had seen a ghost.

"You look just like her," he says at last, his voice barely above a whisper. "Exactly how I imagined she would have looked today."

I stay quiet, revisiting all the little moments between us. The delicate ways he had tried to confirm it, asking about my past and my hometown. I wonder now when he knew it for certain; if it was the second I drove up that first morning, the very second I gave him my name, or if he put it together slowly, carefully. Studying me the same way I studied Marcia and Mitchell.

If it wasn't until last night when I blurted it out, willingly telling him everything he wanted to know.

"Why?" I ask, because it doesn't make any sense. "Why would you even let me stay here? You could have said no. You could have turned me away."

"Because I'm selfish," he says, the answer taking me by surprise as I think about him looking at me during our picnic, that flash of regret like he wished I wasn't there. "And, you're right. I should have turned you away."

I can barely see a few feet in front of me but I realize now that we're heading straight for the shed, that looming structure off in the distance. I swallow, thinking about all those tools hanging up on the wall; the axes and chains and the uncomfortable feeling that rears up in my chest every single time I step inside. We come to a stop before it, finally, Liam motioning for me to move to the side as one hand fiddles with the lock on the door. The gun is still pointed in my direction but I take the opportunity to turn my head slightly, trying to look for any way out. My car is only a few feet away, but I know my keys are inside the guesthouse. Still, I could try to run back, grab them and drive away . . . but then I squint, realizing it looks strange in the soft light of the moon. My car seems like it's sitting way too low to the ground and I realize, with a blow, that my tires are slit.

That even if I had my keys, there's still no way I could escape.

I exhale, panic growing in my chest as the bleakness of my situation starts to set in. I have no light, I have no phone. If I were to scream, no one would hear.

If were to run, Liam could shoot me in less than a second.

"Go ahead," he says once the padlock unhooks. Then I watch as he slips it out of the handle, motioning for me to step inside.

I take the single stair into the shed, figuring that right now, my best chance at survival is to comply. I know I can't risk running, the possibility of Liam shooting at point-blank range, so I watch as he motions for me to sit down at the base of the workbench. The one bolted to the side of the wall. I do as he asks, the moisture from the damp boards seeping into my jeans as I hear the sound of a chain being unhooked from across the room. It's even darker in here than it is outside, only a sliver of the moon illuminating our movements, but I can tell when his footsteps start to walk toward me; the metal of the chain suddenly cold on my wrists as he secures my arms behind my back.

"Why are you doing this?" I ask, a sob seizing my throat. "What are you even doing here right now? It's three in the morning."

I think about the time, the fact that he was in my guesthouse in the middle of the night, and suddenly realize that in the week I've been living at Galloway, I've never once seen Liam leave. I don't even think he has a car. It was always just mine and Mitchell's parked side by side, all my attention on his rusty red truck as I tried to track its movements.

I've never once wondered how Liam gets here or where he goes home to at the end of each day.

I think back to showing up that first morning, Liam emerging from the front door of the house; me returning later that night and smiling wide as he welcomed me in. I had been too relieved at the sight of his face to even wonder why he was still there, what he was doing inside of their house, but now the answer finally sinks in.

"You live there," I say, thinking about how I had crept through their rooms, poked my head into what I thought was a guest room, a checkered blue bedspread impeccably made. "You live there with them."

Liam stays silent as my understanding expands, my mind on Marcia's last entry when she took that test in a stranger's bathroom, hand hovering over her stomach as the new life inside her continued to grow.

"You're their son," I say, the pieces slowly slipping together as I reflect on the similarities between Liam and Mitchell, all the traits they share I'd never noticed before. His knowledge of the vineyard and interest in plants; his voice during our picnic as he ducked his chin low.

That's surprising, he said when he'd asked about a boyfriend back home. *Just, you know. You're very pretty.*

He had been luring me in the same way Mitchell lured Marcia, both of them peeling away at our shells until all of our soft spots were exposed.

"You're exactly like him," I say, a sharp tug on my wrists as Liam tightens the chain around the leg of the bench behind me, my shoulders twisted at a harsh angle. Then he stands up, backing away toward the direction of the doors. My arms are wrapped so tight behind my back now that I can barely move them, but still, I pull. A desperate attempt to yank myself free.

"Were you and Natalie together?" I ask, realizing now that Liam must have been the one she was hiding that summer. *He* was the boy she was always sneaking out to see, returning to Galloway even after she quit.

It wasn't Jeffrey, like the police had thought. It wasn't even Mitchell.

All along, it was his son.

"Did she finally realize she was too good for you or something?" I push, my anger suddenly too big to contain, although I know he's not going to respond. "Did you kill her because she came to her senses and you didn't want her to leave?"

"No," he says, and I yank my arms again, the boards beneath me spongy and soft after forty years of salt water soaked into the wood. "It wasn't like that."

"Of course it was," I snap, watching as his outline retreats farther away. "Natalie and I were both so lost that summer. She was the perfect target for someone like you."

He still doesn't respond, but I sense him hesitate on the other end of the shed until he finally opens his mouth, his voice barely audible in the thick of the night.

"She didn't want you to know."

I take a deep breath, trying to make out more shapes in the dark as Liam sighs like he wants so badly to get the words out, a tug-of-war that he's rapidly starting to lose taking place inside his own mind.

"She was so scared it would crush you," he continues, almost like he's talking to himself now. "But I don't know, maybe it would be better if you knew the truth."

"The truth about what?" I ask, my heart somehow beating even harder as I think about all the strange ways Liam looked at me this week, all the times he started to open his mouth like there was something he desperately wanted to say. "What could you possibly know about my sister that I don't?"

He's quiet, his resolve buckling under the weight of my questions, and I feel my fingers start to shake as I try to prepare for whatever is about to come next.

"We were close," he concedes. "But we weren't *together*. Not like that, anyway."

"Then what were you?" I ask, waiting a few seconds while he clears his throat, a strangled sound like he's trying hard not to cry.

"Natalie and I were siblings," he says at last, his words knocking my world off its axis. "She was my sister, too."

CHAPTER 46

For a few seconds, I can't bring myself to breathe. I have no idea what Liam is saying, his voice muffled like he's speaking through water.

"Siblings," I repeat, though I still don't know how it could be true.

"We met here on her first day at work," he says. "Obviously, I've been here my whole life."

I think back to our picnic again, the way he'd simply nodded and said nothing at all when I asked if he'd been working here long.

"About a week after she started, I brought her and some friends out into the woods. I had found this abandoned old camper a few years back. My parents didn't know I knew about it, but I was a teenager, you know. It was a good place to escape to when I needed to get out of the house."

I swallow, envisioning those pictures of a party deep in the trees; the flash of the camper in the corner of the shot.

"Natalie loved it," he continues, a small laugh slipping out as the memories of my sister start warming him up, her smile always so infectious and free. "She would go in there when no one else would, poke around through all those old things. Then, one day, she told me she found something. An old roll of film and a book shoved between the wall and the mattress."

My breath catches in my throat, the image of the diary flashing through my mind.

"There was a picture of your parents inside," he says as I remember how Marcia had admitted to taking it, slipping the picture between the pages as a reminder of what she might someday have. "And it was so weird, we didn't understand why it would be in there, but then you guys showed up a few days later and your mom freaked out. She made Natalie quit and then, eventually, she finally came clean."

"My *mom* made Natalie quit," I repeat, this new information moving slow through my mind like the steady dripping of sap. "I thought Natalie quit because of their divorce."

"No," Liam says. "I guess your mom didn't realize Galloway was owned by Mitchell. She never even knew his last name."

I think of my mother in the living room my first night in town, the sadness in her eyes as she looked through those pictures like she was reliving some nightmare I couldn't understand. She spent time with Mitchell when she was young, the Annie of those entries all lost and adrift after both of her parents had died. She probably knew how he was, what they did out there, and once she found out Natalie was working for him, she didn't want her daughter to get too close . . . but then I feel my skin grow hot as I finally understand what Liam is trying to say.

"Do you get it?" he prods as I make myself imagine that picture again, the one of my parents on the steps of our porch.

The way my dad had been holding on tight to her stomach, a look in his eyes like he was so proud.

"That can't be right," I say, still unable to process it all as I think about the inner workings of the Farm, all the different girls Mitchell brought back. "My parents got together when they were sixteen."

"Your mom told Natalie they broke up briefly, shortly after her parents died."

I exhale, forcing myself to take a deep breath as I do the math in my head. That picture was dated March of 1984; Natalie was born the following August. That would mean my mom was four months pregnant when it was taken . . . but she had left the Farm only two months before.

"Mitchell was Natalie's father, too," Liam says as a deep heat starts to creep into my cheeks, my head feeling foggy like I'm about to pass out. "Her biological father, at least."

I nod, trying to swallow the rock in my throat as I finally understand why Natalie was so angry that summer, why my sister had been acting so strange.

"I'm sorry," he continues. "It was obviously hard on her when she found out, too."

I close my eyes, thinking about how she had started to avoid me. Her eyes skipping over mine when we met in the hall. It wasn't because she didn't love me, though. Because she didn't want me around. She wasn't outgrowing me; she was *protecting* me. Protecting me in the only way she knew how, burdened by this secret she knew she couldn't share. We were still related, of course, but half sisters feels so vastly different, this essential part of our shared DNA suddenly and inexplicably ripped away.

I was awestruck by her, obsessed in the way only little sisters can be. She must have known it would kill me if I found out the truth.

"She told your dad," Liam continues, my eyes flipping open as I think about the day they told us about their divorce, the fact that it had caught me completely off guard. "That's why he moved out."

I drop my head, remembering how my mother used to sneak

away to her bedroom, locking herself in there for days at a time. The way she would take Natalie's lashes with her lips pursed tight because she knew she didn't have the right to fight back.

"So, when Natalie was coming out here," I say, looking up at Liam again, "what, exactly, was she doing?"

"She was with me," he says. "She would drive herself here and we would meet at the camper, just sit out there for hours and talk. We were half siblings, we had the same dad, but our lives turned out so vastly different."

I picture Liam and Natalie now, cross-legged as they hid beneath a canopy of trees. The steady drone of crickets and a giant bag of scuppernongs burrowed between them as they swapped the stories of their lives in the dark.

"I loved the idea of having a sibling," he says. "I was always so lonely out here, all by myself."

I see Liam's face during our picnic, that look he gave me as he dipped his voice low.

I won't lie to you, though. I'm enjoying the company.

"But for Natalie," he continues, "it was more complicated than that."

"Complicated," I repeat, the sound of her name pulling me back.

"She started to get a little obsessed."

I stare at the outline of his face in the dark, remembering how Bethany had said the same thing.

"I mean, I get it," he continues. "Imagine being eighteen years old and realizing your father wasn't actually your father at all. She was having something of an identity crisis. All of a sudden, she wanted to know everything there was to know about Mitchell."

"So, what happened?" I ask, the cogs slowly lurching as I attempt to work it all out. "That last night she came here, what went wrong?"

Liam is silent for what feels like a full minute before I hear the sudden shuffling of feet, the outline of his body moving back toward the doors.

"Please," I beg, understanding that I'm losing him now. That he brought me in here for a reason and the fact that he just told me all these things means he's not intending on letting me leave. "Liam, please. How did Natalie die? What did she ever do to deserve that?"

I hear the shed doors creak open, the clanking of the padlock as he slips it back in.

"I really am sorry," he says at last. "I just thought you deserved to know."

CHAPTER 47

There's no sound at all but my own breath, rough and ragged as I try to stay calm.

The doors are shut and it's pitch-black in here. The blackest black I've ever seen. Then I hear Liam locking the handles and I attempt to yank my arms out again, though nothing moves as I jerk my full weight against the leg of the bench.

It's bolted to the floor, there's no way I'm getting myself free, and I feel my body start to deflate. The bleakness of it all beginning to take hold.

I close my eyes, open them again. No difference at all in the cavernous black. Now my adrenaline from before is starting to seep out, a slow leak that leaves me grim and alone, and I force myself to take a deep breath. Hands shaking as I decide that if Liam isn't going to give me these final few answers, then at least I can try to piece it together myself.

I lean my head back, trying to concentrate as I imagine my sister sneaking into those very same woods, finding Marcia's diary and that picture of our parents. The roll of old film she never had the chance to develop. Then she had brought them back to our house, tucked them into a box she hid in her room—and now my neck snaps up as I take in the silence around me, the same smothering silence as my bedroom back home, as I think about how I used to lie in the dark, just like this, listening to Natalie's noises from the other side of the wall.

The scrape of her window on the nights she snuck out, the flipping of pages on the nights she stayed in.

Natalie was reading the diary, too.

I picture her body curled up in a blanket, the very same diary as the one I've been reading propped up by two angular knees. Marcia's quaint cursive working its way through her brain like a fever dream that I know so well. Liam said she had gotten obsessed, that she wanted to know everything there was to know about Mitchell, and my body perks up further as I remember that acronym scrawled in the corner, the handwriting so different than every other page. It was written in silver, just like those gel pens Natalie kept in her desk, and now I realize it was a license plate number. She must have jotted it down when she noticed the California plates, decided to search for it later in her quest to learn more.

I imagine her booting up our family computer, typing in the number before coming across the article about Katherine Ann Prichard. The picture of her standing in front of the camper, the BOLO issued for that exact car.

I lean my head back again, trying to wrap my mind around the fact that, twenty-two years apart, Natalie and I have been doing the exact same thing. We've been investigating the same man, coming to all the same sickening conclusions, and despite the fact that I grew up thinking my sister and I were so different, that our appearance was the only true thing that we shared, a wet sob escapes from the depths of my throat as I realize we might be more alike than I thought.

I sigh, my body slumped against the legs of the bench as the warm wet of a tear trails down my cheek. Then I close my eyes, everything about that summer suddenly looking so different. My entire family cast in this strange new light.

All of them had been in on the same, sick secret as I stood on the outside, just trying to peer in.

I think of them now, the irony that my parents are about to lose their second daughter in the exact same place they lost their first . . . though I know my body won't be found, either. Whatever happened to Natalie, the exact same thing is about to happen to me. Mitchell will hide me in the same place he hid her, a fifty-acre grave that will stay eternally lost. Chief DiNello will visit my mother again, ease himself down at that very same table as he breaks the news that another daughter is dead. I should have stayed with her. I should have *talked* to her. I should have demanded we both purge ourselves of our secrets instead of leaving her in that house all alone . . . and then I open my eyes, picturing my mother standing in the living room, that big black cast wrapped around her leg.

I reach down now, dragging my hands across the floor beneath me as I remember the hole in the porch from where she fell through, the boards buckling after years of neglect.

I curl my fingers into a fist, knocking as I hear the faintest echo below. The sound is hollow like there's some kind of open space beneath and I think about the shed's proximity to the marsh, the fact that it must be raised up a few feet.

I knock again, realizing, with a little shudder of excitement, that if the shed is elevated like I think it is, then there should be space beneath the floor and the ground. I had to climb a step to get in here. The water out back floods at high tide. It's probably not much, maybe a foot or two, but if I can rip up the board the leg of this bench is resting on top of, then there should be a gap underneath it for me to slip the chain through.

My heartbeat starts to pick up its pace as my fingers grope around in the dark. All the boards are firmly nailed down but the wood is in such terrible shape, there has to be a crack wide enough for me to get a good grip. Finally, I find a spot that's warped just enough for me to wedge the tips of my fingers through, and I curl them down, trying to pry the board loose, when I feel my nails rip straight from the skin.

"Fuck," I mutter, yanking my hands out as I feel the sharp sting of torn flesh. There's fresh blood dripping down my wrists now, my heartbeat starting to throb in my hands, but I know I have to keep trying.

I know if Liam comes back and I'm still stuck to this bench, there's no way I'm getting out alive.

I stick my fingers into the gap again, curling them around the same edge as before as my nerves scream in pain—but then I stop, realizing that instead of trying to pry the boards up, maybe I should try knocking them *down*. I release my grip, instead flexing my fingers into a fist and slamming it down as hard as I can. It barely does a thing, considering my arms are chained so low . . . and then I look down at my feet.

My feet that aren't chained to anything at all.

I lean back, angling my body so my legs are hovering high in the air. Then I bend my knees, slamming both heels as hard as I can.

I hear a sharp *crack,* the familiar sound of splintering wood, and I twist around in the dark, feeling a pang of panic at how much noise I'm making as I frantically feel around for the board I just broke.

At last, I find it, that small seed of hope starting to grow as I position my body again, bringing my feet down in the exact same spot.

I hear another crack, even louder this time, and I know I made a sizable hole as my heels plunge past the wood. Then I spin around, my fingers shredding away at the floor as fast as they possibly can.

The shards are like razors tearing at my arms, their jagged edges slitting the skin of my wrists, but I do my best to ignore the pain because the wood is disintegrating faster now as I continue to grope around in the dark.

I pry up a large chunk, finally, and I can tell the leg of the bench is just barely hovering in the air, the wood beneath it pulled completely away.

I guide my hands where they need to go, feeling the chain slip into the gap before, at last, I pull my arms free.

I exhale, adrenaline and fear coursing through my veins as I stand up, my hands blindly searching the workbench for something I can arm myself with. There are plenty of options, this place is chock-full of tools, but with the doors shut, I can't even see my hands in front of my face. Still, I glide my fingers across the surface, trying to find anything with some kind of point.

Then I come across something metal and hard, my hands recognizing the shape of the shears I used to work in the garden. The ones with the sharp, serrated edge.

I grab the handle, palms stinging as I run toward the doors before I remember they're padlocked shut. I'm still trapped until Liam comes back—but now that I'm standing here, so close to the wall, I can hear the shuffle of footsteps on the other side.

Someone is out there, walking closer.

I freeze, trying to decide what to do next. If Liam still has that gun, I'd be better off hiding the fact that I'm armed, so I make my way back to the bench, sitting on top of the hole I just made.

Then I twist my arms behind my back, clutching the shears with sweat-soaked palms.

The padlock unhooks, cold sweat coating my skin as the door slowly swings open. Liam is already back from wherever he went . . . but then I blink, the glow of the moon backlighting the body before me making me realize it isn't Liam at all. It isn't even the body of a man.

Instead, it's Marcia, standing in the opening between the two doors.

"Marcia." I exhale, instinctively starting to reach out toward her. I completely forgot that I swapped her drink, had hinted at trying to help her escape. It must have worked. She must have understood me, slipping outside after Mitchell fell asleep, creeping to my car to find my tires were slit.

Then she must have turned to the side, heard all my noises coming from the shed like a panicked animal trapped in a snare.

"Marcia, thank God," I say, a new hope bubbling from the depths of my chest. "We have to go—"

But then I watch as Mitchell steps in from behind her, Liam standing quietly off to the side.

They're all here, all three of them, and I feel the air rush from my lungs as I realize that my attempt to help her escape must have been the thing that gave me away.

"You told him," I mutter, thinking back to how I had grabbed Marcia's mug, slowly swapping it out for my own. The fact that Liam had known to come into my cabin the very moment I was out in those woods. "Why?" I ask, the initial sting of betrayal quickly replaced by rage as I realize that none of this would have happened had I just been willing to leave her here.

That I would have been in my car right now, speeding to safety, if I didn't care enough to help her escape.

"Why would you do that?" I yell. "I was trying to *help* you."

I stare straight ahead as Marcia stands in the moonlight, this puppet stuffed in a box for the last forty-one years. Her tarnish chipping, color fading. Her will to live stripping away.

"You don't have to do this," I plead, thinking about how deeply she must be damaged, how completely she must be controlled. Mitchell pulling her strings for so many years that she's forgotten how to do anything on her own. "I know this isn't the life you wanted. You deserve so much more than this."

She stays silent, a cloud from outside moving away from the moon suddenly amplifying the small sliver of light. Then I watch as her eye catches the beam, that liquid gray staring straight back.

I look over at Liam, envisioning the cerulean hue of his own as comprehension hits me like a punch to the gut.

I think of that picture I just got developed, the one of Marcia gaping into the lens. It hadn't registered before, but I realize now that that's the only picture I've ever seen of her in color. The ones from the paper had been in black-and-white, scanned and archived and grainy on my screen, but now I think of the unease that settled into my stomach when I first took in that image, stared into her eyes.

Something felt off, something felt *different,* and now I finally know what it is.

In that picture, Marcia's eyes had been blue. Not their current, lifeless gray.

"You're not Marcia," I say, everything making a sick kind of sense.

I think about finding that article before studying the woman on the porch before me, noting how different she looked after all the years that had passed. Bethany back in that diner, her hair dyed black and that sleeve of tattoos. Her eyes the only reason I recognized her at all.

The only thing on a person that time can't change.

I reflect back on the diary again, my head rushing as I recall the first entry Marcia had made. Mitchell finding her in the back of that alley, licking his lips as he washed her in praise.

You're very pretty, Marcia. Especially those eyes.

The very first day she arrived at the Farm, smiling at the girl with bare feet in the grass. Marcia had described her irises as the same color as a summer storm, some curious quality to them she couldn't explain—but other than that, the two girls had looked so much the same.

"You're Lily," I finish, watching as the woman before me blinks like she hasn't heard her own name in a long, long time.

CHAPTER 48

I see myself standing at the vanity mirror, begging for a reflection that wasn't my own. Growing up desperate to be someone different and savoring every second I could pretend it was true.

"What did you do?" I whisper, staring at this stranger on the opposite side of the shed as the woman I thought she was evaporates before me, twisting away like a fat plume of smoke with nothing but an imposter left in its wake.

"She wasn't committed."

I tilt my head, Marcia's memories suddenly looking so different as I imagine a teenaged Lily winding through all those houses, flaunting around in heels and fur coats. Trying on lives like masquerade masks, each one infinitely better than her own.

"She had people who loved her," I say, my mind on that picture of Marcia's parents in the paper as the search for their daughter quickly turned cold. "A family who wanted her home. You never had that."

I watch as Lily stands still in a watery pool of the moon and I try to visualize her as a young girl now, a girl who was lost in every sense of the word. Nowhere to live, no one to love, until a man came along and gave her a home.

A home she would do anything to protect.

A quiver of movement steals my attention and I twist to the side, watching as Mitchell steps through the shadows. The clanking of metal keys as he walks, that silver ring hooked into the loop of his jeans.

"You can thank Liam for insisting we do it this way," he says as he kneels on the ground before me. Then I look behind him, the first hint of dawn illuming the shed as Liam stares down at the floor beneath him. "It'll take longer, but it won't hurt."

I look down at Mitchell's hands now, noticing the mug wrapped in his grip.

"Just a little something to take the edge off."

I hear a hint of a smile as I recall him speaking those very same words as I sat in the main house, Liam casing my ankle in gauze as Mitchell offered my only chance of relief.

The way I had taken it, trusted him. All his little persuasions coaxing me into the palm of his hands before squeezing his fingers and cupping me tight. Snuffing out the small voice in the back of my brain that had been whispering all along that something wasn't right.

"You killed Marcia," I say, my voice soaked in disgust as Liam perks up slightly. "The mother of your son. You killed your own *daughter.*"

"Blood doesn't automatically make you a family," Lily says, and I turn to the side, to the place she's been standing, thinking about all the things that Marcia had written. The two of them sitting outside of that barn, Lily twisting those plaits through long, tangled hair.

This is my family. The only family I need.

"I never killed anyone," Mitchell says, his voice firm as he draws my attention back toward him. "And I didn't even know I had a daughter until she showed up that night, accusing me of murder like you are right now."

I look back at Liam, his gaze peeled from the floor as he stares at me the same way he had been staring last night, an intimacy between us as I laid it all bare. How he said he was sorry and how, at the time, I had assumed that was a simple condolence, no different than the string of people that summer who came by with their flowers, their hollow words—but now, I realize it wasn't that at all.

Instead, it was a purging of guilt. An actual apology.

"What happened to Natalie wasn't your fault," I say, thinking about how Ryan had said those same words to me, the shame I had felt for doing nothing, for letting it happen, lifting like a weight had been eased from my shoulders.

"Of course it's his fault," Mitchell says as he lifts the cup higher. "She wouldn't be dead if he hadn't gone against his own family."

Now I feel my mind bend around every single thing Liam told me last night, his emotion so raw it could not have been faked.

Kids are so vulnerable at that age. Like the concept of mortality doesn't even apply.

I picture Liam as a boy growing up in this place. All his remarks about being so lonely, so secluded out here on his own, as a new memory starts to emerge from a forgotten well in my mind: the two of us talking out in the vineyard, the moment I asked about the farthest he'd been and the way he had shrugged, spread his arms wide like he could fit his whole world in that one small space.

He hadn't just meant the state, like I thought. He hadn't meant South Carolina.

He had meant *here,* right here on Galloway. He had meant the island itself.

I open my mouth, an attempt to talk, though my words are

suddenly stuck in my throat as I realize that while I was wrong about Marcia being trapped in this place, there really was someone stuck on the property.

Instead, it was Liam who was unable to leave.

"Come on," Mitchell says, the steam from the mug floating like breath on my neck, although I try to ignore him as I keep looking at Liam.

"You were just a kid," I press, the ceramic edge of the mug now kissing my lips. "You had no way of knowing what they would do to her—"

"That's enough," Mitchell snaps, and I pinch my lips tight, unable to keep talking without him tipping the whole thing back. "Twenty minutes, it's over. It'll be like falling asleep."

I keep looking at Liam, silently pleading as the gun stays clutched in his right hand—although he doesn't move, he doesn't speak, and I suddenly know that it's all over.

I know, at last, there's no way to get through.

I close my eyes and think of my sister, wondering if this is how it went for her, too. In a lot of ways, it's a fate far better than what I originally thought as I spent all those years picturing her trapped in that car, her arms desperately jerking the handle as ten fingers grabbed at the back of her hair.

This, in contrast, almost feels peaceful.

All she had to do was take a few sips, feel a slow warmth filling her up until her eyes closed for the very last time.

I inhale, the smell from the mug making my mind fuzzy and light, and all at once, the loneliness of my life starts to take hold. I think about quitting my job, my failed attempt at making it all on my own. My apartment I can barely afford, my parents with whom I rarely speak. Pushing away Ryan, my one true friend, all because he had been trying to help. He's been so patient, ten whole years of attempting to crack through my impenetrable shell, but now that he's in, now that he's seen all my scars, the rough, ugly tissue I've kept hidden beneath is surely enough to scare him away.

I open my eyes and stare down at the mug, the temptation to take the easy way out building with an irresistible strength. It's the same thing I've always done, simply closing my eyes and sticking my head in the sand. Letting the darkness whisk me away . . . but then I think about Natalie again, her blood-soaked shirt they found in that car, and I know I still don't have all the answers.

I know she must have fought until the bitter end.

I lean forward, closer to Mitchell, the warm clay pressed against my lips, our two faces inches apart. Then I take a deep breath, close my eyes, and grip the shears tight in my hand before swinging them straight into his neck.

CHAPTER 49

The scream that erupts sounds inhuman, practically animal. A high-pitched howl that cannot be natural, a sound created by unbearable pain. It's followed up by a low gurgle, little wet bubbles erupting from the pit in Mitchell's neck.

"Shoot her!" Lily yells, her voice morphing into a manic scream as she runs over to Mitchell now hunched on the floor, her body collapsing onto the ground next to his. "Liam, *shoot her.*"

I scramble to my feet, ready to run, but I'm still cornered in the back of the shed. I take a few steps forward, preparing to dart toward the door just as Liam's silhouette moves between me and the opening. He's blocking my exit, the gun clutched in his grip, and I look back down at Mitchell, Lily's hands grasping the base of his neck as a red glint seeps through her fingers. Hot blood glowing in the light of the moon.

"*Liam,*" Lily yells as I keep backing up, my feet shuffling around as I try to find something to hide behind, some way to block the impending bullet. I can hear Mitchell's chokes transforming to gags, Lily muttering incomprehensible sounds as I keep the shears clutched in my hand, the handle now slick with blood from us both. Liam keeps walking toward me, just a few feet away, and I lift my arm higher, knowing it's no match for a gun, but still prepared to start swinging if he gets too close—but then he kneels, his hands sweeping across Mitchell's body. At first, it seems like he's looking for a pulse, maybe attempting a tourniquet to stifle the blood, though Mitchell is still now, his wet wheezes softening into a rattle until, at last, it all goes quiet—and that's when I realize Liam is looking for something else.

Not a pulse, not something to help, but the set of keys dangling from the loop of his jeans.

"Go," Liam says, his voice bathed in agony as he stands up, Mitchell's key ring clutched in his left hand. "Go right now."

I stare at him, still not understanding until he turns toward Lily, positioning his body like a human shield as he points the gun in her direction, the barrel a few feet from touching her skin.

"*Go, Claire.*"

I look back and forth between them in a slow bewilderment until I finally blink back to my senses, sprinting past them both and bursting my way through the shed doors. The sky is lightening, the slow progression of dawn, and I whip around fast, ready to run back into the trees when I realize that Liam is backing up, too. His arm still raised directly at Lily as her body kneels a few feet away.

"Liam," I say, suddenly understanding what he's about to do. "Don't."

His shoulders tighten, an internal battle raging on. Anger and pain contorting his features as his finger starts to tighten around the trigger.

"Don't let her take the easy way out."

I watch as Lily stares straight at him, marbled eyes asking him to end it all. Mitchell's lifeless body beneath her and any desire she might have had to keep living without him leaching away like blood from a wound . . . and then Liam deflates, lowering himself off the shed step before closing the doors and threading the padlock back through the handles. Bolting Mitchell and Lily inside.

My body is reeling from shock, adrenaline seeping from my pores like sweat as a complete exhaustion slips in instead. Then Liam turns to face me, Lily's screams muffled from behind closed doors.

I look down at the gun hanging limp in his grip, a cold terror starting to climb back in, until he tosses it onto the ground between us, the metal landing with a wet thud.

I stare at the gun, then back at him. This person who, just a few hours ago, was holding that very gun flush to my back. Then I charge forward, grabbing it from the mud as I attempt to steady my shaking heads, wondering what I said that finally changed his mind when it hits me hard, the moment his demeanor started to change.

I think about looking at Michell as I hissed those words—*You killed the mother of your son*—just before Liam had winced, the accusation stinging like a physical slap.

"You didn't know," I say slowly. "This whole time, you thought—"

I stop, thinking back to the diary I know he must have read, too, as he and my sister sat in that camper, learning more about the man who fathered them both—but now I understand that the only reason I realized the woman living at Galloway wasn't the same woman who wrote those words was because of that film I developed.

That picture of Marcia that they never saw, the final piece he and Natalie never had.

"She was never much of a mother," Liam says to me now. "But somehow, I loved her, because I thought she was mine."

I loosen my grip on the gun, looking intently at the lines of his face. For the very first time, I can see the subtle little features he and Natalie share and I wonder if that's why he always felt so familiar. Why it seemed like I knew him the second I met him, my subconscious perpetually searching for her.

He drops down to the grass, his head falling into outstretched hands.

"I told her things," he says, turning to face me as his fingers pull through his hair. "Out in that camper, I told Natalie things I'd never told anyone. How I was born on the property, lived here my whole life. How I never went to school because I don't even have a birth certificate."

My mind flips back to the diner again, to all the things Bethany had said; assuming that Natalie was seeing someone older because he wasn't in school, because they spent all that time in his car.

"I never even realized how strange it was," Liam continues. "I never knew anything else, but then I started to grow up, started meeting people my age when they worked in the vineyard, and it began to sink in. How different I was from everyone else."

I feel a squeeze in my chest as I think about the kids who used to come here that summer, imagining as Liam would watch from a distance like they were some strange species he couldn't understand.

As he would bring them out to that camper, his secret little spot tucked deep in the trees. A meager attempt to try and fit in.

"So, what happened?" I ask, talking a tentative step closer. "That last night—?"

"She went to the police," he says, a single tear springing into his eye. "She told them everything. About how she suspected there was a missing person on the property, that she could connect Mitchell to another from 1983."

I blink, thinking about how I went to Chief DiNello myself and relayed all the same information, though he had acted like he was hearing it for the very first time.

"She told them about me," he continues. "That I was practically a prisoner in my own home. The night she died, she was coming to get me. She brought a bag with her so I could pack my things."

"But if she went to the police, how come they never did anything—?" I start, though the thought screeches to a halt as I think of Chief DiNello again, his fingers twisting in knots as I spewed out all those things that I knew. The way he demanded my proof, dismissing it all when I couldn't provide it.

The only time he paid me any attention at all.

"Montana," I say, the new revelation settling in as I think about how Eric DiNello grew up with my mother, how they all went by some nickname that wasn't their own.

Those pictures I saw framed in his office, the one of him riding a horse with rolling hills in the distance.

He moved here from Missoula a few months back.

"He told Natalie he would go with her," Liam continues, and I think about my sister hoisting up her window, sliding off the ledge and getting into that car—but it wasn't Jeffrey's car, not like we'd been told, but Eric DiNello's. Cruiser doors locking from the outside. "He promised to keep her safe and she trusted him," he says. "She believed him. He was a cop, but instead, he delivered her directly to them."

I exhale, pushing stale air out through gritted teeth. Then I turn toward the water, watching the sun appear on the horizon as it casts everything in an orange glow.

"Did she suffer?" I ask, thinking of what Mitchell had said in the shed.

Twenty minutes, it's over. It'll be like falling asleep.

"No," Liam says, and I bow my head. Relieved, at least, that he was telling the truth about that. "But I wasn't there when it happened. I was still waiting for her in the woods like we had planned."

I glance back at him, registering the faraway look in his eyes.

"Eventually, when it became obvious she wasn't coming, I walked back to the house and found them all there . . . but by the time I arrived, it was too late."

"So, how did she—?" I stop, still unable to say those final few words.

"My parents told me that at first, she ran," Liam says as I imagine my sister tumbling out of the cruiser the second DiNello opened the door. She must have tried to sprint through the vineyard, bee-lining toward the trees where she knew Liam was waiting. "She tried to get away but then she fell in the dark, twisted her ankle and cut her arm bad. Marcia—"

He stops, corrects himself.

"*Lily,*" he continues, "convinced her to come into the house so they could talk. She told her it was all a misunderstanding, that there was an innocent explanation for all of it. Natalie didn't know who she really was. She had no reason to suspect her of lying."

I let myself imagine it now, the scene eerily similar to when I got that bite: Natalie sitting in the living room, maybe even in that exact same chair, her shirt wet with blood from her fall as Mitchell tenderly treated her wounds.

"Honestly, I think she just wanted to believe the best," Liam adds as I imagine Lily walking in from the kitchen next, thrusting out a mug of something hot in her hands. "That her biological fa-ther wasn't the monster she suspected him to be."

"But why didn't you try to leave later?" I ask, although I already feel like I know the answer as my mind revisits all those articles I've covered, Liam being conditioned his whole life to believe he was dependent on two people alone—and in a way, he was.

Without a legal identity, in the eyes of society, he doesn't even exist.

"I was scared," he says, the simplicity of his answer catching me off guard, though I find myself nodding as my mind is transported to my kitchen table, eleven-year-old legs kicking in the air as I willed myself to say silent about all the things that I knew. "They convinced me it was my fault. That it only happened because I went against my family and if anyone ever found out what happened to Natalie, it could come back on me. They had a cop in their pocket."

I think of the pain in his eyes as he led me out to the shed, no doubt believing his life would be over if he allowed me to leave with all that I knew.

"Family," he mutters, the word hissing through his teeth like it has a bad taste, an acrid smack rising up in his throat. "She kept going on about family, how you don't go against your family, but all along, she was lying about that, too. Natalie was more of my family than she was."

A heavy silence settles over us both as I register the silky pink of the sky; the marbled clouds mirrored in the water and the sudden stillness of the wind in the trees.

"You two are so alike," he says as I cock my head. "You and your sister."

"We're nothing alike," I reply, that same line I've repeated to myself over and over and over again.

"Yes, you are," he argues. "Natalie risked her life to help me, you risked your life to help *her.*"

He gestures back to the shed, to Lily, who's gone silent inside.

"Neither of you had to do that. You could have just left, gone about your lives, but you came back to help someone who you could tell was in trouble."

I stay silent, letting myself sit with that belief for a bit.

"If you take me to the police, I'll come clean about all of it."

I glance back at my car, the tires slit, but then Liam holds up Mitchell's keys, his neck jerking in the direction of the truck as I realize the enormity of what he's suggesting.

"Natalie was right," he adds. "This place is the prison. I'd rather be in jail than spend another day here."

There's no movement between us for a handful of seconds, no sounds at all as I let the truth finally settle over my shoulders, the prospect of Liam walking into the station and willingly living the rest of his life behind bars. On the one hand, he's been complicit in so many crimes. He's known the truth about Natalie for twenty-two years and he's hid it from everyone, hoarding the answers all for himself—but somehow, it still doesn't sit right, letting him bear the brunt of it all.

I'm still standing above him, trying to decide what I should do, when Liam perks up beside me, his back lengthening as he turns toward at the road.

"Someone's coming," he says, and I follow his gaze as a cloud of dust erupts from the side, a little black car roaring fast through the gates. Something about it looks familiar and I take a step forward, a small smile emerging as I think about leaving the station yesterday, digging out that picture of my parents before calling my mother and leaving that message. I had admitted to staying at Galloway, demanded answers to the secrets she's been keeping herself, and I watch now as her car creeps closer. Her face twisted in fear on the opposite side of the glass until our eyes meet and I can see her shoulders loosen, her held breath expelled.

I look down at Liam, then back up at her.

"I think I have an idea," I say.

CHAPTER 50

The three of us drive straight to the station—though not in Claxton, not to Chief DiNello, but a hundred miles away in a town called Draper where the disappearance of Marcia Rayburn still sits cold.

We dropped Liam off an hour ago, my mom and I watching from the car as he walked inside. I have no idea how long this will take, how a person even proves a story like his, so we settled into a restaurant a few blocks away, the two of us sitting on opposite sides of a booth as my mother nervously peels at a napkin, my own hands wrapped in rolled gauze. The place feels suspended in time, like we've stepped into some scene ripped from a page in the past. There's a defunct jukebox sitting ignored in the corner, checkerboard tile scuffed on the floor—and then I notice a theater marquee blinking through the glass in the background, red bulbs flashing as I imagine a young Marcia sneaking inside, losing herself in fantasies of some faraway life.

Would it be better to die, she wondered, *than not be allowed to live at all?*

"Claire," my mom says, and I jerk my head up as she cracks the silence between us, brittle and thin. She looks exhausted, two heavy bags the hue of bruises hammocked beneath her bloodshot eyes. "I'm so sorry. I didn't see your message until this morning, but when you said you were still here, staying at Galloway—"

She stops, her eyes filling with tears as she looks down at the table, and I know exactly how she feels. It's the same way I felt when my father first called. That flash of regret, all the things left unsaid, when I thought my mother might actually be gone.

"Should we get started?" I ask, watching as she nods before I tap at my phone. It's been charging in the outlet on the wall beside us and I push it to the center of the table now, red sphere pulsing as our conversation records. "Tell me about Katherine Prichard."

My mother sighs, her eyes slowly morphing to glass.

"She didn't deserve what happened to her," says at last. "None of us did."

"And what happened?" I ask.

"Mitchell happened," she says simply. "Lily happened."

Another tear appears before she wipes it silently, rubbing the moisture onto a napkin scrap.

"You have to understand, Claire, that I was so lost after your grandparents died."

I swallow my response, once again familiar with the feeling, because even though my parents are still alive, there were so many years when they both felt like ghosts.

"I was barely eighteen," she continues. "Way too young to be all on my own. And I had your father, of course, but when your life gets suddenly rocked like that, when the rug gets pulled out beneath you, it's like there's this temptation to tear the rest of it down, too."

She looks up at me now, a real pain in her eyes. A pain I had always brushed off as disinterest, too busy blaming her for all that went wrong.

"So, you broke up with him," I say as she nods her head.

"My first mistake. And then I met Mitchell, my second mistake."

Our waitress appears with two cups of coffee, sliding them both across the table as my mother stares down at her lap. I reach for mine first, a warm pinch on my palms as I imagine Mitchell meeting my mother the same way as the others, sniffing her out as something defenseless and weak.

"Technically, Eric introduced us," she continues once we're alone again. "He was fairly new at school, didn't have many friends, and that made it feel safe, I guess. Recognizing another person out there. Besides, he talked about becoming a cop after graduation and I guess that made me think: *how bad could this be?*"

She grabs a pack of sugar from the caddy between us, fingers shaking as she tears at the slit.

"The whole thing felt like an escape," she adds, a sigh erupting as she dips a spoon in her coffee. "From my life, from the reality of what happened."

"*The escape* being Galloway," I clarify, picturing her blond hair blowing as she rode in that camper, those joints blissfully blunting her sharp edges of pain. It had felt like an escape for me, too. A distraction from all the things in my life that went wrong: my family, my job. Mitchell stocking that guesthouse and speaking as if he understood me so intimately, welcoming me in more than my own mother had.

"Back then," she says, nodding, "they just called it the Farm."

I look up at her now, a new confusion starting to sink in.

"But if you had been there already, then how did you not know Natalie was working for Mitchell?"

My mom twists her head, not understanding.

"We all went there together," I say, remembering how Liam had said our surprise visit that summer was what made my mother realize where Natalie was going; the reason she ultimately forced her to quit. "Even if you never knew his last name, how did you not know that property was Mitchell's if you used to go there when you were young, too?"

"Because the place they live now isn't the Farm," she says. "Not the one that I knew, at least."

I stay silent, the timer beneath us ticking dutifully forward as I think back to the diary again, Marcia describing the first time Mitchell drove her out to his home—a place, I now realize, that was only thirty minutes from her house in Draper, from where my mother and I are sitting right now. Not the three hours away of Galloway today.

"Do you remember how to get there?" I ask, watching as the blood drains from her face. She stares at me for a second, trying to decide how to respond, until her eyes divert back to the table. Fingers grabbing the napkin and continuing to tear.

"There are some things you never forget."

CHAPTER 51

The car is stuffed with a smothered silence, my mom staring out the passenger window as a blur of small towns breeze sleepily past.

"It's just up there," she says at last, pointing to a stream up ahead.

I flip on the turn signal, a courtesy for no one as we curve down a narrow roadway. Gravel dust erupting like smoke from the tires as a decrepit old barn slumps in the distance, four wooden walls stripped down to the bones.

"Welcome to the Farm."

I look at my mother, her voice wilted into a whisper as we come to a stop before the structure, field grass scratching the glass like nails. Then I turn off the car, staring silently at the barn up ahead. Four decades of desertion has made it appear as though it's one wind gust away from crumbling completely but I force myself to slide out, my mother still sitting in the seat beside me as I slam the door shut and make my way closer, coming to stop at the mouth of the entrance.

I peer inside, the barn's hot breath musky and damp as I imagine Lily meeting Marcia in this very same spot, a cigarette balanced between her two fingers as she walked her around on some strange tour. I step inside slowly, taking it in. There are relics of squatters scattered around: an old sleeping bag slouched in the corner and a smashed vodka bottle glinting on the floor. Then a ripple of movement catches my attention and I twist to the side, a strip of pink fabric quivering in the breeze. It's nailed to the wall, just above a window with the glass punched out, and I squint as I turn in a slow circle, eyeing the remnants of a paperback bloated with water. A rogue table leg snapped clean like a femur and the edge of a picture frame, a dull, dirty gold.

I let my hands trail the walls as I walk the perimeter, reading all the words written in paint, graffiti carved with the sharp tip of a knife—and then I come across an etching so old it's barely visible, though my fingers recognize the sentence from all the times they'd felt it before.

Lily was here.

"It looks different," my mom says, and I whip around at the sound of her voice, her silhouette standing still in the entrance. "But at the same time, exactly the same."

I stay rigid before her, taking in the faint whispers of a life lived in this place before I turn back around, my gaze trained on those words still preserved in the wood.

"She never belonged here," my mom continues. "Katherine, I mean."

I feel her come to a stop beside me as my mind starts to sort through everything I've learned about Katherine, a freshman from Berkeley who just disappeared.

"She was smart," she continues. "Had a real future. And it was an escape for her, too, I think—from the pressures of school, a few months of distraction—but unlike the rest of us, she had something to go back to."

I drop my hand, thinking of her picture I found in the paper. Lean body resting against the edge of the camper before meeting a man the same way as the others, a man who said all the things she had wanted to hear. Who persuaded her to bring him along for the summer, the two of them weaving their way across the country before settling down on the opposite coast.

"But Mitchell wouldn't let her," I say, surprised to find my mother shaking her head.

"*Lily* wouldn't let her."

I stare down at her name again, thinking about Lily growing up in the system. The dozens of families she must have known and all of them abandoning her the moment she started to settle. Going about their lives, forgetting her completely. Shuttling her around from place to place until she finally arrived at the Farm and desperately tried to make it feel like a home.

"The summer was over," my mom says. "Katherine needed to get back to school but Lily kept talking about how worried she was that Mitchell would go with her."

I find myself nodding, that familiar fear of being forgotten rearing up its hideous head.

"Though, honestly, I don't think he actually would have left," she adds. "Katherine's camper, it was the only way we had of getting around. He didn't want to lose that, so he was just saying what he knew Lily needed to hear. She was nothing more than a tool in his hands."

"So, what happened?" I ask. "What did she do?"

My mom sighs, the movement so strong her body seems to deflate.

"The night before Katherine was supposed to leave, we were all together, around the fire, and Lily brought her something to drink." Her voice takes on some faraway tone, a placid detachment as she stares straight ahead. "She didn't even ask what it was because we did that all the time out here. Mitchell used to grow things, sell things."

I twist around, staring out at the field behind us as I imagine that steady stream of cars coming and going, Mitchell easing his way onto each seat and walking back out with crumpled bills in his hand.

Lily picking those flowers, tiny and toxic. Rolling the stems between her fingers like needles loaded with a lethal dose.

"And Katherine trusted her," I say, thinking about how Lily had persuaded Natalie to drink something, too, all because they were threatening to break the fragile life she'd created. The home Lily had finally built for herself.

"She got so pale." My mom nods, her voice barely audible as she relives it all. "She couldn't move. Then she tried to start talking but she wasn't making any sense."

She takes a deep, shuddering breath, the tears streaming out faster than she can wipe them away.

"I remember saying we needed to get her to a hospital but Mitchell said she'd be fine, that she just needed to sleep it off. When I woke up the next morning, Katherine was gone, but her car was still there."

She turns toward me now, her skin splotchy and damp, and I watch as she wipes her fingers under her eyes, two black crescents smudging onto her cheeks before her gaze lifts to the sky.

"There was this mound of dirt beneath one of the trees like a hole had been dug and filled back in, and that's when I knew," she says. "I knew what they did and I knew I had to leave, too."

"How did you do it?" I ask, taking a step closer as I imagine the first day Marcia showed up, my mom lying in the grass outside this same barn. Smiling vaguely, keeping her distance. Biding her time as she planned her next move. "How did you leave?"

"We used to go into town for supplies," she says. "None of us had any money so we stole what we needed. Then one day, when we were close to home, I slipped out the back door of one of the houses."

I chew on my cheek, trying to envision my own mother climbing through windows or jimmying front doors. Fingers flipping through closets until she looked around and finally found herself alone.

"I ran back to your father," she adds, drawing my attention back to her. "Of course, he took me right back. He was always too good for me."

"What did he say when you showed up?"

"Nothing," she says. "He was just happy I was okay, then a few weeks later, I found out I was pregnant."

She looks at me, finally, eyes red and wet and begging for forgiveness.

"I knew it wasn't his," she says, and I bow my head, my own eyes drilling into a spot on the floor, because even though Liam told me already, hearing it straight from my mother's lips feels like I'm learning it all over again. "And honestly, I think he did, too, but he was never going to make me face it alone. So, he proposed. Bought us a house. Did all the things you were supposed to do back then."

I think back to the bar, my father's voice on the phone. That desperate desire to keep taking care of my mother even after two decades of being apart.

"I'm so sorry," she says as I remember him asking me to keep our call to myself, that small kindness muddled with shame like he didn't want her to know how much he still cared. "I never wanted you or Natalie to know."

"But I thought she was the one who told him," I say, bunching my brows as I attempt to work it all out. "I thought that was the whole reason why he left."

"She did." My mom nods. "It was. But once Natalie knew, once it was out in the open like that, I think it just became a lot harder for him to pretend."

I fall silent, my mother's dysfunction finally making more sense as I think of how she never wants to accept any help, eternally burdened with the guilt of what she had done.

How she still keeps my dad's picture hanging up on the wall, beholden to the man who gave her another chance—a chance she knew she didn't deserve.

"He loved your sister like she was his own," she says to me now, reaching out to grab my hand, fingers warm as they weave through mine. "Him leaving, it was never about her, but he spent eighteen years staring straight into the face of my lie. It was time he moved on from that."

"So, you knew all along," I say, thinking about how Eric Di-Nello showed up the morning Natalie vanished, looked my mother square in the eye.

You know how girls can be.

"When Natalie went missing," I continue, realizing that moment between them held so much more weight than I ever could have known. That his words were never meant to be a comfort, an encouragement that her daughter would turn up all right; instead, they were an intimidation, a threat. A warning to stay silent about all the things that she knew. "You knew there was more to the story than what he was saying."

"Not exactly," she says. "All the evidence pointed to Jeffrey. I couldn't prove anything other than that. Besides, I had another daughter I had to protect."

I look down at our hands, our slack clasp, and feel my squeeze tighten as I think about all the things my mother has done. The lies she's told and the secrets she's kept, all of it an attempt to take care of her daughters.

To give us a better, safer life.

"They found me," she continues. "A few months after I left, I came home and I could tell Lily had been there."

I look up at her again, imagining a chewed-up core dropped in the sink. A picture missing from the face of the fridge and those phantom words reemerging on the mirror as soon as the room filled up with steam.

"It was like she was tapping on my shoulder," she says. "Always reminding me that they were there, what they were capable of."

I stare at my mother, trying to process the weight of her secrets. The fear she's been carrying for twenty-two years keeping her cornered, holding her down.

"Why didn't you tell me any of this?" I ask at last. "Why did you keep it all to yourself?"

"Because you were a child," she says. "Then you grew up and left and never came back. I love you, Claire, but it always felt like you were safer when you weren't here."

I stare at my mother, realizing, now, that in the same way Natalie pushed me away in an attempt to protect me, my mother has been keeping me at a distance to help me stay safe.

"I wrote you a letter," she says, a stitch in my chest when I remember what Ryan had said a few days ago, flipping through my mail to find my mom's name. "After you left, I realized I was going to lose you for good if we couldn't start being honest with each other. So, I tried," she says, dropping her gaze to the ground. "The best I could, at least, to get all these things out that I never knew how to say out loud."

I nod, tears filling my eyes as I glance down at our hands.

"I just need a minute," I say, pulling back as she smiles softly. Then I let myself take one last look around before making my way toward the barn doors. It's midday now, the summer sun singeing the nape of my neck, and I pull out my phone, snapping a few pictures of the barn, the brook. The weeds and wildflowers and sweetgum sprouting its spiny gumballs, a drowsy willow weeping at the edge of it all.

I walk back to the car, sliding inside. A blank stare as I peer through the windshield. Then I twist around, eyeing my bags I had grabbed from the guesthouse floor.

My brown briefcase slumped on the seat, the maroon spine of the diary peeking out of the pocket.

I reach out and grab it, draping the book across my lap. I have five pages left, and while I'm going to turn it in, its contents corroborating all the evidence I've collected, giving credence to the things I know Liam will say, right now, I can feel the temptation to finally learn how it ends vibrating my bones like a rattling wire.

I crack the spine and stare down at the words, that familiar blue script faded and worn as the ink starts to run dry. Then I take a deep breath and lean back in my seat, allowing myself to live the last moments of Marcia Rayburn's fleeting life.

CHAPTER 52

SEPTEMBER 1984

Marcia stretched out at the edge of the marsh, her baby boy asleep at her side. Her diary was propped up on her knees, only a few pages left until the whole thing was full, and she rolled the pen between her slick fingers. A smear of blue ink staining her skin as she gazed out at the dock just ahead.

A sound from behind stole her attention and she spun around quick, recognizing the slap of the screen door in the distance. Then she watched as Mitchell emerged from the main house before making his way into the budding vineyard beside it.

She turned back around and eased down on her elbows, reliving the day they arrived in this place. It was a moment that would be forever ingrained in her psyche, a moment that would mar her dreams and mold her nightmares: standing in that house, five months ago, a pregnancy test hot in her pocket as she looked down at the body on the bedroom floor.

"Come on," Lily had muttered as Marcia stared down at the eyes starting to glaze, crimson blood seeping into the carpet as Lily held that gun in her hand. "We have to go."

Everything about that day had taken on a foggy quality like submerging your whole head underwater and hearing nothing but the thump of your heart in your ears, blinking to find all your surroundings blurry and bent. It happened so fast it felt impossible to process—she and Lily were alone, then they weren't; that woman had been alive, then she wasn't—but there was one thing Marcia could remember perfectly, one little thing that seemed to transpire in slow motion: looking around the room in a faraway haze until her eyes landed on that film Lily had dumped on the bed. Her mind rewinding to the flash she had seen when she walked out of the bathroom, her face frozen for one single incriminating second as the camera's timestamp placed her smack in the center of a crime.

She remembered walking to the mattress in a numb detachment, cupping the roll in her damp hands before sliding it into her pocket. Then she had turned around, trailing Lily as they tore down the stairs, their bodies bursting through the front door.

"What did you *do*?" Montana had hissed, eyes swelling as he saw them both coming. The gun was still clutched in Lily's right hand, the metal bouncing back and forth as they ran.

"*Drive,*" Lily had said, Montana cranking the camper before they could even climb in the back seat. "Just drive."

Marcia took a deep breath now, the salt air cleansing her system as her eyes stared down the length of the dock. It was understood immediately they couldn't stay at the Farm. Lily had killed a cop—a cop who had been watching them, learning them, who knew where they lived—so they left that afternoon, the four of them piling into the camper before driving three hours south. She could still feel the bounce of the tires as they took their last turn, the tangled trees surrounded by a moat of a marsh and a large white house standing tall in the distance, an identical cabin just beside it and acres and acres of untouched land.

"Where are we?" she'd asked as a man appeared on the porch. Mitchell didn't answer; she knew he wouldn't. Instead, he simply parked at the base of the stairs just as the man started to descend—and that's when Marcia realized she knew him. He was familiar, a face she had seen so many times before, but it was primarily his posture she recognized: the way both hands were punched in his pockets as he watched them all stumble out of the camper, dirty and disheveled without a possession to their names.

The way his shoulders stayed slouched like he was trying to make himself small, the same twitchy demeanor as all those times he had waited for Mitchell to slide inside of his car.

That's one of our regulars, Lily had told her. *Some rich guy who just inherited a fortune and doesn't know how else to spend it.*

Steven had welcomed them in without question, droning on about how his father had passed, how he had moved onto all this land by himself because there was no one else in his family alive to claim it. He didn't know anyone on the island and he had clearly been lonely, inviting Mitchell to visit during all the times he had stopped by the Farm. Those little bags that he bought the only things to keep him company, the drugs blunting his boredom like a dull blade.

"What are you doing?"

Marcia snapped her neck up at the sound of a voice, Lily making her approach from across the grass.

"Nothing," she said, slipping the diary beneath her legs as she pictured Lily bursting into the guesthouse the day they arrived. Opening up closets and pulling out drawers before grabbing a knife from a block on the counter and scratching that sentence in the depths of a desk.

Mitchell, of course, had set his own sights on the property's main house. Then he had started planting things, picking back up on his business. Slowly spreading his tentacles wide as his fingerprints touched every inch of the place until it started to feel more like his every day.

"Pretty eyes," Lily said as she sat down beside her. Marcia looked down, realizing her son was awake, staring up at them both. "He got those from you."

She smiled, taking in their deep, cerulean blue.

"How are you feeling?" Lily asked next, long fingers playing with the thin strands of his hair. "All healed up?"

"Getting there," she said, crossing her legs.

"Mitch has some yarrow flowering out back. It should help with the bleeding."

Marcia stared at her, trying to decipher her words like she was speaking in code. Ever since that day in the closet, the two of them looking down at the strip in her hand, Marcia swore she could feel the girl watching her, studying her. Those cold gray eyes trained on the side of her face like she was waiting on Marcia to make some kind of move.

"I'll have to try that," she said simply, looking down at her lap.

"I'll make you a cup."

Marcia opened her mouth, about to protest, but Lily stood up before she could respond. In truth, she had no idea if she should trust her. On the one hand, Marcia couldn't forget the look in her eyes as she held that gun, her total lack of remorse for taking a life—but on the other hand, Lily hadn't told Mitchell that Marcia wanted to leave. She had kept quiet, kept their conversation a secret. Still, Marcia never mentioned leaving to Lily again; instead, she spent every moment of the last five months watching, waiting. Staying poised and patient as her stomach started to grow. Honestly, she was terrified, because while this place was certainly more comfortable than where they were living before—they had real beds and bathrooms, actual space to themselves—they were completely cut off now, dozens of miles from the nearest neighbor. Nowhere to run to; no one to hear if she screamed for help.

They never even went into town anymore, that very last thread keeping her tethered severed the second they stepped into this place.

She glanced down, studying her son on the grass beneath her. His mouth gaping open and closed like a fish. She had known she couldn't risk leaving when she was still pregnant, her unborn baby relying on her heart to keep beating, her lungs to keep breathing, her mind flashing back to that woman bleeding out on her bedroom floor every time Marcia wondered if she should try. That little life inside her had become her everything since the moment she learned of its existence; it was her reason for being, her motivation to finally make her escape. That baby deserved so much more than the life it would be born into, so she had waited until he was safely on the outside, putting on a face for the others while counting down the days until they could both finally leave.

She turned around now, watching as Lily disappeared into the house before pulling the diary out from under her legs. Then she clicked on the pen that was now almost dry as she scribbled into its pages for the very last time. Her plan was solid, but just in case anything were to go wrong, she still felt the need to write it all down just as she had written down every detail of the last ten months. They would be leaving that night, she and Liam, the two of them slipping out of the guesthouse as soon as the sky was swaddled in dark.

Then she would take her son, the diary, and the film she had stolen, before starting the long walk toward town.

She flipped the book shut, scooping her son from the grass before turning toward the line of trees in the distance. The camper was out there, slowly getting swallowed by vines and leaves, and she made the walk as quickly as she possibly could, her scheme running through her mind like an endless scroll. Despite her isolation, her lack of connection to the outside world, the one thing she knew for certain was that the police were looking for Lily. She had listened to the stories Montana brought back, the reward money mounting for information about the murder of a cop named Carmen. A single name scratched into a headboard the only evidence her killer had left behind. Over the last few months, Montana had become their sole source of information, taking Steven's car when he left for training before bringing back news when he came home. He was working to become an officer himself, an irony as bitter as all those teas Marcia tasted—though she was starting to realize it was all a part of some plan, Mitchell giving himself an extra layer of protection he knew that only a cop could create.

She reached the camper, finally, opening the door and climbing inside before making her way to the bed in the back. Then she wedged her diary between the wall and the mattress, the same spot she'd been hiding the roll of film.

The same spot she once found that sweatshirt, the very spot she'd return to later that night once everyone else was in bed, collecting her evidence before she and Liam would make their escape.

By the time she emerged from the trees, there was a cluster of clouds gathering in the distance, a sharp chill in the air as the sky grew dark. Then she looked down at her chest, at her son asleep against her warm skin.

When she looked back up, Lily had appeared on the porch, a large, white mug clutched in her hand.

She watched as Lily hoisted it higher, beckoning Marcia to join her inside. Then she smiled, waved, and tipped her head back. A single drop landing on her cheek like a tear.

"One more time," she whispered into the wind, because she knew, at last, it would be over soon.

EPILOGUE

It's live.

I turn to the side, the buzz of my phone pulling me from sleep as I stare at the screen alight on the table. Then I reach out to grab it, squinting as I try to make sense of this text from my father until I bolt up in bed, a stitch in my chest once I understand what he means.

"Ryan," I say, shaking his shoulder. "It's live."

He sits up quick, a sleepy smile spreading across his face. Then he gets up and pads across the room, grabbing his laptop from on top of his desk before bringing it back to the bed.

He hands it to me, my fingers tapping away at the keys.

"Front page," I say, leaning forward as the article loads. "It's on the front page."

The first thing I see is *The New York Times,* the logo big and bold at the top of the screen. There's a picture of Galloway just beneath it, that goldenrod shot I took on my first night there when the lighting was all eerie and still.

I read the headline next, a few sentences of summary, before eyeing my byline printed prominently below.

"Well?" Ryan asks, climbing back under the covers as I take a deep breath and start to scroll. "What do you think?"

I begin reading, this unbelievable story I pieced together. The story that not only revived my career but, in the process, my whole life. It's a strange sensation, all this death, and me being the one to uncover it all the only reason my job was given new life—but at the same time, this is the whole reason I chose this profession.

To make sure lost girls are never forgotten.

My eyes start to water as I take in their pictures, the dedicated sections about each one—and not just a few sentences, not only how they met their ends, but all the wonderful ways they spent their short lives. Their plans and passions, hobbies and homes. Scanned excerpts from Marcia's diary and those pictures of Natalie I found in that shoebox. The shot of Katherine in front of her camper next to the one I took out in the woods as it sat swallowed in that sea of bright blue.

"Forget-me-nots," Liam had told me, calling to mind those petals I once found crushed in Natalie's pocket. He had planted them for her in that secret spot they had shared, an effort to honor her memory the only way he knew how—and then they had spread, invasive under the right conditions. Irrepressible and wild, just as my sister had been. "They were her favorite."

I keep scrolling, drinking in the various shots of the property. The plants and the shed, yellow tape wound around its busted-down doors. My mom and I arrived back at the station in Draper just as Liam was being led to a cruiser, blue lights blinking as he ducked in. Then we had pulled out behind them, trailing from a distance as we wound down south.

I think about pulling into Galloway now, finding the place crawling with cops like a colony of ants drawn to dropped fruit. Easing to a stop in my regular spot as an officer made his way toward us, gesturing for me to lower the glass.

"You can't be here," he said, elbows resting against the side of the car. Then I had glanced to the side, to Lily handcuffed in the back of a cruiser; Mitchell's body veiled beneath a white sheet. "This is an active crime scene."

"My name is Claire Campbell," I said as I leaned over, one hand on the wheel as the other grabbed the diary from the floor of the car. Then I had thrust it toward him, his head cocked as he took it in. "This is my mother, Annaliese. We have some information you're going to want to hear."

I stared straight ahead as he looked down at the diary, then back up at me, before motioning for us to get out of the car. Then he had led us into the living room, Liam perking up as soon as we entered as his body sat slumped in Lily's old chair.

"Where did you get this?" the officer asked, holding the book up in the air.

"I found it," I said. "Pushed into the back of a vent in the guesthouse."

"And how did it get there?"

I still remember that moment so clearly, my voice withering in the back of my throat as I realized, for the first time, that if Marcia never put the diary in there, then I had no idea who did.

"I hid it," Liam said as I turned to face him, his gaze pulled to his hands clasped in his lap. "As a safeguard, I guess, back in 2002."

I stared at him then, the very last piece clicking into place as I imagined him sneaking into the guesthouse after Natalie had died. Pulling the diary from the depths of her duffel—their shared secret, his sole piece of proof—before walking to the vent and removing the cover, sliding it back as far as it would go.

"Nobody ever went in there," he added. "Not until we started using it for workers a few years back."

I blink back to the present, to Ryan's warm body sitting flush by my side.

"Well," he asks again, nudging my shoulder as I think about how I came back to the city six months ago, moving out of my apartment and in with him as I spent every second piecing this story together. Ryan giving me his room while he crashed on the couch until slowly, silently, he started to sleep in here, too. "Are you happy?"

"I'm happy," I say, actually meaning it for the very first time.

I turn my attention back toward the screen, all the pictures of evidence the police pulled from the floor. Every single item stuffed inside of that bag had belonged to a person who had long been gone: Katherine's sweatshirt, Steven's license and deed. The gun registered to a cop named Carmen who had been murdered back in the eighties, her cold case finally closed. Then they had moved into the shed next, ripping up the rest of those bloated old boards to discover the remains of three separate bodies, just as Liam had promised they would.

One of the bodies belonged to Marcia Rayburn, a cheek swab provided by Liam proving they were mother and son. The second belonged to Steven Montague, the rightful owner of the land known as Galloway Farm before Mitchell stole it away.

The third body belonged to Natalie Campbell.

I stare at the picture of my sister now as I remember the strange sensation I had every time I crossed the shed's threshold, the way Liam always hesitated before stepping inside.

How it felt like I could physically *feel* her at Galloway, a closeness between us I couldn't explain.

We held a funeral for her, a proper one this time, and Jeffrey Slater was exonerated after twenty-two years spent sitting in prison for a crime he didn't commit. Bethany came forward, claiming Eric DiNello had coerced her testimony, leading her with questions designed to make her think that Jeffrey was the one my sister had been sneaking out to see—and it made sense, she said, because Jeffrey Slater had been in their system for years. He was a drug dealer, a criminal. A known acquaintance of Natalie's and an older man with a car, a car Bethany had seen her sit in before.

He was the simplest, most logical explanation.

I scroll down to his mug shot now, Eric DiNello's, his crimes ranging from planting evidence in Jeffrey's car—that blood-soaked shirt from Natalie's fall, a single blond hair he had ripped from the root—to helping cover up an illegal drug operation and being an accomplice to five murders over the span of forty-one years. Ironically, Mitchell hadn't been lying when he told me he never killed anyone—not directly, at least. It had been Lily, all of it: Steven and Marcia, Carmen and Natalie. Katherine, whose remains were found buried beside a decrepit old barn after my mother brought the cops there.

I look at Lily now, the very last picture at the bottom of the screen. Those bleak gray eyes staring blankly into the lens. I may never know if Mitchell was actually drugging her—if it was yet another method of his control, those teas tranquilizing her into a placid oblivion—or if she drank them of her own free will. The police are still trying to piece her together, this neglected girl who simply started to rot.

Living her life behind a series of masks and stealing so many things, including a name, because she left hers as evidence at so many crimes.

I feel my phone buzz again and I look down at my side, the sound nudging me out of the moment. Then I reach out and grab it, swiping up to find a new text.

Turns out I'm named after my grandfather. Who would have thought.

I watch as a picture comes through next, a picture of Liam next to William and Jane Rayburn, both of them older but very much alive. They're standing in front of a house, 1629 Hickory Road. The address I had found and passed along to Liam, urging him to meet his family.

The family he didn't even know that he had.

I pinch my fingers to the screen and zoom in on his face, blue eyes crinkled as he squints into the sun, and think about how he kept his every last promise, backing up my claims of self-defense and spending a few weeks behind bars as the police worked to confirm that his story was true. It had been hard to prove, of course, but based on the dates in Marcia's diary, the timeline constructed from his mother's own words, he was determined to have been born a month *after* Natalie, in September of 1984, still making him a minor on the day she had died.

It's a good name.

I type back, smiling as I think back to the diary's first entry, the single sentence that started all this.

I guess I'll start with my name, Marcia, because most days, my name feels like the only thing that's mine.

ACKNOWLEDGMENTS

As always, there are too many people to thank and not enough space to thank them all, so I'll do my best to keep this brief.

To my agent, Dan Conaway, for your endless patience and trust. This book tested me in ways I hadn't yet experienced, but you never wavered in your confidence that I could get it right (and if you did, don't tell me. You hid it well!). You have a unique ability of stretching me in the moments when I need it the most, and for that, I am incredibly grateful.

To my editor, Kelley Ragland, for the grace you extended during the many, many months I spent writing this book. You made a particularly chaotic time of my life feel significantly less stressful with your steady insistence that it would all be okay—that, and your insights made this book a hell of a lot better. Thank you, for all of it.

To everyone at Writers House, including but not limited to Sydnee Harlan, Peggy Boulos-Smith, and Maja Nikolic. I'm so lucky to have you.

A special thanks to Jen Enderlin for swooping in with the perfect title, as well as everyone else at Minotaur Books, St. Martin's Press, and Macmillan who made their mark on this book in every conceivable way: Katie Holt, Allison Ziegler, Sarah Melnyk, David Rotstein, Paul Hochman, and Ken Silver, among many others.

To Julia Wisdom, Lizz Burrell, and the entire team at Harper-Collins UK, who continue to bring my books overseas.

To Sylvie Rabineau at WME for your dogged efforts to bring my stories to the screen.

To my husband, Britt, for patiently waiting four books to finally have one dedicated to you! None of them would have been possible without you, of course, but *this one* probably would have been deleted out of existence had you not been there to encourage me through it. You are the best partner, the best dad, the best friend, the best everything.

To my sweet, sweet Avery. From balancing my laptop on my growing belly to bouncing you as I attempted to tap out a few lines, you were with me every step of the way. Thank you for showing me a love I didn't know could exist.

To the rest of my family, including but not limited to my parents, Kevin and Sue; my in-laws, Laura and Alvin; my siblings, Mallory, Brian, Lindsey, and Matt; and my niece and nephews, Reese, Stella, and Everett. Thank you for being my people, always.

Thank you to Mako, my canine coworker, for forcing me to occasionally step outside. Our daily walks bring me my best inspiration.

Thank you to my friends, near and far, for keeping me sane.

Thank you to my fellow authors who have turned into colleagues and friends, as well as to every bookseller, librarian, blogger, and reviewer for taking the time to share your praise.

Last but not least, a heartfelt thank you to my readers. You have changed my life in more ways than I can count. None of this would be possible without you.

ABOUT THE AUTHOR

Mary Hannah Harte

Stacy Willingham is the *New York Times, USA Today,* and internationally bestselling author of psychological suspense. Her books include *A Flicker in the Dark, All the Dangerous Things, Only If You're Lucky,* and *Forget Me Not.* Her debut, *A Flicker in the Dark,* has sold over one million copies in North America alone. It was the winner of *Strand Magazine*'s Best Debut Award and a finalist for the Book of the Month's Book of the Year Award, Goodreads Choice Best Debut Award, Goodreads Choice Best Mystery & Thriller Award, and ITW's Best First Novel Award. Her work has been translated into more than thirty languages. Before turning to fiction, Stacy was a copywriter and brand strategist for various marketing agencies. She earned her B.A. in magazine journalism from the University of Georgia and M.F.A. in writing from the Savannah College of Art and Design. She lives in Charleston, South Carolina, with her husband, daughter, and dog.